81/10

A SEASON TO KILL

23rd May 2024

In conspect
wants R.H place
to depart

Q voll up — S. Killers (??)

not quite
descriptory

A
SEASON
TO
KILL

NIC WINTER

PROLOGUE

Thursday, 17 October, 5.35 p.m.

THERE HAD BEEN NO warning of the approaching storm. Mother Nature herself had provided a perfect backdrop to the cruel and ugly plan.

The car door swung open, and the hunter emerged.

The heavens opened, allowing rain to pound down mercilessly upon the village—as though a punishment was being delivered from above.

The hunter gently pulled up the zipper and adjusted their black hood with deliberate care and attention.

Perfect.

Slowly, carefully, the hunter turned full circle, scanning the road, taking everything in. Watching the verdant evergreens thrash from side to side sparked a thrill of excitement. Scarlet and bronzed leaves tore from large oak trees gracefully lining the road, never quite reaching now muddied ground. Instead, they swirled and danced before being carried away into the frozen night air.

Ripped apart and gone forever.

Stalking Elle for the past few weeks had been surprisingly simple and entering the Bradshaw house undetected would be a breeze. Predictably, Elle Bradshaw had excelled in her focus on the aesthetics of her property, seemingly unburdening herself from the practicalities of a security-conscious mind.

Too easy.

Euphoria hit like a shot of amphetamine—dizzying, out of control. Just a few more hours and she would be gone, scrubbed from memory. Sins would be cleansed and washed away.

To be the judge was satisfying.

To be the executioner was almost too much to bear.

Almost…but not quite.

Tonight would be a good night.

Superlative.

Only one question remained: play with her for a while or just snap her neck?

Decisions, decisions.

Thursday, 17 October, 5.42 p.m.

Elle Bradshaw stared out of the large bay window in her bedroom, craving a Grey Goose on the rocks with a splash of fresh lime. Maybe a double. She was desperate to crawl into her Olivia Van Halle pyjamas and forget the day had ever happened. The softness of the décor—white with splashes of lemon—and the vase of fresh yellow roses bursting with life would usually have soothed her.

Not tonight.

She breathed out, almost gave in to the urge to smash the vase against the immaculate wall but she knew she couldn't be bothered to clean up the mess.

Darkness cloaked the picturesque Scottish village. She stared out into the abyss. *So much anger.* The emotion so strong it seemed to be leaving a bilious taste on her tongue. When she found out who was behind her recent misery, she would dismantle them piece by little piece.

But most disconcerting was the other emotion lurking in the background—fear. Most peculiar, because she couldn't recall ever having feared anything, or anyone.

Ten phone calls today; many earlier in the week.

Each one more frightening than the last. Either static, the low whistle of a nursery rhyme, or the voice. A voice, an ugly voice—full of mania, and just a hint of disgust.

What dirty, filthy little secret had the caller been referring to? It had to be the one buried so deep she'd almost forgotten its existence. There was only one other living soul who knew of it, of that she was sure—or at least she thought she was. Still, it had left her with the sense that something catastrophic was hurtling towards her.

The phone hadn't stopped ringing all day—the same withheld number.

Taunting her. Backing her into a corner.

The envelope had arrived in the mail several weeks ago, and the second she'd torn it open a Pandora's box of stifled emotions had exploded. That shame had been hidden many years ago, hadn't it?

Wrong.

Everything had changed.

Next, the doll had arrived.

Elle swallowed painfully against the memory—how her elation had spun into horror as she'd lifted the kid's toy from the package, its plastic eyes gouged out. That doll had cemented her fear.

Someone out there knew everything.

Someone was hunting her.

She'd begun to sleep with the light on, a childish habit she thought she'd left behind a long time ago.

Fool.

Standing straight, she smiled at her reflection in the mirror. Patted at her impeccable caramel-and-toffee balayage hair. Inspected her skin. Despite the lack of sleep, the little top-up of fillers appeared to be doing their job. Heads always turned to watch her. Ice-blue eyes, high cheekbones, and an athletic figure, today shown off perfectly in the pale-pink silk Prada blouse and Hugo Boss tailored grey pencil skirt. The new Stuart Weitzman nude peep-toe five-inch heels showcased her long, toned, tanned legs.

She skimmed her hips, patted her non-existent stomach, and took a deep breath.

At fifty, she looked damn good.

Her mind flicked through memories, grasping for a happy event, but each one floated away as soon as it was within reach.

Charles…

Her marriage had been a car crash from the second she'd tossed her bouquet into the air. His touch had made her skin crawl by the second night of their honeymoon. Everything about him was impotent. His only saving grace was the money he made, and he made a shitload.

Money. The only reason she'd crawled into his bed.

So many nights she'd staggered there, relieved that Charles was sleeping but too damn drunk to bear being alone. She'd realised quickly she'd hated being a wife and had been a lukewarm mother to Cole when he was born.

Marriage had been pure hell, but her little flings had allowed her to settle into a satisfactory routine. She tugged at a memory. Her *friend*, Cat Henderson, arriving on her doorstep one night—a hot mess, sobbing over the possible collapse of her marriage. Cat's husband was upstairs, tangled in Elle's bedsheets.

With indifference had come power.

Pure unadulterated power.

She'd craved it, wanted it as badly as a junkie needed a hit.

How she ached continually for the little thrill of euphoria when she'd seen the flash of jealousy in her friends' eyes and the lust in their husbands'. Power eradicated the agony. It washed away the misery she'd carried from the second she'd allowed *him* into her bed—when everything had turned painful and real and ugly.

Elle held the memory for a little longer, then let it float away like all the others.

Call Jonathan. Jonathan Mitchell might have worn a minister collar, but he was a devoted friend—that's how she'd played him so many times before. But this was a gamechanger. Only one thing to do—make him believe she was the victim. Manipulation came as easy as breathing to her, but dismantling reputations was where she excelled.

Her finger wavered over the green connect button. Damn it! He'd said he'd be at the hospital with the McGill family giving solace.

A smile tugged at the corner of her mouth as she fired off a text to Bill Henderson. *Give him something to think about.*

Elle opened the walnut box rammed with old photographs, only one of which held any special meaning to her. As she snatched up the prized photo, anger, sadness and disgust surged through her. The twist of emotions made her nauseous—just as she'd intended.

The trill of an incoming call startled her, and the photograph brushed the bed and fluttered to the soft, wool, oatmeal rug. She hesitated then reached for the phone.

"Hello, this is Elle." She spoke quietly, uneasily.

"Elle? Is that you?"

"Oh, Maddie." She tried to conceal her impatience. Failed miserably.

"How's things? I'm soaked through—just back from a run."

Shut up. Silly little bitch.

Maddie was younger, prettier, and enjoyed a seemingly happy marriage. Elle despised her for it.

"Thing is, Elle, here we are, no accounts in my hand," Maddie's tone sharpened, "you need to get them to me—now. I thought we'd agreed this has gone too far. Give Olivia the benefit of the doubt."

Elle gripped the phone until her knuckles turned white. "I'm warning you, Maddie, don't play me. I don't know why you're sticking your neck out for Olivia Miller."

Money had gone missing from the parish funds and Olivia was the only one who could possibly know what had happened to it—she was the treasurer after all.

"And remind Olivia I've sent a gorgeous little snap of her doing the walk of shame last Wednesday. She might like it—slut."

"I don't appreciate you threatening my friend, Elle," Maddie said, her tone low. "Delete whatever shit it is you think you have on Olivia because she's been through enough. If I don't calm myself down in the next thirty seconds, I'm going to land on your doorstep where we can continue our pleasantries."

Elle disconnected and exhaled. She looked at the patio door, but the rain-spattered glass displayed only her own reflection. Pepper, her Finnish spitz, scampered down the hallway and snuffled at the door.

"Out you go."

Shit! The gate.

One look at the driving rain made the decision for her. She opened the door and took a step out, shielding herself from the cold sheet rain.

The phone trilled again, ratcheting her anxiety, and forcing her back inside.

"Hello?"

Nothing.

Panicked, she disconnected the call and moved towards the stairs.

Pepper erupted into a volley of barks. Elle's head snapped around, the muscles in her neck screaming. The spitz never growled. She reached the top step and stopped dead.

She felt the presence before she turned.

No longer alone.

That knowledge came like a punch to the gut.

No time to run.

And no one to run to.

She spun around.

Her heart hammered, trying to catch up with itself.

It couldn't be.

The realisation brought an urge to vomit.

"Hello," the voice sang. "It's me."

And she knew.

This was her end, her last moment on this earth.

Time's up.

And how she wanted more. Time to talk, to laugh, to cry. Time to change who she was and who she'd been and what she'd done. But it was too late—the ugly decisions she'd made in the past had rippled forward to what she now knew was inevitable. And Elle would have given anything to be spared.

The visitor lunged, grabbed at her hair and neck; shook her like a rag doll.

A sickening crack rang out as a fist connected with her cheek. Elle's head thrashed from side to side like the evergreens bending outside in the wind. White-hot pain exploded in her head and lanced down her neck.

The figure tossed her like garbage down the stairs, and she tumbled onto the cold, wooden floor.

Darkness enveloped her. She welcomed it.

Elle Bradshaw didn't want to remember anymore.

CHAPTER ONE

Friday, 18 October

"**C**HRIST ALMIGHTY!"
    I threw off my duvet, swung my legs around, teetered and clambered out of bed, hurling a few expletives at the alarm. Harry rolled over in bed yawning, oblivious to my cursing.

Get to the shower. Get to the shower.

It was my morning mantra, after which everything would fall into place. I yearned to glide out of bed and straight into ten different yoga positions, hair billowing around my shoulders, but no, not I, not Darcy Sinclair. Instead, I had mastered the art of staggering to the bathroom and turning on the water, of scrubbing my face and brushing my teeth.

Pat on the back for me.

Hand to God, I used to be a morning person but that was B.C.— Before Children. My two kids and my husband were the loves of my life, but my morning routine rivalled a Navy Seal boot camp.

I let the warm water course over me.

A few minutes later, my brain had defogged and I was human again.

I was me.

Humming, I rinsed out shampoo. Neil Young was still searching for a heart of gold in my head. Music could enhance my mood, happy or sad, and it wasn't uncommon for me to kill a perfectly good tune while in the shower or cooking or driving.

It also helped me shake off feelings that I didn't want to feel.

A little trick I'd learned as a kid.

Another ghost from my past.

This morning I didn't want to think about my impending meeting with Elle Bradshaw. And I sure as hell didn't want to think about my mid-morning appointment with a client whom I was certain was a psychopath.

I'd long since learned that the monsters don't live under your bed—sometimes they stand beside you and wear a smile.

So, I scrubbed away the prickle of anxiety off my skin with a vigorous rub of shower gel.

Wrapped in a fluffy white towel, I crept back to my bedroom so as not to wake the kids. I treasured these silent and sacred moments—*just me*—before everyone woke and the house became at best a cacophony of noise and on trying mornings a battleground.

Twenty minutes later I'd completed my make-up. The process seemed to take longer with each passing month, seemingly slowed by the blossom of new wrinkles.

My hand wavered over my hairdryer. Not today. I'd let my auburn hair air dry. It wouldn't take too long despite the length, now way past my shoulders thanks to a desperate attempt to grow it after my hairdresser had had a hell of a bad day. I always tried to straighten the natural wave out of it. It never worked.

I liked my eyes better—hazel with flecks of green, bright but warm. At five-foot-three I was on the small side and carrying some much-loathed extra pounds—blame the kids—and it was nobody's damn business just how many.

Now it's coffee time, I thought, doing a happy dance.

Right on cue, there it was, the thump, thump, thump on the bedroom floor that drove fear into the hearts of tired parents everywhere.

And so it began.

An hour later my hands flew across the chopping block, slicing and dicing, until two lunchboxes were packed with sandwiches, water and fruit. Georgie and Henry sat at the kitchen table, inhaling their cereal, hypnotised by the banality of the blaring television.

I turned it off. "No television when eating breakfast, guys. How many times do I have to tell you that?"

My just turned eight-year-old daughter rolled her eyes and her six-year-old brother kicked her under the table. My head began to throb.

"Mummy!" Henry yelled, even though I was literally a foot away. He hadn't quite mastered the art of an indoor voice. That little quirk was from my side of the gene pool. "Are zombies real? Like, could one turn up at school?" His little face looked thrilled at the possibility.

It was a tricky question because I was sure I'd met a few zombies in my life. We all knew the kind—dead behind the eyes with one flickering brain cell.

"No, Henry, zombies aren't real."

His face fell, the sprinkling of freckles across his nose scrunching up. Tall for his age just like his dad, his enormous blue eyes shone with a mixture of curiosity and mischief. With a mop of nutmeg brown hair and two front teeth missing he was as cute as a button. A natural show off, tormenting his big sister was his favourite pastime surpassed only by his love of playing football.

Georgie was tall and gangly, all legs and arms, her shining crown was dark-auburn hair that lightened over the summer months and framed her huge blue eyes. She, too, sported a smattering of freckles. One night as I was tucking her into bed, Georgie told me she wanted to scrub them away because she hated them, and it had broken my heart. My daughter was a sunny, fiercely independent little girl with a kind heart and a heck of a lot of smarts.

The kids' happy squabbling was a gift delivered every morning. I'd come to savour it.

My own beginnings had been far humbler. Growing up in a ramshackle tenement in a worn-down working-class neighbourhood in Glasgow, my past was a jumble of happy and awful memories that had taken me a long time to separate.

Maybe I was still trying.

Forced to observe my father's profound narcissistic tendencies and paranoia complex blow up, with the help of alcohol infused self-pity marathons, had left me pessimistic about my relationships.

Domestic violence. Two ugly little words with huge ramifications.

Shame and *fear.* Two ugly little words that continued to destroy a person long after the physical scars had begun to heal.

Being an unwilling audience member had left me nursing emotional scars that were still scabbing over.

Occasionally they still bled.

"Mummy, can I have more milk, please?" Henry said.

I snapped out of my reverie and bustled around the kitchen—tired, but happy and content. I'd been dealt a rough hand, but I didn't like to linger in the past. It wasn't healthy and it can be a hell of a place to fritter away time that is better spent in the present. After all, compared to some kids out there my childhood had been a Disney film.

Still…

Our family history had awarded me a legacy of too many flaws to count. While I laughed off my little eccentricities, what most people didn't know was that they'd been cultured and grown like a bacterium under a microscope throughout my childhood.

The infection was still raging.

"Darcy! Have you seen my phone?" Harry bellowed from upstairs.

Different morning, same slapstick routine.

We used to savour our hot lattes in the morning while discussing the world at large. Now we foraged through laundry baskets, hunted down missing socks, swallowed lukewarm instant coffee, and ate breakfast in a standing position because sitting down to eat in the morning was a luxury of time that we didn't have.

Harry's thumping about upstairs on a pointless quest for his missing phone and the kids in a full-blown yelling match edged me towards a strip of migraine relievers. I downed one tablet with a slug of diet whatever and breathed, gazing around my cosy kitchen. It rewarded me with instant calm.

My safe place. My happy place.

I could have said I'd earned the right to call the house my own through grit and determination, but I'd have been lying. I hadn't scrambled my way up a thousand corporate ladders and scrimped and saved—I'd inherited it.

Eight weeks after finding out I was expecting Georgie, my great auntie Annabelle had passed away. Her death left me devastated. Then I'd discovered she'd left me her house...her last act of pure kindness. She'd done her best to protect us during my dad's darkest episodes when my mum knew she might not survive the night. That's when the three of us would land on Annabelle's doorstep, seeking shelter.

It had been more than a home to my mum, brother and I; it had been a place where we could breathe.

All grown up, I'd returned the favour by doing everything I could to protect Annabelle when dementia had wrapped its cruel fingers around her brain.

"Mummy, are you sure zombies aren't real? I mean, they have zombies in *Minecraft*."

I didn't have time to dwell in my dark place, so I shook off my memories like raindrops and crammed lunchboxes into school bags.

A trail of soggy cereal almost took my feet out from under me. The kids bickered as they left the room, affording me the luxury of a few mumbled obscenities at my clumsiness as I wiped up the mess.

Clumsiness was woven into the very fibre of my being...but at least I'd made peace with it.

"Now where did I put my phone?" Harry asked no one in particular. He landed a quick peck on my cheek and ruffled my hair until it flopped over my eyes.

He strode to the other side of the room and struck up a conversation with the home smart device. At least she'd answered him. The robotic voice drove me nuts, but I'd learned to tune her out. Unless she could make coffee or get the hoover out, she was of no use to me.

If my metabolism was giving me the middle finger—eating Doritos straight from the bag and having two kids will do that—Harry's was giving him the thumbs-up. Being six-foot-four, running daily and playing football will do that.

Harry's walnut-brown hair was thick and permanently tousled, which afforded him a casual aloofness that I secretly adored. A few flecks of grey had begun to appear, but rather than age him it blended perfectly with the crinkles around his bright-blue eyes. Although five years older than me, he looked younger. And it took him less than three minutes to get dressed in the morning. Damned irritating didn't come close.

"Who's dropping the kids at school this morning?"

"Dammit. You, please. I have to pop over to Elle Bradshaw's," I said, trying to recall where I'd stashed the draft minutes to the previous meeting from hell.

Harry splashed coffee into a cup, then glanced at the residue of the cereal on the floor. "Why do you let yourself get roped into these things? I mean, committees and fundraisers? Really? Not your style, Darcy. Elle is a nightmare—I don't know how you can stand her."

I rolled my eyes and shrugged. "I can't, but I promised to help Jackie McPherson with these minutes. You know she's terrified of Elle and according to her it's a torturous nightmare every time she sits in a meeting with Cedarwood's queen bee. She's my friend, Harry, and I don't want to let her down. If I don't get them to Elle this morning, I'll never hear the end of it, and I'm not starting my day off in a dust-up with Elle. I might just kill her."

Elle bloody Bradshaw. We all knew the type—spoilt lady of leisure who believed the gleaming silver spoon in her mouth made her DNA shine that little bit brighter. Yet here I was about to hand-deliver minutes of a meeting I didn't care about.

Idiot.

Harry sighed. "Just don't come home with a dossier of work to do for her."

A whiff of burning toast infiltrated my nostrils. Rather than snapping back a witty retort, I checked the toaster wasn't about to explode.

"I have a meeting at half ten with Richard Bradshaw, so I can't stay at Elle's for more than five minutes anyway. Surely even she can't rope me into some community nonsense in five minutes."

Harry found his phone underneath a tea towel. "A meeting with Ted Bundy? What about?"

"Harry! Will you stop calling him that?"

Richard Bradshaw was Elle's brother-in-law. Our local handsome narcissist who treated women like disposable toilet wipes. The kind of guy with enough charm that you just knew when the door closed behind you the mask would slip—and you'd have nowhere to run to. I knew this from whispers shared between some of the local ladies over a glass of wine at the local pub, but I'd figured out Richard all on my own from meeting him several times.

I liked to think I can spot malignant charm a mile off—it might have been the one gift that my dad, the sociopath behind closed doors, had given me. After all, I had watched him consistently fool everyone over the years with his good looks, erudite persona, and flamboyant charisma.

Until the last person had left the party.

Until the door locked.

That's when my dad's mask would come off and get tucked away until he needed it again and my mum would prepare herself for another battle.

Richard was one of the most sought-after bachelors in town. I never understood that, but sometimes a handsome face, plenty of cash and good sex is enough to ignore blazing red flags and disregard gut intuition. He usually paraded a different woman on his arm every week. His little black book was full, and he had more friends that I could ever accumulate.

So maybe my amateur psych evaluation was way off?

But I doubted it.

"Richard is Bob's client. Nothing to do with me usually, but Bob's been out of the office what with Grace, his mother-in-law, being in hospital. They think she's close to the end."

A familiar lump rose in my throat.

Don't start.

"No clue what it's about but I'll just be taking instructions. I doubt Richard thinks I can count past five."

"So, what time do you think you'll be home?" Harry asked, cramming a slice of burnt toast into his mouth. "I have to pop into the office for a couple of hours, so I'll not get back until after four."

Harry split his IT consultancy work between Glasgow and home, which allowed him to help with the kids. It also allowed him not to get under my feet on my days at home.

That alone was priceless.

I dropped a kiss on the top of Georgie's head and told Harry I'd be home after five o'clock. Eyeing the French press longingly, I knew I didn't have time for more than a cup of instant. As I waited for the kettle, I savoured the view of my garden—a carpet of fiery red and burnished bronze, the trees practically stripped bare following last night's storm.

My favourite time of year. Shed everything, let go and look forward. Rolling hills embraced our little village like Mother Nature's protective arm.

"Darcy! Are you listening? Who's picking up the kids after school?"

The toast had disappeared, and crumbs littered the floor. My patience began to fade. "My—eh, I mean, Isla." Tears gathered behind my eyes, and I released a breath. It felt like a punch to the gut.

My mum.

She'd been gone ten months, but it was still raw. A wound I wasn't sure would ever heal.

Like dominos waiting to be toppled, the second Harry and I had made the decision to move to Cedarwood everything had fallen into place. I'd nailed a position as a dispute resolution lawyer in the litigation department of a local law firm. With the end of my city career at Richardson Summer and one leg down the corporate ladder, gone was my anxiety about every motion lodged, every writ signed off and every billable hour. One month later, my mum moved close by. Finally emancipated, finally separated from my dad. She, too, had made it to safety, and I could breathe.

But of course, all good things must come to an end.

And it hurt like hell.

Harry nodded. A flash of empathy passed over his face as he shuttled the kids out. "Shoes on, jackets on and line up at the door."

I rolled my neck and squared my shoulders.

Get it together, Darcy.

"Martin McAllister just texted me," Harry yelled from the door. "Hurry up Darcy, let's hustle! Martin said not to take Oak Bridge Road. Two trees came down last night in the storm and it's a mess."

I found the minutes and stuffed them into my new chocolate-brown tote. They were crumpled, meaning Elle would look down her perfect patrician nose at me in disapproval. Screw her! She'd be lucky if I didn't beat her over the head with them.

Halfway down the driveway, I felt a nudge against my ankles, and I steadied myself from falling flat on my face. *Another lost soul.* Our adopted cat Indy had appeared one bitter winter afternoon a year earlier, bedraggled and painfully thin. A decent diet and a bucketload of love were all she'd needed to plump her up in no time. The kids had named her after one of the coolest guys to ever walk the earth, Dr Indiana Jones. I'd made sure to sit them in front of *Raiders of the Lost Ark*—no way in hell was I calling the cat Sparkle.

I fed her and scooted back to the car, now out of breath, covered in cat hair and wearing the alluring scent of mackerel—perfect for a meeting with Elle Bradshaw.

Five minutes later—though it felt like five hours—Harry dropped me at my destination on Mapleway Road: Everbrook. Elle's house had a name. Of course it did.

I braced myself for the meeting ahead, but I knew I had a ten-minute walk into the office afterwards to calm myself down.

It was all good.

Birds twittered, grey squirrels ran amok, a huge ginger cat strolled towards a red sandstone house with ears twitching, and my shoulders relaxed as I breathed in the fresh morning air.

And then a gleaming white Range Rover sped by, spraying me with freezing muddy rainwater.

"Bloody hell!" I stared heavenwards, looking for divine intervention.

Of course, there was none.

Miserable, shivering and covered in dirty rainwater, I should have taken it as a sign.

Even the most ordinary of mornings can turn to hell in a heartbeat.

CHAPTER TWO

"**D**ARCY! DARCY!"

I turned so fast I wobbled on my heels. Seconds before, the tree-lined street had been deserted; all the movers and shakers were already on their way into the city. The remaining residents, those fortunate enough not to be bound to the daily rigours of work, were either snoozing, sipping espressos, watching the news, or preparing for yoga classes.

Maddie Clement. Where the hell had she sprung from? We were great friends, but she was a chatterbox, and I was already leaking time.

"Maddie! Good to see you."

She drew me in for a full embrace and I stifled a sneeze—far too many bursts of Chanel Coco Noir.

"Are you skipping work, you naughty girl?" Maddie said, her New York accent lyrical to my ears. "How's that handsome hubby and the little ones?"

The words were the right ones but the inflection wooden, her vibe jittery. Something was off.

"All fine. How's Dave?"

"Oh, you know Dave, never out of his scrubs." She waved her hand, dismissing my question. "Anyway, what are you doing over here at this ungodly hour?" She stared towards the entrance of Everbrook.

Smirking, I cocked my head towards the house. "On my way to see Elle. I've been summoned."

Something flickered over Maddie's face – fear, or anger, I wasn't sure which. It was so fleeting I thought I'd imagined it.

"What are you doing out this morning?" I asked.

"Oh, just out for a stroll, bit of exercise, adjusting my zen, you know…"

Bullshit.

She wasn't in her usual tight running clothes. I'd often see her racing through the village, long legs, earbuds in, ponytail swinging like a pendulum. While even the beautiful people had to work at it sometimes, they probably didn't do it in five-inch knee-high tan leather boots and a camel belted cashmere coat. Who even strolled at nine in the morning dressed like that? Not me. I wanted to rip the beautiful coat from her body and stuff it in my tote, but I remembered the task at hand and stuffed away my fantasy instead.

"Maddie, I couldn't pull that outfit together this early in the morning if you had a gun to my head. Girl, you look good!"

She was an American beauty with huge shining green eyes framed by a mane of glossy raven hair. Crosby, Stills and Nash's *Guinnevere* played in my mind when she was near. The lilting music matched her slender, graceful movements and the lyrics fit her classic features. Beside her, I felt like a gargoyle. Those familiar insecurities had a habit of visiting like an old friend, and sometimes they'd settle in for a spell. But that was all on me.

Only a few years older than my ripe old age of thirty-seven, Maddie managed to look like she'd been dressing herself in couture since birth. Her make-up was flawless—naturally. Just-so highlighter glistened along the planes of her high cheekbones, subtle bronzer contoured the hollow of her cheeks and rosebud-pink gloss sparkled on her full lips—sultry but fresh. I'd have killed to look that good at any time of the day never mind this side of breakfast.

"Maybe I just have too much time on my hands these days, Darcy. I'm all dressed up with nowhere to go."

What? I peered a little closer. No doubt about it, Maddie looked…I wasn't sure. Troubled? Melancholy?

"Is everything alright?"

"Oh, don't mind me. What's that saying? Idle hands?" She blew a sigh from her glossed lips, not quite as put together anymore. "I don't know, I'm at a little crossroads right now. Need to make some changes. I miss my old job. Darcy, I was born to create, to illustrate. Not sit at home fluffing damn pillows all day. But look, you don't have time for this right now. Let's have a glass of vino later and you can counsel me."

"Is it Dave?" I hated my abruptness, but I had to know if my friend's marriage was going down the toilet.

"No, he's fine. We're fine." Her laugh evaporated into the cold morning air and my shoulders eased a little.

I was torn between reaching for Maddie's hand and telling her I would help with whatever was bugging her and getting to Elle's. I made a production of looking at my watch. "Well, I'd love to chat Maddie, honestly, I would, but I've got to hustle; need to catch Elle then get my backside into the office. But let's have that drink later when we can chat properly. Promise?"

"You know, I think I'll come with you, have a catch-up. What is it you lot say? Have a blether."

Wait, what? Maddie could barely tolerate Elle's company for a second longer than I could. This little pantomime was getting weird, and I felt a pinch of unease. I had no idea why, but, the feeling was there, nonetheless.

Maddie chattered as we walked through Elle's wrought-iron gate. I tuned her out because I'd landed in Elle's garden without an interrogation. *Huh.* The gate was open. No intercom required. Usually visitors were buzzed in, or Elle greeted you at the gate. She'd once told me she closed the gate every night at eight unless she was entertaining.

Given our arrangement, perhaps she'd opened it for my arrival. *Lucky me.*

I trudged toward the house like a prisoner being dragged to the gallows.

Even in my depressed state, I couldn't help but marvel at the home—not quite Pemberley, but it was gorgeous. Bronzed sandstone, huge bay windows and a gleaming black door showcased the five-bed-room house. The manicured garden was the perfect cherry on top.

There were no kid's bikes, discarded hula hoops, deflated footballs or adopted stray cats with little pink food bowls littering this lush paradise.

A frantic barking erupted from somewhere to the left of me and a pang of dread bubbled in my stomach.

Pepper. Elle's dog. Alone.

I'd long since learned that I loathed the derailing of routine.

Where was Elle? Why was her gate open? Why was her dog running around outside? A heaviness settled across my chest. Maddie quit prattling.

"What's wrong?"

"Sounds like Pepper. He's out here somewhere. Can't you hear him? He's going nuts."

"I'm not deaf, Darcy. Of course I can hear him." Maddie pointed. "Look! Over there, by the trees. What's he doing outside?"

I squinted at the house.

No sign of Elle.

No sign of life.

I was torn. Part of me wanted to run, but I couldn't shake a perverse desire to find out if my fears were founded.

Move, idiot, move! Do something!

"Pepper! Pepper! Come here boy." Maddie slapped her hands against her thighs. Pepper ran across to her, still barking and dancing in circles.

Imprinted deep into the golden copper fur on his right hind leg was the tread of the boot print. The hot flash of anger came first. Then the crawling fear. *Blood.* On his front paws. I couldn't stomach cruelty, but fear won the battle. For now. I wasn't ready to move nearer to the door just yet.

Coward.

I leant into the dog and laid long reassuring strokes over his coarse head. "Shh, Pepper, it's alright."

Ears pricked, his head moved between us and the house, telling us a secret.

I straightened. "Maddie! Look! Pepper's got blood on him. Shit! Do you think Elle's alright?"

She blinked three time in a row, like a nervous tic. "Darcy, why do you always panic? Everything's fine. Chill out, you'll have a stroke before you hit forty!"

Pepper raced ahead.

We landed at the front door.

It was ajar.

Time to panic.

Inhaling a deep breath, I nudged the door open.

Table lamps emitted a soft but eerie glow across the oak floor. *Shit. Why were they still on?*

Scanning the hallway, I felt her presence before I saw her, and froze.

"Elle!" Her name escaped my lips in a sob.

It was futile. The black liquid oozing from her head told me so. It wasn't just the blood—her bowels had emptied too. Her head lay at an agonisingly unnatural angle, her beautiful face front down on the cold floor. I was glad I couldn't see it; I didn't want to see the damage that had been done.

Hot bile filled my throat. I heard a gasp from behind me. Maddie. I'd forgotten she was there.

I knelt beside Elle.

I can't do this again. No more death.

I instantly felt ashamed.

Trying to chase the memories away, I shook my head, before they planted roots and stayed with me for the rest of the day. Because this wasn't about me—this was about Elle.

Blood had spattered the edge of several stairs and had drenched part of the wall; black, crimson, ghastly against the soft eggshell white. Elle must have struck almost every step on the way down.

I stared at the bloodied wall. My eyes widened, taking in each drop of blood, each spray, so out of place in such a beautiful home.

Feeling the tremble in my hand, I knew a hit of anxiety was coming for me.

The memory slammed into my brain, and I couldn't do much to stop it.

Six years old, barefoot, wiping sleep from my eyes and squirming against my bursting bladder, I crept into the bathroom where my mum was wiping her own blood from the wall.

'*Oh Darcy, silly mummy! I fell and bumped my head. Go back to bed, pet.*'

The sound of smashing plates erupted from our kitchen, and I banged the bathroom door shut. Drown out the noise, keep mum safe. *I could make it better. I* could make it all better if I cleaned everything up and then got to dad first. Stop him coming in for round two. Kneeling beside my mum, feeling the urgency to go to the toilet turn to a painful throb, I ignored the aching and scrubbed.

Stop this. Please not now. No time.

Cramming the memory away, I knew it would resurface later but I would cross that damned bridge when I came to it.

I breathed.

Fuck.

What must have been thirty seconds later, something else hit me— the floor was muddied with heavy boot prints. Not Elle's...these were far larger than her dainty feet.

Peering closer at Elle, I instantly regretted it. A dull-pink froth had dried around her mouth, like smeared lipstick. God, she'd have hated being found like this. Elle had craved perfection.

Closing my eyes I turned away, but I couldn't unsee it.

Elle, what happened?

"What should we do?" Maddie whispered.

Despite the bronzer, her skin looked jaundiced. She held her phone limply in her hand.

"Call an ambulance. And the police."

No response. I waited two beats.

"Maddie! Do you want me to call?"

"No, I'll call," she said somewhat mechanically. "She must have fallen."

"Maybe."

"But…oh, hello." She turned away from me to speak to the operator.

I studied the abstract mess of muddied prints on the hallway floor and felt the hairs on the back of my neck bristle. *Who had been in here?* Drying mud clung to the gleaming stairs. Elle's shoes told a different story. There was not a hint of dirt; in fact, the soles were immaculate.

Bloodied prints left behind from Pepper were dotted all around Elle's head like a dark crimson halo.

Sounds erupted all around me.

Maddie talking to the emergency services.

The wind picking up outside.

Pepper whining and pushing his wet nose into Elle's hand.

All I wanted to do was put both hands over my ears and drown out the sound of heartache. I couldn't stand it.

Turning a full circle, I took everything in. Trying to memorise each detail. It was an old habit I couldn't shake—left over from the days of making sure nothing was ever left out of place or in the wrong order because that was bad. There would always be consequences, so my memory always had to be damn near perfect.

Oh. My. God.

Could someone else be in the house? Had someone else been hurt? Upstairs maybe? Elle lived alone, but my gut told me to check. I nudged open the living-room door and searched for Maddie.

And found her furiously rummaging through papers on top of Elle's side table.

What the…

"Maddie?"

She reared back as if I'd struck her with a cattle prod. Our eyes locked, and I knew that whatever came out of her mouth next would be a lie.

"Just looking for a tissue."

My bullshit radar pinged off the charts. No tears filled her beautiful green eyes.

Liar.

Turning my back on her so she wouldn't see my expression, I cuddled then coaxed Pepper into the kitchen with some kibble and shut him in.

The stairs.

Should I? Should I check upstairs?

Tick tock.

Climbing carefully, I froze midway. Spray and drops of blood and possibly body fluids were everywhere. My gag reflex began working overtime. My hand wavered as I reached to steady myself on the banister. *Don't touch.* I took one more step, my decision made. Treading meticulously, trying to avoid any potential evidence. Evidence? Was I jumping to conclusions as usual? I'd always had more than a passing interest in human behaviour. In psychology. In true crime. The reasons why I yearned to understand the bad things people do weren't hard to fathom.

But maybe I was seeing shadows that didn't exist. After all, the horror of seeing Elle's body up close and personal was causing my heart to thump at an alarming speed.

Mud, dirt, and leaves had been ground into the floor on the landing, screaming that a scuffle had taken place. *Shit, I really shouldn't be up here—why can't I leave things be?* If something bad had happened, I would be in a world of trouble for walking about upstairs. But I'd already made one bad decision, had already contaminated the scene, hadn't I? I was a lawyer for God's sake! Litigator yes, but I still knew better. What the hell was I thinking? Forward or backwards? I didn't know which way to go. I looked down at the hallway. Elle's crumpled form looked even worse from the vantage point of where I stood.

Move, Darcy.

I could feel my blood pulsing in my ears as I shifted between the various rooms, making sure to only look and not touch anything.

I entered what I assumed was Elle's bedroom.

Soft, feminine accents of lemon. Nothing out of place.

Except the photograph lying on the floor.

I picked it up. Without my reading glasses, it was difficult to see the subjects clearly, but Elle was the star of the show. The shot had been taken in a lush garden on a hot summer's day—the abundant rose bushes in the background told me so. One hand lay on her pregnant tummy, and although she was staring off into the distance, a little smile seemed to tug at her full lips. Someone stood behind her, slightly off camera, and another—possibly in a kneeling or crouching position—stared at the ground.

Squinting at the image, I tried to focus. Elle was beautiful. I imagined her mouth not quite so hard, her eyes not so cold. Had Elle been looking at that photo, reminiscing about her life, only to plunge down the stairs a second later?

Only Elle Bradshaw didn't seem the type to reminisce over old photographs.

I'd better get out of here.

I joined Maddie at the open front door and the cold October wind bit at my face.

"Should we call anyone?" she said.

It dawned on me then how little I really knew about Elle. Charles Bradshaw, Elle's husband, had died a little over two years ago. Her only son, the remarkably accomplished Cole, was currently making a ton of cash somewhere across the globe. I knew this because Elle had told me so, repeatedly. What was strange was that I couldn't recall him ever visiting. The local gossip had gone into overdrive when Cole hadn't manifested at his dad's funeral.

Her relationship with Richard was fragile at best, fractured at worst. And then there was Jonathan Mitchell, Cedarwood's local minister. Perhaps Elle's one true friend.

"Jonathan will know. I'll call him later," I said.

There'd be the usual suspects—a ton of ladies who lunch. Elle would have had them on speed dial, but I wasn't touching that with a bargepole.

And then I remembered—I was due to meet with Richard Bradshaw in less than an hour. *Damn.* I called Laura at the office and explained what had happened.

"Tell him I'll reschedule, that I've been detained by an emergency. Whatever you do, don't mention Elle."

Laura was a gossip, and this was not the time for idle chatter. They might have been unable to stand each other but it wouldn't be right for Richard to hear about Elle's death from a receptionist at our office. Better it came from the boss. Or the police.

"And give Bob a buzz, too. Elle was his client for years, but he knew her on a personal level. He'll be at the hospital."

"Will do, Darcy." She sounded a little breathless, perhaps excited, as if she couldn't wait to get off the phone and indulge herself in being the bearer of news, bad or otherwise.

Maddie stared off into the distance. "I can't believe it. Poor Elle."

All the right words had come from her lips, but her expression? I swear I saw relief.

CHAPTER THREE

"**S**HE'S IN HERE," I said to the paramedic. "We found her about ten minutes ago. There isn't anything you can do, is there?"

Of course, there wasn't. I was already welcoming the grief with open arms.

Several beats passed and the paramedic stood. "I'm sorry, she's gone. Why don't you take a seat in the living room while we wait for the police?"

Once more I found Maddie rummaging, this time through a drawer in the sideboard.

She spun around and slid the drawer closed. "Er, I was just looking for an address book or something with numbers in it. I couldn't see Elle's cell phone anywhere."

Two damn lies in the past twenty minutes. *Why?* But I couldn't muster a shred of energy to argue with her.

"Maybe her phone is in the kitchen," I said. "I don't want to open the door and let Pepper out until the paramedics are finished."

Pepper's whining and incessant barking had reached a distressing crescendo, but I couldn't risk him bolting. Instead, I eyed the couch and considered falling face first onto it. Finding Elle had brought a wave of unwanted memories back to me with such clarity I wanted to rip my hair out.

Three years earlier, just before Christmas, rather than opening the presents while visiting my dad, we'd argued. Ugly and desperate. He'd already begun drinking before I'd arrived. As I always did, I wondered what the hell I was doing there in the first place. It was a hopeless task, but I tried. Pathetic perhaps, but I'd always yearned to make everything *right*. Whatever the hell that meant. Lord knows I'd hoped the years had mellowed him.

Bickering spun to arguing. Rewriting history will do that to a family. It becomes just like every other lie people tell themselves every day—*I am happy. I love my wife. I could never cheat on my husband…it wasn't my fault.*

The same old script, one that started with pleasantries. Add one drink, dig into the past. Second drink, the truth began to warp. Third drink, the warp became an ugly lie that pinned the blame on my mum, my brother, me or even the postman—anyone would do.

Twenty minutes into the argument and the fourth or fifth double measure, a massive stroke had taken him right in front of my eyes. Funny how people seem so large in life and yet so small in death. That's the thought that had struck me as I'd tried to cover him with a blanket while waiting for the authorities. What if we hadn't argued? Would it have made a difference? Another cross to bear. Another burden to shove in my already-full bag.

"Darcy! You look like you're going to throw up!"

But Maddie's concerns weren't enough to drag me back to the present quite yet. Emotional turmoil had become my default setting from the split second I'd tightened my hands around my mum's the day she'd received her terminal diagnosis of ovarian cancer to the minute she'd taken her last breath. I'd been grieving for her whilst she was still with me. I'd found watching her fade away in front of my eyes to be the cruellest punishment. Calling that memory painful woefully underplayed the hurt.

My mum, my best friend, my biggest cheerleader, and my confidant had gone. I missed her every day since and still wrapped guilt around myself like an unwanted blanket. *Why couldn't I save her?* Long ago, I'd stepped into the role of her protector, but I couldn't save her when she most needed it.

Self-flagellation had become my favourite pastime. When you lose someone close, the void remains black. You can try and stuff as many rainbows in there as you want, but the light never shines through. The godawful truth? You must find a way to live with it— simple as that.

The landline rang, snapping me out of my dark meanderings. Shaking off the past, I answered.

"This is Elle's phone."

"It's Cat. Cat Henderson. I'm next door at Sandhill. What's going on? Who am I speaking to? I saw the ambulance. Is Elle alright?"

Cat Henderson. Damn. It would be all over the village before lunch. Too many questions to sort through. Did she really care if Elle was alright? Or just want in on the action? I figured it was the toss of a coin. I also wondered why everyone on this road referred to their house by name.

"Hello, are you there?" Her shrill voice was jarring to my ears, and I wanted to reach through the phone and throttle her.

"Cat, I'm sorry but there's been an accident and the authorities are here. I can't talk now."

"Darcy? Darcy Sinclair? Is that you? What the hell's happening?"

I hung up, massaged my temples and gave myself a full three seconds of steady breathing. A soft knock echoed from the hallway and a uniformed policeman entered the room followed by a forty-something year old man in a smart navy suit, light-blue shirt and navy tie. A tablet was tucked under his left arm.

We shook hands.

"Morning," the man in the suit said.

His voice was gentle, and my shoulders eased a little. I didn't recognise him which was strange. Cedarwood was a small enough village that most people knew each other, even if Harry and I were still considered relative newcomers. *No proper bloodlines.*

I introduced myself and Maddie.

"Dave Clement's wife?"

Maddie presented him with a heart-stopping smile. "Yep, that's me. Sorry, do I know you?"

Being a fellow Glaswegian, Maddie's husband Dave was one of my favourite people. Our favourite pastime was poking fun at several of the stuck-up locals.

Dave's orthopaedic clinic had a waiting list a mile long over at the university hospital and he ran a successful private practice specialising in sports injuries and rehabilitation. My brother, Adam, had thought him a God after he'd helped our football team's best striker back on his feet in the middle of the season after a particularly nasty ankle injury.

After guest lecturing at Columbia University one fall semester, he had returned with Maddie on his arm. Hot and heavy, fast and furious, caution was thrown to the wind, but I'd never seen Dave happier. Maddie had uprooted her entire life, marrying Dave ten months after she landed at Glasgow Airport.

Three years later and, oh my, the tongues were still wagging.

"Oh, I know Dave from the golf club. I'm Detective Inspector Reece McDonald, but please call me Reece."

My curiosity piqued. Why was a detective inspector attending a sudden death?

He was attractive, with thick, cropped sandy-blond hair and engaging, light-blue eyes that reminded me of someone I couldn't put my finger on. His demeanour relaxed me. Unusual from what I would have expected from an officer of the law. His sympathetic gaze told me he was going to listen very carefully to everything I was about to say. Faint lines around his eyes indicated he could smile a lot. The platinum wedding band glinting on his finger was highly polished, like he cared about it.

The uniformed officer standing next to him cleared his throat.

My twenty second psych evaluation told me this guy was pissed at the world, like smiling would be alien to him. Angry people in positions of power made me incredibly nervous and I itched to look anywhere other than straight at him.

With a deeply furrowed brow, he threw open his notebook. "Mrs Sinclair, Mrs Clement, I'm Sergeant Jim Burns."

His voice was deep and gruff, and instinctively I took a small step backwards. He had yet to make eye contact with us, and that bothered me. I eyed his tight uniform and neon vest stretching over the paunch of his stomach.

Jim took our names, addresses and contact details as we made ourselves somewhat comfortable.

"What relationship do you have to Mrs Bradshaw?"

Oh, God help me. "Friends?" It came out sounding like a question. Elle and I weren't friends, acquaintances yes, but not friends. He didn't have to know that though.

Maddie offered me a look of sympathy.

Jim raised a thick eyebrow. He had caught my slip.

Excellent start, Darcy.

"What time was it when you found Mrs Bradshaw?"

"Just before nine this morning," I said.

The officer checked his watch and continued to write. "And why did you come here this morning?"

The question hung in the air.

Jim looked at me with an intensity that made me wonder whether he was deciding whether to drag me off to a max-security black site for a good interrogation.

"Elle was expecting me at nine," I said. "I was dropping off the minutes of a meeting before I went into the office."

"Where do you work?"

"Anderson Jones. The law firm."

He threw a me a look as if I'd named a strip joint. *Okay, not a fan of civil lawyers then.*

"And what do you do there?"

"I'm a lawyer." The answer sounded sarcastic even to my ears. I didn't intend to piss him off, but my gut told me that I had. The air in the room felt a little tight.

He paused scribbling for two beats then resumed.

"Minutes?" The sergeant's brow furrowed deeper.

"Sorry, what?"

He sighed and repeated himself. Alright, so we were doing the whole dumb-chick routine.

Got it.

"From last Tuesday's committee meeting—a fundraising committee." A bizarre sound emitted from my lungs, and I chided myself for my perverse desire to laugh in uncomfortable situations.

"For what?"

Why did he need to know this?

The truth was I didn't want anyone to know about my dirty little secret, which was that I'd been at a fundraising committee to discuss the Cedarwood Christmas decorating project.

Hand to God.

Though I had been *coerced.*

"Did you not understand my question? I asked what the minutes related to."

A gleam of malice drifted across his face, like he was getting a weird kick out of this. My cheeks burned. Right there and then, I wanted to be anywhere else but sitting on Elle's sofa.

I blew air from my nostrils. "Well, Elle chaired the committee on how the village decorates the town square at Christmas. You know, the Six Village competition."

Villages and town squares? I was not a Stepford Wife. *This. Was. Not. Me.*

Every year the other five surrounding villages would compete to win first prize in the Six Village competition. Simply put, which village was best dressed for the holiday season. The first prize was nothing more than winning the title and a write up in the local papers, but it was intended to be an event that would bring communities together. *Festive family fun* was the super original tagline. Elle had worked for Cedarwood to win each year like an athlete would train for an Olympic gold medal, turning the meetings into a war council.

It was neither festive nor was it fun.

Jackie McPherson had cornered me last month, begging for my help with the set-up of the room and drafting of the damned minutes. Oh, how I'd wanted to tell her to get lost, but Jackie was a friend and tired of being terrorised by Elle. Given that Elle's favourite MO had been to subject her prey to humiliation in front of an audience, the odds of surviving the night unscathed had not been stacked in Jackie's favour, so she'd enlisted me as her backup.

Politics, small-village or otherwise, have been known to make me lose my cool—it wasn't pretty. My first foray into Elle's committee-led world just over five years ago hadn't exactly gone according to plan. I'd been the rebel with a damn good cause, suggesting we could support the nearest woman's refuge shelter. rather than squandering more funds on erecting another bizarre and abstract sculpture at the entrance to Chestnut Park. That outburst had cost me my potential political career in my new hometown, and Elle had blackballed me from any future gatherings.

Pity.

Still, I couldn't stand saying no to someone when they begged for my help, so I'd allowed Jackie to drag me into the Bradshaw Insurance boardroom, where Elle had held us hostage for the evening.

Oh my, it had been an eventful three hours. An aerial map had been set up, onto which Elle had proceeded to poke multicoloured pins and flags from her position at the head of the table while she lectured us. It had been ridiculous, self-indulgent, and I'd loved every damned minute. Sarah Evans had fought Elle at every step, simply for the sake of it. Two so-called pillars of the committee had recreated a production of *Dangerous Liaisons* for all of us to see. There had been innuendos, raised eyebrows, side whispers and veiled threats. Consequently, I'd suffered a pang of disappointment when the finale to the evening had not involved both queen bees bitch-slapping each other over the conference table.

"Why didn't you just email the minutes?"

Jim clearly wasn't buying what I was selling.

"I already had, but there were so many corrections we had to meet to discuss them! Elle was meticulous about presentation and every word had to be verbatim. As she remembered it."

His mouth curled into a smug smile and my temper flared. *Shit.* Exactly where he wanted me.

"Are you related to Martha Burns?" Maddie asked suddenly.

I gawped at her.

"My mother," he replied tersely.

A lightbulb went on in my head. Easy to see that the rotten apple hadn't fallen far from the rotten tree. Martha Burns, gatekeeper to hell, stood guard at the library counter, shushing kids and swapping spiteful chatter with her cronies. Truth be told, Martha was a nasty piece of work.

Jim's beady eyes slid over to Reece then back to me. "How did you gain entry?"

"The door was open...well, ajar."

"Ajar?"

Wondering if I was speaking a different dialect, I faltered for a second. "Yes, it was ajar. And the gate was open. That was strange, but I dismissed it, thinking Elle had left it open for me."

Reece retreated into the hallway, and I could hear him moving about, checking the front door. He came back in, pulled at the blinds on the huge window, and studied the window frames.

Looking for points of entry? My history of true crime obsession told me so. A little shiver snaked up my spine.

"What about you, Mrs Clement? Why were you here this morning?"

About time someone asked her that.

I turned towards her to see if another lie would fall from her mouth. Maddie flicked her wrist, dismissing the question. "Oh, I was just out for morning walk and bumped into Darcy. Thought it would be nice to catch up with her and Elle. You know, just friends having a coffee together."

"Where were you this morning prior to meeting with Mrs Sinclair?"

"At home. I live just a few houses down. I was up at seven, said goodbye to my husband as he left for work, ate an egg white omelette and drank two expressos. Got dressed and left the house just prior to nine? Anything else you need to know?"

Maddie sounded pissed. Not her usual carefree self. What the hell was bugging her this morning?

"Where were you going?" Jim asked glancing up at her.

"Just out for a walk. Nothing nefarious."

The officer dragged his eyes up and down Maddie, perhaps wondering the same thing as I had. Very well dressed for a casual wander around the neighbourhood.

"Just out for a walk?" he parroted.

"Yes," she answered aggressively.

Silence hung in the air.

"I'm sorry. I've a splitting headache. This has been a hell of a shock."

"When was the last time you spoke with Mrs. Bradshaw?"

"Eh, well, I don't know. A few days ago, maybe? Why?"

Reece McDonald still hadn't uttered a word. He stared at Maddie in a way that made me think he hadn't believed one thing out of her mouth.

Neither had I.

CHAPTER FOUR

JIM TURNED HIS ATTENTION back to me. I told him about the mark on Pepper's leg and my suspicions that he'd been kicked. The officer couldn't have looked less interested, and that made me mad as hell.

Reece started typing on his tablet. The man still hadn't uttered a word.

My big mouth continued to flap as I recounted my observations of mud all over the floor and the ground-in leaves at the top of the stairs.

"Why did you go upstairs?" Jim snapped, his thick black eyebrows knitting together like he wanted to waterboard me.

My heart rate accelerated. "Sorry if I shouldn't have done that—I promise I didn't stand on anything. Honestly, I wanted to make sure no one else was hurt, and I was freaking out. I know Elle lived here alone, but…I just feel like something's happened here. The mud and leaves? It's weird. It looks someone came in from the garden wearing soaking-wet work boots. Elle would never have done that."

"Something happened here? Did it really? If you have information, Mrs Sinclair, now is the time to tell me. Otherwise, it's not really your job to speculate, is it?"

Reece cut Jim a sharp look, which appeased me a little.

Jim shifted in the chair. "Looks to me like Mrs Bradshaw took ill and fell down the stairs."

"I don't have any information," I said. "I've told you everything I know. But the front door wasn't locked, Pepper was running about in the garden and there's mud everywhere."

Jim sighed. "And?"

"Elle would never have made a mess like that, sometimes she even asked you to take your shoes off if it was a dry day let alone a wet one. Her shoes were spotless, so how did she track mud everywhere? Look at the size of the treads!"

Jim pinched the bridge of his nose and shot a look at Reece as if wondering whether he'd noticed the crazy in the room. "Her shoes? Why were you examining her shoes?"

"I wasn't *examining* her shoes!" My voice rose a few octaves.

Jim resumed the nose-pinching. "Go on."

"That's it. Maddie called the ambulance and we waited."

"Alright." He stood and made a production of stretching his legs. "Do you know who Mrs Bradshaw's GP is?"

"Sorry, no."

His radio crackled. He left the room and a sigh of relief escaped me.

"For what it's worth, you make a good point about the floor, Mrs Sinclair," Reece said softly.

I jumped at the sound of his voice. Jim Burns had sent my anxiety through the roof. *Damn him.*

"Last time I was here, I could have eaten my dinner off the floor," he said.

"Oh, I didn't realise you knew Elle."

A small smile played across his mouth. "Not well. Civic council meetings and the like. A few charity shindigs here with my boss. Mrs Bradshaw knew how to throw a party."

She certainly had. Elle had embraced the hostess role like a queen would a crown. She'd always catered, always served the best champagne, always invited just the right guests to her home. I'd never enjoyed myself once.

What would happen to Everbrook? Elle had loved the house, that much I did know. It was perhaps one of the few things she had loved.

A head popped around the door. Dr Phillip Mavers, or Dr Phil as his patients called him behind his back. I didn't know him that well, but the cloud of arrogance he carried was as unmistakable as an expensive aftershave.

"Hi all. Terrible news."

Real sincere.

He dipped his head towards the DI. "Got a minute, Reece?"

They left the room but stood just outside, close enough for me to earwig. I was on my feet in a heartbeat.

"I've administered a quick exam,' Mavers said, "but obviously can't sign off the death certificate until we get her over to the hospital. Given it was a sudden death we'll have to ask the family if they want a post-mortem or a view and tell. Either way I'm fine."

"Well, I'm not fine, Phil, not at all."

Mavers continued as if Reece hadn't spoken a word. "Looks to me like a simple fall. She's been my patient for years. Had an appointment only last month. Seemed perfectly fit and healthy. It's a hell of a surprise but that's the way it goes."

Rolling my eyes heavenwards, I thanked the universe that Dr Phil was not my GP.

"Why are you here anyway?" Mavers said. "Bit over the top, no?"

"The boss thought it might be good for me to be on the scene. Glad I am. A PM is a good idea, so I'll be requesting that."

"On what grounds?"

Mavers's clipped delivery told me he didn't appreciate Reece second guessing his one-minute examination of Elle's body.

"On the grounds that I say so. Phil, there are questions that need answering here, and you can't do that for me, can you?"

I loved this guy.

The silence stretched.

"Thought so," Reece said. "Look, this is going to end up on the procurator fiscal's desk, so I need one of their officers here now, before Mrs Bradshaw is moved. Tell me about her recent medical appointments."

"Not much to tell other than some menopausal issues and adjusting to HRT, which is common for her age. She wasn't on any other daily medication, but that'll have to be verified."

"How long do you think she's been lying there?"

"Twelve hours give or take."

"So last night?"

"That would be my best guess at this stage, yes."

Reece called out to Jim who I could hear moving around upstairs. "Sergeant, contact the PF office now so we start can working this together."

"But—"

"Then when you've done that, get the outside taped up and secured."

"Are you serious?"

"Do it now Jim and make it quick before anyone else walks through here."

The sound of a laboured sigh as he stomped away told me he was pissed at his orders.

"So Phil, any idea where the son might be?" Reece said. "Understand he's the next of kin."

"Cole? Haven't seen him in years, not since he was a kid. Heard he's done well for himself though, the prodigal son and all that."

Exhaustion crawled over me. Simon and Garfunkel's "Sound of Silence" had begun to loop in my head and my brain felt as if it was ready to implode. I needed the comfort of my own home, to cuddle my kids. *I wanted to talk to my mum.* This morning had burst open a barely healed wound and it was oozing everywhere.

Maddie stood. "Let me see if we can leave and I'll drive you home, Darcy. You can't go into the office; you look like crap."

"What about Pepper?" I couldn't stand another minute of hearing him so distressed. "You know what? I'm taking him."

I found Jim and told him. He had other plans.

"I'm contacting the SSPCA. They can deal with him. Not my job."

I almost stamped my foot like a child but reined myself in. "The hell you are. Detective McDonald, I need to speak with you, please."

Jim's beady eyes held mine as Reece appeared. I put forward my plea to take Pepper with me and the sergeant started with his rebuttals.

Reece held his hand up. "Not exactly protocol but we can ignore it this once, can't we, Jim? Poor chap's been through enough already. Could you find his leash? I can't have the witnesses touch anything further in the residence."

My smile faded as Jim settled into a staring match with me.

But still...round one to me.

***

I slipped on Pepper's leash and he strained against it, pulling towards Elle.

Maddie yelled from out front. The car was ready.

"Be at peace, Elle," I whispered, and Pepper released a mournful whine.

I needed to get the hell out of the house, which now felt like a mausoleum. We both did.

Reece talked into his phone as I coaxed Pepper into Maddie's car. I could just about make out his words.

"I need the techie and SOCO guys out here now. Scene's been secured, but we've already had two witnesses, the paramedics and a dog walking all over it, so the quicker the better."

This was serious. I fiddled with Pepper's leash, loitering so I could hear more.

"Don't know, sir. Something's off. I need every inch of the house photographed and the forensic guys to measure and cast the prints. If I'm right, I'll request a phone dump."

Jim came out of the building, scowling and rapping his notebook against his hand like the bad Sheriff in a TV movie. I wouldn't have been surprised if he'd practised the move in front of a mirror. On any other day I'd have belly laughed—but not today. Instead, I listened as the church bells tolled. Eleven chimes, each one more morose than the last.

Mourning, longing. Get a grip, Darcy.

This was no time to fall into a well of self-pity; if I did, I'd settle in and stay a spell.

Closing chapters of my past was crucial to my well – being in the present. Just as some words were better left unsaid, some memories were better left behind. After all, you can't seek answers from someone after they're gone. I'd made my peace—or a version of it—with my dad's failures to nurture, nourish, and protect. They say the cycle of abuse can continue; well, I was making damn sure it was laid to rest right alongside my dad. He'd let his inner demons consume him and, in the end, it's difficult for monsters to have loving family and friends.

I shook my head and walked up behind Maddie. She was typing so furiously on her phone she didn't notice me settle beside her. I glanced the message: *I'm almost home. Call me. It's about Elle. It's bad!*

She swiped the screen and I shuffled backwards and gazed everywhere but in her direction.

Who had she been messaging? Dave? No, that didn't feel right. We climbed into the car and she cooed at Pepper like a mother with her new-born.

"Are you good to take him? I would, but Dave's allergic to animal dander. And he can't go to that monster Richard."

The undercurrent of her words startled me. It hinted at intimate knowledge of Richard that I'd not known she had.

I was about to ask her what she'd meant but her phone rang. There was a tremble in her hand as she flipped it screen down. *Still ringing.*

Maddie Clement was either hiding something or feared something. *Take your pick.*

"Tonight's not the night for that drink. Maybe tomorrow?"

"Sure Maddie. But, uh, are you alright?"

"Alright? Of course I am," she answered. A little too high pitched. "Yes. No. God, I don't know Darcy." She thrummed her fingers on the steering wheel. "What a day, huh."

Rubbing my forehead, I hesitated. Stay or go? Pepper started to whine, and I had my answer.

"Take care, Mads. Call you later."

Back in my kitchen, I chugged back three paracetamols to ease my pounding headache.

My ghost-like reflection staring back at me from the mirror. Eyes sunken. Pale-red lips dry and cracked. I scrubbed at what was left of my make-up and let the tears fall until I felt raw.

Enough punishment for one day.

My hands trembled, so I sat on the edge of the chair, gripping the table to steady them. I hadn't felt anxiety like this since my mum had passed.

Chest heavy, angry all over again. Why had she died so young? Hadn't she been through enough in her life? It was so unfair; I couldn't stand it. She never had a chance to enjoy much of life before she was forced back into sickness and pain. I'd never quite made peace with it, but acceptance would have to do.

It's done, Darcy. That was then. This is now.

I couldn't change what had happened no matter how often I lingered in the past, but I could make a difference in the here and now.

After ten deep breaths, I forced my brain to go back through Elle's house from the second I'd walked in the door and mentally noted everything I'd seen. I visualised Maddie's face when I caught her raking through Elle's drawers, the marks at the top of the stairs...

Everything.

Clear as day.

Then I let every emotion I had been holding in for the last two hours escape from my body.

My hand wavered over my phone as I considered calling Harry. I needed to hear his voice.

Harry. He'd saved me in more ways than he'd ever know. They say every little girl dreams of her wedding day. It's not true—not when you believe you're already damaged goods. Not when you've witnessed your mum's head slammed into a wall because dinner was late. Not when your six-year-old self sits wide eyed and frightened in a cold and chaotic Accident and Emergency Department gripping her bedraggled teddy bear whilst her mum gets her latest head wound stitched and broken nose checked out.

Maybe the milk wasn't the right brand.

Maybe there wasn't enough bread left to make toast.

The reasons didn't matter anymore.

I'd had no intention of handing my life over to someone else, someone who might destroy who I was piece by little piece. But one night had changed that. Partying at a club, drunk as a skunk, mascara smeared halfway down my face and hair frizzing from the heat of the bodies crammed at the bar—that's the moment I'd met the love of my life. Not the greatest romance story ever told but it was my story to tell.

After seventeen years together, we still made a hell of a team. Harry practised mindfulness and meditation while I bellowed at the top of my lungs and spiked my blood pressure into the hypertension zone. I revelled in my childhood borne OCD and my temper could fly from zero to one hundred in a heartbeat. Harry, though, was always set at a slow burn.

Apparently, we have balance.

As he always did, Harry let me talk.

Let me bare my soul.

Made me feel better.

Eventually, I was all cried out, so I did what I'd been dreading all along; I called Jonathan and told him.

*****

Shit.

The hunter's fists rained down on the steering wheel. When that provided no relief, they pinched at the flesh on their arms, twisting and twisting until the beautiful pain began.

Ever so slowly, the rage began to dissipate.

Stupid, so stupid. Anger had undone the meticulous preparation. A post-mortem could smash that perfect plan into a thousand pieces.

They snatched a pocket-knife from the glove compartment, sliced the skin ever so slightly. Blood oozed from the tiny wounds. Euphoria coursed through every muscle. An intoxicating blend of arousal and the excitement of things to come...

CHAPTER FIVE

AGAINST MY BETTER JUDGEMENT, I answered the shrieking phone. "Ms Sinclair!" The words were delivered haughtily but with a hit of plain old nasty. "Richard Bradshaw here. Have you any idea how important my business is to Bob's firm? I don't appreciate being stood up at the last minute. I'm a busy man and I needed that meeting this morning."

He doesn't know.

"Mr Bradshaw, I'm terribly sorry about this morning but... I, I'm afraid I have some really bad news. You see, I was over at Elle's and—"

A sound came through the line. Contempt? Disgust?

"I know about Elle's death," he snapped. "Next time we have a scheduled meeting, please be there. I'll be contacting Bob, *your boss*, regarding this matter and rescheduling at my own convenience. Don't get too used to your office."

The line went dead before I could respond.

"Compassionate bastard."

I sent the phone skittering across the counter and reached for Pepper. Maddie hadn't lied when she'd said that the dog was safe with me and out of the hands of a borderline psychopath.

***

A cacophony erupted. Isla McAllister had arrived with my kids. Who'd just clamped eyes on Pepper. I chided myself for not anticipating this moment just as Henry threw himself on the floor and tried to roll underneath Pepper. The dog erupted into a volley of sharp but happy barks.

"That's enough kids!" My tone was a little sharper than I'd intended but my nerves were frayed.

The kids knew I wasn't messing about. So, it seemed, did Pepper. The dog and my son sat to attention on the floor, both squirming with excitement. Isla dropped the two backpacks, a look of sympathy on her face.

Georgie thrust her hand in the air, a habit she'd picked up from school. "Mum, is this our new dog? Can we keep him? What's his name?"

"Zombie! Can we call him Zombie?" Henry yelled.

I held my hand up like I was directing traffic. "Guys, this is Pepper."

"Sergeant Pepper?" Isla snarked behind me.

"Why is he called—"

"Henry, I'm still talking so you should be listening. Pepper's mum is in hospital...with a broken leg, so our job is to look after Pepper until he's ready to go home. We have to be gentle with him, and most importantly we have to be..."

Blank stares. I waited.

"Anybody?"

Georgie launched her hand into the air again. "We have to be kind!"

"Well done, Georgie! Yes, we have to be kind to Pepper." I clapped my hands together. *So proud.*

"What happened to his mum's leg? How did she break it?"

"That's not important right now, Henry."

"Did she trip over Pepper? Did her bone poke through her leg? Was there blood? Was it gross?"

"Henry, can we forget about the leg? So, as I said," I glared at my son "we must look after Pepper, be kind and make sure he's happy. Now, take him on a tour of the house. Then we can take him for a walk after dinner."

The squeals that followed made the moment feel like Christmas morning had arrived, and a rush of emotion overcame me. For the hundredth time, I wished I could freeze this single moment and smother myself in its comfort...but the kids thundered past me, whipping Pepper into a frenzy, and the magic was gone. Time had given me the middle finger once again.

"Well, you've just added another level of crazy to your life, but the dog is a cutie." Isla smirked and barrelled past me. "Latte?"

"Add a shot of tequila, will you?" I joked. "It's been a crappy day."

"What did Harry say about the dog? Was he cool with you dragging another stray home?"

"Bless him, Isla, he didn't mind at all. I called him as soon as I got home and cleaned myself up. He was pissed that they were going to dump the poor pup at the SSPCA. You know Harry, he's a softie."

"So, what on earth happened?"

I unburdened myself, and Isla blew a low whistle.

"Elle Bradshaw. Didn't see that one coming."

Recounting the events had left me chilled to the bone and I cradled my cup, savouring the warmth.

"The bottom of the stairs, huh? Jesus. I just can't get my head around it. For all the places in the world I thought she'd end up, dead at the bottom of her stairs was not one of them."

She stared somewhere past me.

"You knew her a long time, didn't you?"

"Did I ever! She was hard to like." Isla rubbed her forehead. "I'm sorry, it's just...I'm rattled. That news, it shocked me. After Robin, I get sensitive when I hear bad news, even if it's concerning someone I can't stand."

Isla rested a large hand on my arm and squeezed. "Finding her the way you did would've been a shock for anyone, Darcy, but you're still in the thick of grieving. Want to talk about it?"

Her blue eyes searched my face for an answer but the one I delivered wasn't truthful—far from it—but I didn't want to drag her down memory lane any more than she wanted to meander there herself. Isla had suffered enough heartache to last two lifetimes.

Four years ago, she and Martin had received the knock on the door that must be any parent's worst nightmare. The one that can only bring pain and destruction. The one that will change everything forever. Robin—their daughter—her husband, Thomas, and three-year-old Hope had been involved in a fatal two-car crash on the M6. Only Hope had survived.

Six weeks later, Isla was still trapped in a dark and desperate grief. One night, when Isla was three quarters of the way through a bottle of gin, Hope had awoken to another nightmare. Isla had managed to get the little girl back to bed, but something in her had changed. She'd gone to the bathroom and vomited, held her face in freezing-cold water until she could stand it no longer, and then chucked the last of the gin down the drain.

Done.

"I didn't have a problem with alcohol, Darcy. I had a problem with grief," she'd told me.

And at forty-three, she'd quit her journalism career to become a full-time guardian to Hope. Four years on, she'd transitioned the little girl into a confident, funny kid who surely had all the love in the world she'd ever need.

"You're not telling me everything, Darcy. Spill it." Her eyebrow arched.

"Jesus, go join the Spanish Inquisition, Isla."

"I would but I'm not that damn old. I could always tell when Robin was holding back on me, so tell me what's up before I ground you for a month."

A lump formed in the back of my throat. Isla had been there for me while I'd navigated the pain of my mum's terminal illness, and I loved her dearly for it. Just less than a decade older than me, she regularly showered me with motherly advice. She was big too; quarterback big, which for some reason always made me feel safe. And she was as funny as hell, cunning as a fox, and smart as a whip. Which is why she'd seen through my façade.

"I think someone was in the house with Elle last night. I think there was a struggle. I think that's how she ended up dead at the bottom of the stairs."

Silence.

"I'm not losing it, Isla. That's what I think."

Isla blinked. "Alright, let me ask you this. Why?"

I knew my audience. Isla always wanted the facts. I kept it short and sweet.

"And here we are."

"Here we are indeed." Isla stretched her legs and chewed her bottom lip. "I swear, I really don't get a kick out of speaking ill of the dead, but, well, Elle Bradshaw was a bitch. Let's not dress it up. She was an awful human being. Can I see someone *wanting* to pop her one? Absolutely? But murder? Here?"

She let the question hang. The enormity of it seemed to suck the oxygen out of the room.

Cedarwood was so different from my own childhood home. Harry knew I'd been running from my past and from the desolate and deprived street I'd grown up on. Poverty, drugs, alcohol—take your pick, I'd been surrounded by them all. One can destroy a community; all three can be a death sentence. Over time, the houses I'd played in had been boarded up, windows and brick walls covered with meaningless scrawls. Familiar faces had been replaced by the haunted vacant stare of the drug addled. Neighbours replaced by alcohol-ravished bodies with just a hint of rage simmering underneath. Before I'd hit puberty, I knew where my future could lead me—down the dark, dead-end path of leaving school early, what was left of my self-confidence dragging behind me, marrying a monster I barely knew who'd use me as a punching bag when he needed a little ego boost.

"Crack your books open, Darcy," my mum had told me.

And I had.

One law degree (and a husband and two kids later) and here I was. *On another planet.*

Cedarwood was an old-money neighbourhood. Ugly though that might be, it was the truth. Houses had been passed down the generations, and that's the way the locals liked it, thank you very much. It was only once long-time residents had been carted off to their final resting places that riffraff like me were able to infiltrate the village.

Old oak trees lined every immaculate pavement edging its winding roads. Long driveways rambled up to large traditional red-brick houses. The ruddy sandstone of the elegant parish church gleamed in the sunlight, and the soaring steeple watched over those who'd been laid to rest in the small cemetery.

Adjacent to the church sat the primary school where my kids were enrolled. The structure might have been a gingerbread house in another time, plucked straight out of a fairy tale, complete with a manicured lawn as lush and smooth as a bowling green. And, of course, the shiny cherry on top was the Cedarwood Country Club. I'd thought country clubs only existed in towns where debutantes twirled in their pretty gowns.

Silly me.

I rubbed my aching forehead. The squealing, yips and barks coming from upstairs had reached a crescendo.

"Evil lives everywhere, Darcy, even in places with fancy houses and manicured lawns. Sometimes, especially there. So let me give you a little history lesson." She gazed out of the window. "I bet you didn't know that my Martin dated Elle briefly...years ago, before I knew him. He told me she had every guy in the village following her around like a puppy dog, desperate for her attention. She'd stare at you like she wanted you, even needed you, but of course it didn't take Martin long to realise she wasn't really looking at him at all. She was staring right through him—a real piece of work. We were invited to her wedding, you know. It was a beautiful day. Stunning location, the bride stole the show, of course, but she seemed so...disinterested. I can't explain it."

She thrummed her fingers on the table and I urged her to continue.

"Well, I don't recall her ever holding Charles's hand, or smiling...
with her eyes, I mean. It was all just a show, a big, pretty, expensive
show. Fast forward two years we were invited to the club to celebrate
her second wedding anniversary. I was bored stiff, begged Martin to
leave early. We were both buzzed, it was a beautiful summer's night,
and I didn't want to waste it celebrating a fake marriage. So, there
we were, staggering about the car park, laughing and fooling around,
and then we saw her. Elle was passed-out drunk at the wheel of her
friend's car, one six-inch heel lying on the ground of the country club
carpark, driver door lying wide open. I'll never forget it."

I released a low whistle. "Go on."

"Ten minutes to shake her awake, five more to get a coherent
sentence out of her. Long story short, Elle hated her marriage, and
she was pregnant. We took her back inside to one of the staff rooms
and plied her with coffee, then Martin found Charles and he drove
her home. I made up some story about Elle feeling ill. When the
tongues started wagging the following week, she told everyone it was
morning sickness. Naturally, she collected sympathy like handbags.
And that was that. She went on to deliver Cole and, well, let's just
say I never got the feeling that motherhood came naturally to her.
Not exactly Mommy Dearest, but I always felt a lot of sympathy for
her kid. Not that anyone's seen him for years. She packed him off to
some posh boarding school up north as soon as he was off the sippy
cup. Never really saw him again. A damn shame is what it was." She
leaned back and titled her head. "So, you see, I have a little history
with Elle. Not exactly in her inner circle but I knew enough to back
the hell away."

Well, my God.

"So," Isla said, "whoever trailed mud in from the storm last night
wasn't wearing a size-three peep-toe."

"Exactly. Granted the treads were smudged, but they looked like
a print from a working boot or something similar."

I wondered what forensics would make of the accidental

characteristics—in the case of footwear these were physical characteristics of a sole resulting from the wearer's gait and movements.
They'd be looking for unique wear patterns as well as material caught
in the sole that could create a unique impression. *Like a fingerprint.*
The true crime documentaries I'd watched had taught me a thing
or two.

"Then again," I said, "maybe she simply had a friend over last night
and, like the rest of us lazy arses, decided to wait until the morning
to clean the floor. Then she had a heart attack, or she slipped. Maybe
I'm beginning to sound like a nutcase."

Isla smirked. "First of all, I doubt Elle ever cleaned her own house
in her life. Second, what did your mum teach you?"

"How to be a smart arse?"

"To always trust your gut instinct. Stop second guessing yourself.
Have a good long think about what you saw this morning and write
everything down. Everything. I always find that little trick useful." She
stood and reached for her coat. "As sick as it is, if anything sinister did
happen to Elle, it would be the most exciting thing to happen here
since Cat Henderson fell down pissed up at the club last Christmas.
Hand to God, the whole side boob was on show. That was a doozy."
She snorted and grinned.

"Damn, I missed that."

"All kidding aside, Darcy, if anyone did hurt Elle then I'll bet you
it's close to home. You mark my words."

"You think it's possible?"

"Christ! Don't be naive! Of course, it's possible. Like I said, don't
be fooled by the pretty houses with the pretty people living in them,
there's darkness all around us. Now write everything down and we'll
speak tomorrow. It's way past Hope's dinner time."

She charged past me and out the door before I could reply.

I went to the window. The gnarled tree branches were naked and
raw, stripped completely of their halo of brightly blushed leaves.

What happened to you Elle? Who was watching when you fell?

And then Isla's ominous words played over, and my breath caught a little...*evil lives everywhere.*

***

Tired and despondent, Jonathan swallowed most of our couch that evening. A bear of a man, at almost six foot three he'd have made an imposing figure if it hadn't been for his lopsided grin and the smile in his eyes.

Harry placed a bottle of Ardbeg malt and a glass on the table. "Neat or with ice?"

"I'll pour, thanks."

And he did. Three fingers. *Shit.*

He tugged at his silver hair. "The police are still there. Isn't that a little weird? Something's off."

I stole a glance at my own empty glass. Would it be unseemly to be half in the bag when the minister was sitting on my sofa? My own selfish needs won over social politeness, and I asked Harry for a small refill.

"I can't know for sure," I said, "but I have a weird feeling."

"What do you mean, weird?"

Me and my stupid, big fat mouth. I wished I could take the words and stuff them back down my throat. Jonathan had paled and Harry shot me a death stare.

"You can't be suggesting that..." He stared somewhere past me. "But Elle's been, I don't know, different these past few weeks. Jittery. Not herself. I can't put my finger on it. Tell me exactly what happened. What did you see there?"

Against my better judgement, I told him the truth as I saw it.

"Thing is," Jonathan said, "Elle, was...different. Like every guy in town, back in the day I followed her about, begging for her attention—so many years ago now. It makes me laugh to think about it. Sally and I could never have children...that devastated Sally and almost destroyed us. So, when Elle gave birth to Cole, Sally was only too happy to babysit. But it turned into something more than that. Elle began to drop him off almost every day. She was just so distant, so self-absorbed, she didn't care much about anything else. She'd say she needed a break and Sally would snap back, 'You need to do a day's work to need a break.' Charles never left the office and I have no idea how Elle filled her days, but it certainly wasn't mothering Cole. For the first two years of Cole's life, it was pretty much the three of us. We loved that boy. But then, once he became a toddler, he turned sullen, and the tantrums were something else. So spoiled. You see, the cycle continues, doesn't it? And that was that. He was soon off up north, and we never really saw him again after that. Broke Sally's heart. Even when he came home for the holidays he never visited, never left his parents' house."

My heart ached for Jonathan in that moment. He seemed a little defeated after unburdening himself.

"Was Cole close to Elle later in his life?"

I already knew the answer but was interested in Jonathan's perspective.

"No, never close. She chose to portray him as the prodigal son—he had perspicacity, the ability to make everything he touched glitter with gold. What people didn't know is that Cole loathed his parents. Or at the very least had no interest in them."

Jonathan continued. By using illusion and misdirection, Elle had crafted a lie big enough to explain why Cole hadn't attended his own father's funeral. How she'd vowed never to forgive him. How, as with all unattended wounds, their relationship had quickly blistered and turned poisonous.

And now she was dead.

***

I shut the door behind Jonathan once he'd taken his leave and turned to Harry.

"What did you give me that look for?" I whispered.

"What look? And why are we whispering?"

"The death stare you threw me when I told Jonathan about what I saw at the house."

Harry failed to hide his smirk. "Are you kidding me? You are so weird. Did you see his face? You nearly gave the guy a heart attack. Dead bodies, howling dogs, footprints in the mud. Really?"

"You're making it sound like an episode of *Scooby-Doo*! I know what I saw, and I'm telling you—"

Harry held up his hand, a white flag. "I know. And for what it's worth, I trust your instinct. Look, it's bugging you. But they're going to investigate, aren't they? So why don't you call that guy you spoke to this morning?"

"That idiot Jim?"

"No, the other guy. See if you can get any information. It might put your mind at rest."

I opened a bag of crisps and tucked in. Eating was a habit that I indulged in when I was thinking, pondering, stressed, relaxed, upset, happy, hungry, not hungry and everything in between.

Should I call Reece McDonald? I knew I'd pick up the phone. Not because I owed Elle Bradshaw anything.

Because it was the right thing to do.

It was also an ugly scab that I had to pick at until it bled and faded away.

Even if it caused me pain.

CHAPTER SIX

Saturday, 19 October

WITH A PIPING-HOT COFFEE in hand, I leaned against the garden table and drank in the autumn morning. Foliage clung to some of the trees and shrubs in a glory of colour. Berries glistened with morning dew. Plump chestnut-brown acorns lay scattered across the grass.

Breathing in the cool, crisp air, I felt a sense of renewal. And with renewal came hope. Hope of piecing my heart back together after losing my parents. Hope that I could forgive my dad. Hope that my memories of my mum would be of love and laughter rather than illness and death. Hope that I would feel whole again.

And hope that I could find out what had really happened to Elle Bradshaw.

"Mum, my bag's packed up, but Henry can't find his shoes." The sunlight bounced off Georgie's hair, creating a halo of fiery auburn. Just then, she looked so much like my mum that it soothed me. Perhaps I was beginning to shed a little of my grief just like the trees were shedding their dead weight.

This is good.

I planted a kiss on her head. "Uncle Adam and Auntie Emma will be here soon so Henry can go in his slippers for all I care."

Georgie smirked. "His room is a mess and I'm not helping him clean it up. He still owes me pocket money from last week for picking up his laundry. He's so gross." She scrunched up her face and went looking for Indy.

My time for reflection had been flushed down the toilet so I went inside to find the missing shoes. Maybe sending my son to his uncle and aunts in his slippers wouldn't quite cut it.

***

An hour later I'd found the shoes and emptied the house. Now I was sprawled out on my sofa, the television on mute, listening to The Pixies. I flicked between channels and brushed leftover chilli Doritos from my hands. Next up was a true-crime documentary on Netflix. TV addiction is a terrible thing.

Pathetic much?

My phone rang and I closed the music app and paused the TV. 'Unmasking a Killer' would have to wait.

"Hazmat guys are all over Elle Bradshaw's house. Put me in a rain-coat and call me Columbo!"

Gia's staccato dialogue should have been jarring to my ears, but it wasn't. My good friend danced to her own beat and if you didn't like it, you could go to hell.

"What? What are you talking about?"

Had she partaken in a liquid lunch? I could picture Gia at her kitchen table, vibrating with excitement to pass on some salacious gossip. She was only five-foot tall but made up for it with sky-high heels, a heck of a lot of attitude and green eyes that could roll faster than any I knew, which, made me laugh because I was a self-proclaimed master of the eye roll.

"The. Hazmat. Guys! Like on *CSI* or whatever crap it is you watch."

"It's *NCIS*. I don't watch *CSI*. When would you ever see a forensics expert with—"

"Whatever! The point is, they're all over Elle's house, like in a movie." Gia sounded positively gleeful. "Carla Bellingham called me because she was out for a run on Mapleway Road. She's still trying to lose the baby weight, although I think that ship has sailed. Have you seen her recently? Anyway, there they were. Suits. Gloves. The whole enchilada. So, she called me for a gossip, and I decided to go for a wee walk."

"Since when do you walk?"

Gia snorted. "I walk when I'm told there's a full forensic unit crawling about a dead neighbour's house!"

"For real?"

A little thrill of something passed through me. Excitement, maybe? Shame on me if it was. I suspected it was likely fear.

"Are you deaf? There's even police tape all over the garden. It was creepy, like one of those true crime documentaries you watch, you freak. Do you think they found anything?"

I stared at the pixelated TV screen but said nothing.

Maybe I wasn't so crazy after all.

***

Thirty minutes into the documentary I realised I hadn't retained a single piece of information. Instead, my mind churned over the horror I'd discovered behind Elle's front door.

The doorbell rang and Pepper yipped and scampered down the hall. Muffled voices from the hallway piqued my interest. Harry stepped into the room, his face a mask of concern. DI Reece McDonald appeared behind him. *Ah. Got it.* My cheeks burned at being caught watching a true crime show. I scrambled to my feet, grabbed the remote and hit the mute button.

"Hi again." I thrust my hand out, nerves fluttering in the pit of my stomach.

"Hi, Mrs Sinclair." He smiled and his blue eyes crinkled at the sides. *Hint of Daniel Craig meets...*

So *that's* who he reminded me of —it was all in the eyes.

"Would you like a coffee?" Harry said. "I was just making one for Darcy."

A blatant lie. Harry had been heading out for a run, the running shorts and earbuds gave him away.

Reece nodded and put in his order for black with one sugar. I waved him over to the sofa, cringing as he stared at the TV. Why hadn't I just turned it off? An artist's sketch of the Golden State Killer cloaked in a black ski mask loomed on the screen.

Perfect.

My phone buzzed from a text I'd received, and I snatched it up. Carla recounting the hazmat story.

"That was a hell of a case."

"Sorry, what?"

Reece nodded towards the screen. "The serial killer in California. The Golden State Killer. I watched it a few weeks ago. So many victims."

"Yeah, I've just started it, but I did read a lot about it. Absolutely horrendous."

He must think I'm a ghoul. Or really weird. Yep, probably weird.

"So, Mrs Sinclair, I was—"

"Please, call me Darcy."

"And please call me Reece," he said, and flipped open a notebook. He settled his tablet on the table but held his pencil over the notebook.

Ready or not.

"Walk me through yesterday morning, from when you got up."

Admittedly, I can talk. However, today, I was stumbling over my words like a fool. There'd been a knot of anxiety in my belly since I'd found Elle. The possibility that something violent had happened to her scared the hell out of me—too close to home, too real.

"Just relax. Tell me about your morning, your thoughts, everything."

My thoughts? My thoughts had been on strangling Elle for making me traipse over to her house to comb through the now loathed document of minutes.

I took a few deep breaths and began.

As I talked, Reece's pencil tore across the page, and I quelled an urge to snatch the book from his hand and see what he was writing. *Suspect? Nosy neighbour? Nutcase?*

"When you arrived on Mapleway Road, did you see anyone? Any vehicles? Commercial vans?"

Only Maddie. "A white Range Rover sped past me. In fact, it soaked me. But I assumed it was someone late for the school run or work."

"Good. Think back. What direction was it coming from?"

"I was facing north so it must have been coming from Cedar Walk. But it was just another massive shiny car, like all the others you see around here."

"And nobody except Maddie Clement was on the street?"

Except Maddie Clement.

I shook my head.

"And when did you last speak with Elle?"

"On the Wednesday night, the sixteenth, probably around eight p.m." I scrolled over the call-history page on my phone and handed to Reece.

"Any texts or other messages from her?"

"None since the night before the committee meeting, so about two weeks ago."

Harry came in with two mugs of coffee. "Is everything alright, Detective? Darcy got a hell of a shock yesterday. Do you have any idea what happened?"

And there it was. The question I'd been too cowardly to ask. What the hell had happened to Elle Bradshaw?

"It's early days," Reece said.

A politician's answer. A statement with no substance or detail. Harry nodded and set his watch for the track he'd run and said he'd be back in an hour.

"Do you run daily?" Reece asked just as Harry had reached the door.

Harry grunted. "I try, but the kids outrun me."

Reece chuckled. "I used to run every day, loved it, but…it's been a year." A flash of emotion passed over his face, sadness perhaps. "Just started back up two weeks ago. Knees are killing me."

"Mine get the worst of it too. Brutal," Harry said, and was gone.

Reece turned back to me and held my gaze for a beat too long. I wanted to squirm.

"Yesterday, you made a big deal about the prints on Mrs Bradshaw's floor. Why was that?"

A migraine was building, ready to pack a punch later. "I wasn't in Elle's intimate circle of friends, but I'm certain she was rigid with her routines. I'm the same way and I can spot it a mile off in other people. Her gate was open—unusual. Pepper was in the garden—no way would she have allowed that, especially with the gate open. The door wasn't locked. I imagine her to be security conscious, like me. And then…" I cleared my throat, "after I found her, and the shock had cleared a little, it was the mud and leaves that screamed something was off. The storm was on Thursday night, so the prints must have been left then."

"How do you know she didn't leave them herself?"

"The treads. Her feet were tiny, size two or three. Her soles were immaculate, so she couldn't have been wearing them outside, not that night." I looked at the floor. "If someone was in there with her, and she'd fallen ill or had an accident, why didn't they call an ambulance?"

"But it's speculation, isn't it?"

Fair point but I wasn't ready to back down just yet. "Doubt she'd have chucked on boots several sizes larger than her own feet. Did you find any that matched?"

Reece shook his head. "We did not. Was Elle in a relationship?"

"Like I said, I wasn't in Elle's circle of friends, so not that I'm aware of, but I'm fairly sure you'll hear about it soon enough. Secrets don't stay quiet around here for long."

The pencil scratched at the paper, and I couldn't stand it a moment longer.

"Was she murdered?"

"Truthfully? I don't have the answer to that yet, but I will. I don't let sleeping dogs lie, Darcy. You might come to find I can be a right pain the arse, but only when it counts."

That was good to know. I was same way. "Will there be a post-mortem?"

"In the morning."

And then we'll know.

Sadness, even pity, washed over me. Beautiful Elle lying in the morgue, surrounded by stainless steel and the stench of death. Only the last time I saw her she hadn't been beautiful anymore. My eyes closed against the image, but it didn't eradicate it from my brain.

"I've heard there are crime scene guys at Elle's right now."

"Never seen so many people out for a walk on one road in my life." He grinned. "Almost had to send Sergeant Burns out to direct traffic."

"Damn, I would've paid to see that."

"So, tell me, what did *you* think of Elle Bradshaw? What kind of things did you hear about her?"

Victimology.

Picking over her bones.

The directness of the question caught me off guard, but the man sitting opposite me was taking no pleasure in my discomfort.

"Honestly? I didn't think much of her. I feel shitty saying that given what's happened but it's the truth. She had a very cruel tongue and enjoyed an audience when she unleashed it. Hand to God, if I repeated every story I've ever heard about Elle, you'd be sitting here until Christmas. You're asking the wrong person, Reece. Check her inner circle. They'll know where the skeletons are hidden."

"Got it."

Her intimate circle. Her trusted friends. Her loved ones. Is that where the danger had lain waiting for her?

My gut was screaming at me to start looking there.

"I didn't see any sign of a break-in though. Am I right?"

"No sign whatsoever."

Anxiety settled over my chest causing little pinpricks of fear to ripple on my skin. "So, if the unimaginable did happen then…"

"Then she either let them in or it wasn't a stretch for the person to gain access."

Damn.

"Did you reach her son in the States?"

Reece nodded.

"Is he coming home?"

"He's been working in London recently; that's where he is at the moment, so he'll be here later today or tomorrow." He stood and handed me a business card. "Thanks for the coffee. Look, if you think of anything else, give me a call."

I clutched the thin, white card as if somehow it would protect me.

Against what, I wasn't sure.

CHAPTER SEVEN

COME AS YOU ARE by Nirvana was blaring in my kitchen and *Dexter* was paused on the TV. My spicy butternut squash and lentil curry sat atop the cooker, mushy and abandoned. My focus was shot to hell. I needed quiet and switched off the music app.

The sudden silence jarred.

I was damn sure Reece McDonald didn't believe that Elle's death was a result of misplaced footing or sudden illness. Someone had been in that house with her when she'd died. Cold blood or accidental rage? Either way, the statistical possibility of the killer being someone I knew was reasonably high. My logic led me by the hand and took me to a very dark place.

I moved over to my abandoned pan and began to sing. It was a little trick I'd learned as a kid to drown out the noise. The screaming, the shouting, the crying, the ugly sound of a fist connecting with bone. *Old habits die hard.* As I stirred the sizzling vegetables I ran through a list of names.

Elle would have made many enemies over the years.

Petty jealousies. Vicious comments tossed into the air.

But enough to result in her lying in a pool of her own blood?

And yet, here we were.

***

The people in white forensic suits had become local folklore by the dying hours of the afternoon; the conjecture ran rampant, and each telling was more embellished than the last. Human psychology told me that this story would be the narrative told over every kitchen table in the village come early evening.

But it was my work colleague Carla's phone call that piqued my interest the most.

"You do know she was sleeping with Bill Henderson for years?"

"Cat's husband?"

"The very one. That guy has been around this village more times than flu in the dead of winter. Cat knows it but pretends she doesn't. I'd have done him in years ago."

Bill Henderson. Our local lothario, who considered himself the greasy prize every woman would be lucky to win.

"Are you serious? I'd heard he was a player, but Elle? How do you know?"

"Och, I heard it ages ago. It went on even when Charles was still alive and kicking. Plus, Sandy Olson, you know her, Elle's neighbour across the road? Well, she saw Bill creeping out of Elle's house at weird times...if you catch my drift."

The village idiot could have caught her drift.

"I thought Elle and Cat were the best of friends. What the hell was she thinking?"

Carla snorted. "Friends? Elle didn't have friends. Anyway, doubt she was thinking with her brain if you know what I mean."

"Yep, I think I got it, Carla. I wonder if..."

The chime of the doorbell interrupted me from further meanderings about Elle Bradshaw's extracurricular activities; I told Carla we'd speak later.

When I swung open the door, I nearly dropped to the floor.

Cat Henderson stood on my doorstep, her eyes puffy and red.

I welcomed her in, Carla's words replaying in my head.

What the hell was she doing here?

"How are you doing? I'm so sorry about Elle—I know you were good friends."

How easily the lie had come.

She swept past me and headed straight for the kitchen. "I could really use a drink, Darcy. Not tea. Vodka if you have it. And go easy on the mixer. I've had a hell of a day."

We knew each other well enough because her twin girls were in the same gymnastics school as Georgie, but we'd never been sofa-martinis buddies. She hung out with the private-school crowd that her girls went to, so I was more than a little confused by her visit.

Cat settled at my kitchen table as I scrutinised her. Early to mid-forties, espresso-brown hair shining with gorgeous caramel highlights strategically placed to frame her pretty face. I couldn't for the life of me understand why her husband Bill allegedly had it away with every girl in town.

"Sarah Evans is a cold bitch," she hissed.

I flinched and, sensing the approaching storm, poured myself a drink. "Here, take a sip and catch your breath."

She knocked back the drink with practised ease, pursed her glossed lips and shook the glass at me. "I needed that. Can I have a top-up?"

Mightily impressed, I refilled her glass, although I eased up on the alcohol measures a little. I didn't want to have to pick her up off my kitchen floor later.

"What's happened, Cat?"

She stared out the window into the fast-approaching dusk and let out a troubled sigh that came from somewhere deep inside of her bones. "It's all over town. Everyone's talking about Bill sleeping with Elle. I'm so sick of it. Sarah's been dispensing gossip as easily as she knocks back her champagne. And I've just had a call from some Detective McDonald. Wants to speak with us as soon as possible."

Five blinks later, my brain kicked into gear. Cat Henderson was stripping her soul bare in my kitchen. Should I tell her about my conversation with Carla? Confirm her worst fears that everyone was indeed talking about her husband? *Damn it.* No. I couldn't do that to her. I didn't have it in me to watch someone fall apart. But why sit in my kitchen? Why come to me?

"Tell me everything you saw yesterday morning," she said. "I know it was you and Maddie that found her. I spoke to you on the phone, remember? I'm begging you, Darcy. Cut the crap and just tell me. Who killed her? You must know something."

And there it was. She wasn't reaching out to me. She didn't need a friend to talk her troubles over with. She needed information.

"I don't know anything. Maddie and I found Elle and we called an ambulance. The police took our statements and that's the end of the story. All I know is she fell down the stairs. I don't know what happened before that."

She slammed her glass on the table. "There's a forensic team out there, for God's sake! The cops are starting to canvas the street. Something's up!"

I took a small step back from the table. Her pupils were like saucers.

"Did you see anything weird?" she said. "I don't know, like men's clothes lying about or anything?"

What the hell was she talking about?

"I…I don't know what you mean. Why would…" The shiny little penny dropped. "You mean Bill's clothes?"

Her pained face begged me for an answer.

And in that split second, I yearned to toss her right out my front door. There were countless women out there scrambling to escape the most horrific domestic situations, scraping together pennies to buy their children a square meal or patching up their cuts and bruises to face another day. Cat had places she could escape to, money to burn. But I knew it was the accumulation of the last twenty-four hours that had me on edge, so I dug deep and readjusted my attitude. I'd heard rumours about Bill here and there in the past. I'd paid them no mind. Truth was I felt rotten for Cat. I felt sad for her little girls. If the rumour mill was true and Bill and Elle had engaged in an affair, then Cat would have every ounce of support I could give her.

Rather than judge her, I appraised her with a cool eye. Skin flawless, not a hint of physical abuse. And yet the emotional scars were etched all over her face. I could have reached out, hugged her, indulged her a little. Instead, I settled my hand on her arm, and squeezed gently, delivering my empathy. Wanted or not. After all, I knew better than anyone the pain that someone will endure to keep a family together.

"No, I didn't see any clothes lying about, and it didn't look like Elle had been, well, entertaining anyone."

"You sure? No champagne or glasses or anything? Was her bed made?"

Why do people put up with this kind of crap? "No, nothing like that, Cat. I swear. Don't let your mind wander into places it doesn't have to. You'll make yourself ill."

"You would tell me, wouldn't you? If I had anything to worry about?" She grabbed at my hand, her touch ice cold against my skin."

"Of course I would. Look, I don't even know how she died. She was at the bottom of her stairs and that's all I can tell you."

She finished her drink and slipped her perfect mask back into place, hair tumbling around her shoulders in a way mine never could and produced a wolfish smile.

"Don't believe what that cow Sarah Evans is telling everyone. She's always been jealous of me, always been after my Bill."

Ah, the legendary Bill. Six-two, thick, black hair that was always just so; wide, easy smile lodged permanently on a smug but pleasing face, a physique that screamed he worked out at least five times a week. And I'd have guessed that every photo on his phone was not of his wife or daughters but himself—in different work-out poses. When he wasn't at the gym, he was running around the village, literally and figuratively so it seemed.

"I don't listen to gossip, Cat; doesn't interest me in the slightest," I lied. "No one is talking about you or Bill."

"Thanks, Darcy, you're a good pal. You know Sarah, she's such a bitch sometimes. She told Rob Bellingham that Bill had been at

Elle's on Thursday night. She's probably told half the village. Can you imagine?"

I could very well imagine. Rob's wife had just recounted that very story to me not five minutes earlier. I could see why Reece McDonald was going to land on her doorstep.

"He was with me on Thursday night. The things I could tell you about Sarah. And her husband Eric. Did you know that—"

A grating noise erupted from her handbag, and I wanted to kick it away, so she'd continue to spill her grubby stories about the Evans's.

The phone banged against her diamond earrings. "I'm not in the mood, Bill. You better take me out somewhere for dinner tonight, and somewhere pricey. This is going to cost you. I'm at Darcy's. What? Who's looking for me?"

A little fear crept into her voice and the hairs on the back of my neck stood to attention.

"I never went near Elle's house that night! I was only out for a walk to clear my head. You know I was only out for ten minutes. I got soaked through and turned back. I didn't see her!"

Wait. What?

"Who the hell told Jim Burns that crap? Sandy Olsen? It's not true, Bill!"

The doorbell chimed again. I so wanted to ignore it but thought better of it and headed down the hall. And who should greet me but Bill Henderson, his phone to his ear and a sheepish smile plastered on his face.

"Sorry! I was nearby. Can I come in and see Cat?"

He sauntered over the doorstep and into my kitchen as if he had all the time in the world.

Cat narrowed her eyes and stood. "Did you think I wouldn't find out? I warned you. That last time, I warned you, Bill. My God, did you think I was joking? You're pathetic." Although her words dripped with disgust, there was a tinge of sadness mixed up in them too.

Bill fiddled with his phone and scanned the room as if unsure where to place himself. I offered him a seat.

"Come on, Kitty Cat," he said.

The words were practised, designed to pacify and deflect. I recognised the manipulative technique a mile off because my father had deployed the exact same tactic. Time after time. I could only hope Cat would call his bluff and spin on her heel.

"Nothing was going on with Elle," he said. "I swear to you. Didn't I promise you? Look, Elle texted me about business. I swear to you. Why the hell would I need her when I have you and the girls?"

He traced his fingers across her lips and tugged at her hair. Feeling awkward at witnessing intimate moment, I moved to make a hasty exit out of the room, but Cat beat me to the punch by blocking my way as she stepped out of Bill's reach.

"If I find out that any of these rumours are true, if you've mixed us up in this nightmare, I'll make sure you don't have a pot left to piss in. I'll burn your world to the ground. Understood?" She snatched up her bag and reached for her coat. "Darcy don't leave on our account. This is your house and Bill shouldn't have come here."

She turned back to Bill as I hesitated in the doorway, unsure where to turn.

"You better organise a table at Nick's and a babysitter for the girls. Then first thing tomorrow you speak to Sandy Olsen and let her know I was not in Elle's house on Thursday night. Do you hear me?"

"I hear you," he said.

Even under Bill's tan I could detect a hint of pink on his cheeks. The man wasn't used to being reprimanded by his wife. Maybe Cat had had enough. Maybe she'd do what she should have done a long time ago.

Witnessing the interplay between the Henderson's reminded me how grateful I was for Harry. Maybe I was one of the lucky ones after all.

Emotionally scarred yet healing.

Messed up but trying my best.

Funny how life turns out.

Cat's laugh was as fake as Bill's honesty as she turned to me. "Thanks, Darcy. And apologies for our little domestic! Let's go out sometime. I'll buzz you during the week. We can organise something and I'll fill you in on what that detective has to say."

Oh, please do.

I closed the door behind them and slumped against it, exhausted. *What the hell?* Talk about witnessing an emotional bomb exploding in my kitchen. So, if Bill had engaged in a tryst with Elle on Thursday night, then what? Had it got out of hand? An argument that had ended with Elle at the bottom of the stairs? Or was it Cat who'd been there that night instead?

Darkness had fallen and a sliver of unease crawled over me. Pepper bounded in and erupted into a volley of barks, his tail thumping against the floor. Friend, not foe.

Then came Harry and two yelling and giggling kids.

And all at once the dread popped and fizzled away.

Silly me.

CHAPTER EIGHT

M Y PHONE BUZZED. EVERY fibre of my being screamed at me to ignore it, but I grudgingly answered.

"Hi, Darcy, it's Jonathan." His deep mellow voice was so distinctive he needn't have identified himself.

"How are you feeling, Jonathan?"

"Sad, but a little time will ease it. Listen, will you and Harry come for lunch tomorrow? I just spoke to Cole! I haven't heard his voice in twenty-odd years." A touch of melancholy tinged his words. "I've invited him, too. He's arriving tomorrow from London, and I think he should have people around him when gets here."

I doubted Harry and I would be of much comfort to Cole Bradshaw but jumped at the chance to meet the prodigal son.

Harry responded to the news with a grumble and feigned needing to read an important email on his phone. I glared at him for several minutes and the charade crumbled. I am a sensei of the glare. I understood it though; Harry liked Jonathan well enough but hanging out with the local minister wasn't exactly on his list of fun ways to kick back on a Sunday. Or any other day.

Truth be told, I wasn't in any mood for socialising either. My morning high had long waned, but it was the right thing to do. Still, I couldn't help but wonder what Cole would be like. His father, Charles, had been a meek man, a shade of unremarkable grey—the kind of man you never noticed was in the room, even if he stood right next to you.

Unlike his wife.

***

Sunday, 20 October

We dropped the kids at Isla's, and Jonathan led us into his cosy home. I was glad to get inside; the biting wind had picked up.

"I'm just making bruschetta; I have enough fresh basil to entertain half of Rome," he said, ushering us into his large kitchen like stray sheep.

The space had been recently remodelled—a splash of red and white high-gloss, modern. Everything gleamed. A huge pine farmer's table sat proudly in the middle of the room and lent the room some warmth.

"Where else do people feel more at home than round a big kitchen table?" Jonathan said.

I couldn't argue. Harry and I both knew we were welcome around Jonathan's table anytime even though we didn't attend church; it just wasn't our thing. I'd stared down the barrel of many a dark night and survived. My prayers for inner strength were my own business.

Jonathan splashed Prosecco into flute glasses, and I hid a smile— the local minister pouring drinks at lunchtime! There was sparkling water, too, but I disregarded it. It had been a crappy week and I'd rehydrate later.

He took us into the living room. Classic rock music played softly in the background, and I asked who else was coming.

Jonathan clapped his hands. "Cole, of course, Maddie and Dave, and Richard Bradshaw."

I choked a little on my drink at the mention of Richard's name. He was the last person I wanted to hang out with, especially after his snide comments on Friday. Still, he'd just lost his sister-in-law, and regardless of whether he cared, I should at least put on a show of sympathy.

"He's not my first choice by any means," Jonathan said, "but Cole should have his uncle here; they haven't seen each other in probably twenty years or more. I just about managed to dodge Sarah and Jessica Evans, so I'd call that a win."

He excused himself and I glanced at the remaining Prosecco still fizzing away in my glass. Guilt washed over me.

Enjoying a drink and anticipating a nice lunch? Really? We'd gathered to meet the son of a woman who'd just died—a death that hadn't even been determined as natural and might never be.

I wanted to make my excuses and leave. My throat felt tight—*too much death, too much grief.* Images of Elle's blood sprayed on her wall, seeping through her floor, flooded back to me and I felt a little lightheaded. I turned to Harry, intending to let him know it was time to get the hell out, and right on cue the doorbell rang.

Feeling cornered, I stood and painted on a smile for Maddie and Dave.

"Sorry to hear the news, must have been a hell of a shock to find her like that," Dave said. "Maddie took it pretty hard."

Had she really? Her duplicitous behaviour at Elle's house swam back to me, adding to the unease I was already feeling. I looked around for a refill. Like a genie floating out from a bottle, Jonathan appeared and topped me up. *Perfect.*

"I got a visit from DI McDonald yesterday. Did you?"

Glossy raven hair bounced as Maddie nodded. "And that Sergeant Jim Burns was with him. What's up with that guy? He never cracks a smile. Honestly, he gives me the creeps. Anyway, I couldn't add much more than what we'd already told them both on Friday."

"That officer certainly gave you a grilling about the call you made to Elle on Thursday night, didn't he?" Dave turned to me. "Maddie clean forgot she'd spoken to Elle on the night she died, and Jim didn't like that one bit. Thought he was going to cart her off to a cell." His smile died on his lips as he caught Maddie's death stare.

Huh. Maddie usually avoided Elle like a dose of the plague so why had she called her? And why not mention it when we found her on Friday morning?

"What was the call about, Maddie? If you don't mind my asking," I asked. Harry's eyes widened like saucers at my abruptness. Cringing inside, I still held Maddie's gaze.

"Oh, nothing really. Just about that committee meeting you were at. Thought I could add some ideas to it, that's all. No big deal."

Not one word rang true. Maddie hadn't even been seated at that meeting and so the likelihood of her reaching out to help Elle was slim to none.

I couldn't hold it in anymore. "There was a forensic team out at Elle's yesterday. Seems odd if she simply fell downstairs. Maddie, you were there, what do you think?"

Her eyes widened. I'd never claimed to be a body-language expert, but she was worried. Hell, in that moment, she looked cornered and ready to bolt.

"So, it's true? A few people texted me, but I thought it was just the usual gossip and Dave and I drove down Firmont Road on the way over here, so we didn't even pass Elle's house. Surely the police only send out forensics if they think something bad happened?"

Dave cocked his head. "Forensics?"

I mustered up the courage to drop my bombshell. "I think the police have ordered a post-mortem. So, either the family have requested one to find out what killed her, or the police believe something else is going on. My best guess is the second option."

Before Maddie could respond, Richard Bradshaw swept into the room. The temperature must have dropped at least ten degrees. He merely glanced at me, but I still blushed at the memory of the reprimand I'd received from the arrogant prick. Of course, I pretended everything was fine and mumbled my condolences.

The man was attractive. Some might have said very attractive. Late forties, early fifties, although he looked younger. Tanned, strong, slender physique. Piercing dark-brown eyes that were almost black. He was groomed from top to toe, too. His hair was thick and stylish in that silver-fox way, and he wore a perfectly tailored charcoal suit with a brilliant white starched shirt—worn casually without a tie. Relaxed yet completely in charge. *Richard Gere in his glory days.*

I couldn't stand being in his line of sight. His eyes raked over me, possibly weighing up what I was like in the sack. The gleam in his dark eyes told me he liked what he saw and that made my skin crawl. The ultimate alpha male. And just in case we all hadn't received the memo, he shrugged out of his cashmere coat and handed it to Jonathan without a thank you.

Harry, in his worn jeans and rumpled checked shirt, looked puzzled as he took in Richard's suit.

The forced social niceties petered out and Dave turned to me.

"Bet the kids are loving having Pepper."

"Pepper?" Richard said. "Oh, you mean Elle's dog. Well, I can't keep it—no use for the bloody things." His lip curled.

I glowered. Even after seven years in Cedarwood, I often still felt out of place—the great pretender. Those little doubts of self-worth usually crawled to the surface around people like Richard. I wanted to tell him that I wouldn't have let him look after a disease let alone a defenceless animal, but of course I left the words unsaid and that stung. Had my courage disappeared down the drain along with my confidence?

"So, when is the golden boy arriving?" Richard asked.

Jonathan, a dishcloth over his shoulder, brandished another bottle of Prosecco. Richard waved it away.

"Do you have any good whisky, Jon? Make it a double."

No please, no thank you. Just hand it to me.

The doorbell rang and we all froze. Nervous laughter bubbled up inside of me. Any more of these charades and I was going to lose it. I tried not to look at Harry, who seemed to have discovered something of great interest on the ceiling.

Jonathan gabbled at the door, and I craned my neck. After what felt like hours but was just a minute, Jonathan came back in and beckoned towards the door.

The man who sauntered in was quite simply stunning; he stood around six three and was broad in the chest but with a lean, tight physique. He wore a wide, easy smile that dimpled his cheeks and showcased straight white teeth. And those eyes—almost liquid black. He eased into salutations as if he'd known us for years. I caught a pleasing trace of sandalwood and cedar as he leaned towards me, and I had to restrain the urge rush to the bathroom and check my make-up.

He hugged Maddie next and lingered just a beat too long. Enough that Dave's tension was visible.

This guy was the *real* alpha male in the room.

He knew it.

We knew it.

Even Richard looked on in awe.

"Uncle Richard!" His voice was soft but strong. "I'm sorry it took this long to come home."

They shook hands, then Richard took a step back, appraising Cole, seemingly pleased with what he saw.

"My God, Cole, you look great! I'd never have recognised you in a million years! Great to have you home but bloody awful circumstances."

Cole shook his head. "I'm still in shock. Couldn't believe what I was hearing when I got the call from the police. Did you know they're sending Mum for a post-mortem? I'm just sick about it. She would've hated that. And wasn't it just a fall?"

Harry and I locked eyes.

"That can't be right? You sure?" Richard asked.

"You mean you don't know? Reece McDonald told me. Didn't sound like I had much of a say in the matter either. He's the one that's ordered it, but truth be told I was in too much shock to question it. So, he thinks what? Someone did something to her? Hurt her?" His hand flew to his mouth.

Shuffling from foot to foot to ease my building anxiety, Harry rubbed the back of my shoulders, I was grateful for his touch. Breathing in through my nose and exhaling through my mouth settled me a little. Cole's open grief was a punch to my gut and I wanted to run. Anywhere.

Dave cleared his throat. "Sometimes this is standard procedure with a sudden death, particularly if the person's youngish and in seemingly good health, much like your mum."

Cole nodded and his shoulders loosened. "Makes sense I guess but, still, it's a hell of a thing. It's just…I hadn't seen her in so long. Hadn't even spoken to her and now it's too late and I can't fix it." He scanned the room as if seeing us for the first time. "I'm sorry, everyone. I shouldn't have brought that up, not in company. I'm just, well, I'm numb. For the first time in a long time, I haven't a clue what to do."

We all spoke at once, waving off his apology. Jonathan pushed a drink into his hand and urged him to take a sip if it would help settle his nerves. Half the glass disappeared.

"How are things here, Richard? I barely recognise the village." He turned his head, and his mood went with it. "I can't believe it's been this long."

I couldn't stand the awkward silence and decided to fill it.

"Jonathan's been so looking forward to seeing you again. He could barely contain himself earlier."

I offered him a kind smile and Richard glared at me as if I were a simpleton.

"What's going on with business?" Richard asked.

Cole seemed to relax. Inane conversation. Safe and solid ground.

"Well, as you know, I was out in the East Coast for some time, but I've been in London for almost a year now which has been great, felt more like home. I can take things a little easy now." He shrugged, as if making enough money to semi-retire in your late twenties was an everyday occurrence.

I vaguely recalled that Cole had studied for a PhD in applied mathematics at St Andrews. It must have bought him a ticket into the big league.

The gorgeous submariner watch glinting in the weak sunlight told me his wrist was probably worth more than my annual gross salary.

I glanced at his wedding finger—no ring, but he probably had a model or two stashed away somewhere.

A few minutes later we sat down to lunch. If I'd been expecting a sombre undertone, I was mistaken. Everyone appeared to be having a thoroughly better time than we should have been given the circumstances.

Cole was gregarious, erudite, charming, and confident. In no time at all he had everyone eating out of the palm of his hand. Perfect... maybe too perfect, but who was I to judge? A fractured relationship that had never had a chance to heal before his mum passed. That was some load to carry. Let him be the star of the show.

"Remember that fateful day I was coaching the Boys Brigade football team, Cole?" Jonathan said. "Everyone, I'll have you know I was quite the striker back in the day, cracking goalkeeper too. Anyway, I used to coach a few of the local teams—"

"Why don't you coach now?" Harry said. "Henry's coach could use the help. Trust me, his team's a shambles."

Jonathan shook his head. "My knees are shot."

What was it with middle-aged men and their knees? Maddie and I exchanged a smug grin.

"Anyway, there I was, playing like Messi, and Cole wandered away, bored, and almost lost his finger on this old, rusted slide that should have been demolished years before! And little Sean Martin threw up everywhere because of the blood and the metal sticking out of Cole's hand. Half your fingertip was hanging off, Cole, and Sean was screaming his head off. All I had was a single tiny piece of gauze! Nightmare. Do you remember screaming at the nurse when you got the tetanus shot, Cole?"

Cole smiled.

"You still took an infection. Oh, the scarring! Between Elle scream-ing and Sean's mother yelling at me, I thought I was going to have a heart attack. Packed a full first-aid box ever since and always made sure I had an assistant coach with me."

Cole looked down at the table. "I remember it well, even now. Man, that hurt! Thanks for spending the time with me that you did when I was a kid. More than my dad ever did. If it didn't involve a maths equation, he wasn't interested. And my mum and I didn't really do much together. Ever. But you and your wife were always great fun. Where is your wife?"

"She passed. Cancer."

An uncomfortable silence settled over the table as Cole offered his apologies. Richard seized the opportunity like a hungry lion and took us on a self-indulgent journey through the pretty courtyards of St Tropez, Cannes and Monaco. We learned about money spent, the select hotels he'd graced with his presence, the women he'd met, his insanely good golf handicap, and even his stunning ability to select the most expensive wine thanks to his extensive vineyard-hopping.

After a short while I began to feel a great sympathy for the good people of France, wondering what they'd done to deserve this idiot. My interruption—yes, Harry and I had taken a few holidays in the south of France—was met with a look of withering pity. Perhaps if I poked him hard with a fork, he might shut the hell up. Instead, I yawned. Big mistake. It brought the windbag's monologue to a crashing halt.

But he wasn't done with me yet.

"Have you spoken with Bob about the meeting you failed to attend on Friday? The last lawyer at your firm who didn't move quick enough for me doesn't work there anymore." His lip curled.

"As a matter of fact, I spoke with him yesterday. Told him exactly what I told you, I couldn't make the meeting because I was talking with the police after finding Elle's body."

Cole slumped and guilt washed over me. *Damn.* I couldn't keep my stupid mouth shut.

"Just to be crystal clear," I said, "Carla Bellingham is currently on maternity leave. She handed her files over to Stephen Barnes before she left. You didn't have her fired, Richard, and I don't appreciate the suggestion that you did. Nor will Bob."

A slew of emotions crawled over his face, settling on shock with a hint of anger. Richard didn't enjoy a woman biting back. *Shame.* My two-minute psych evaluation of dear Richard told me I'd been right all along; he appeared to enjoy at least two traits of the dark triad because his narcissism and Machiavellianism had been on full display all afternoon. I couldn't imagine lasting another five minutes in his company.

"Cole, Maddie and I found your mum at home on Thursday. We called the ambulance, but it was too late. I really am sorry." I twisted my napkin under the table. Over and over until my fingers throbbed. Despite the pain, I continued to twist.

Cole nodded and sighed. Jonathan patted his hand and topped up his drink. Question was, would anyone mention the forensics unit crawling all over Elle's house? I'd lost patience with all the social nonsense and wanted to chuck all the cards on the table, but the gift that was Richard Bradshaw just kept on giving.

"Are you planning to stay at the house, Cole?" he said. "If so, I'll send my housekeeper round to do whatever's necessary. She won't mind."

I bristled, thinking the housekeeper *would* bloody mind.

"Well, the short answer is yes. I was going to drive straight home this morning, but Reece McDonald asked me to wait until later this afternoon, he said there were still officers at the house this morning." Cole shrugged.

As casually as I dared, I tossed in my verbal hand grenade. "I think they're still processing things over at the house. I understand the police have also been canvassing the neighbours."

All eyes swivelled towards me. I could have sworn even the ticking of the clock stopped.

"Processing what?" Richard snapped.

"I don't know. Maybe you should ask Reece McDonald! Didn't you know there was a forensics team out at Elle's yesterday? The whole village knows."

"Bullshit! I don't believe it. Why the hell would there be a forensics team at my sister-in-law's house?"

I didn't respond.

"*Well?*"

Maddie jumped, while a childish part of me relished his fury.

"Pick up a phone and call Reece," Harry said coolly. "Get your answers from him and watch your tone when you speak with my wife. Next time I won't be so polite."

I squeezed Harry's hand under the table and turned my head away from Richard.

"Forensics? Is there anything I need to worry about? Is this why the police are insisting on a post-mortem? I knew something was wrong. Jonathan, do you think something bad happened?" Cole said, now looking very wary.

"Honestly, I don't know Cole," I interrupted. "Perhaps the police are just doing due diligence, but I think you should have a chat with Reece. Here, I have his card if you want his number."

Cole waved me back into my seat, stood, fished his phone out of his back pocket. "Don't worry. I've already got his number. I've to go meet with him and give him my statement and whereabouts over the last few days. If I could take back the last few years and fix things with my mum, I would do it in a heartbeat. Do you know what I mean?" he asked no one in particular.

Jonathan scrambled out of his chair, gripped Cole's hands and pulled him into a bear hug. "Your mother would be so proud. I wish she could see you here with all of us, back home where you belong. In fact, I know she can see you."

I couldn't help it—my eyes flicked heavenwards. A smile played across Harry's mouth. One of my inappropriate nervous laughs threatened to escape.

We finished lunch and milled about the front door saying our goodbyes. Harry's hand pressed into the small of my back, nudging me out the door, desperate to escape. I turned to thank Jonathan, but Maddie was talking to him. He frowned, then stared beyond her into nothing. What had she said to him?

She walked off, and I went over and tugged on his arm. "Are you alright?"

Jonathan gazed at me as if he'd never seen me before in his life. "What? Forgive me, Darcy. I was a million miles away there." He grasped my hand as if clinging to a lifeline. "I'll call you later."

Then he scuttled inside and slammed the door in my face, leaving me feeling like an unwanted interloper.

CHAPTER NINE

Our usual family Sunday afternoon routine kicked into gear—Henry begging to play football, Harry trying to usher him into the shower, me searching for backpacks, homework, reading books and school shoes.

I rubbed at my aching back but forgot the pain the second my nose welcomed the aroma of roasting veggies. My thoughts turned to one of my favourite hobbies, eating.

"Before you ask, dinner will be five minutes. Grab the plates?" Harry asked.

As I crammed a piping-hot parsnip in my mouth, the phone rang. As so often happened, the second I picked up a fork or a cup of coffee, someone called. It was a conspiracy, I was sure.

I ignored it and got the kids seated at the table. Pepper scampered in and stationed himself under the table, waiting for scraps the kids would pass him. We made it through dinner, and once I was satisfied that the kitchen no longer looked like it had been raided by a Viking army, I made a pot of decaf and listened to my voicemail.

Jonathan's voice was breathless and laced with fear. He needed to talk about something *odd*.

I called him and waited. It went to voicemail. I tried again. Same thing. And a third time. I paced around the kitchen. Eight minutes crawled by before I couldn't stand it any longer. I struggled with overanalysing, but let it run wild anyway.

"Harry!" I yelled with enough urgency to drag him off the sofa. "I think we should go over."

He shook his head. "Have you lost your mind? I know you're hyper-vigilant, but this is ridiculous. It's Sunday night and we're all in our pyjamas. If Jonathan wanted to talk, he'd have called back. Get a grip."

"Nope, I can't settle. Something's off."

He looked heavenwards for divine inspiration that didn't come. "You're driving me nuts."

I snatched my keys from the kitchen counter and said over my shoulder, "I'm going over there. If he's not in, fair enough. I tried."

Harry sighed, told the kids we were going on a jammies-journey, and held his hand out for the keys.

I'd learned a long time ago to trust my gut instinct. When the little voice inside my head talks, I listen closely. When she screams, I pay attention.

But if I'd realised what lay ahead, I'd never have left the house.

***

Jonathan's car was parked in the driveway, so Harry pulled up on the pavement. Slamming the car door behind me I took a hit of air. Spruce Drive was empty, the cold night warding off walkers and joggers. The moon peeked through bare branches and night frost glinted on the pavement like scattered glass. On any other night I would have embraced the beauty of it. Breathed in the freezing air. Not tonight.

Every dread-filled step dragged.

Get a hold of yourself, idiot.

I rang the bell six times. The silence was deafening. Was he sleeping? Snoozing on the couch? I didn't think so because the door chime mirrored Big Ben.

Maybe he'd walked over to the church. *Bingo!* And now I felt like a damned fool. Harry was right all along. My hypervigilance had finally crossed over into paranoia. My pyjama-clad husband and kids, huddled in our car, proved it.

There was one more thing I could do. I called Jackie McPherson.

"Sorry, but I haven't seen Jonathan all day," she said. "I've just left the church and he's not there. Is everything alright? Didn't you see him this afternoon?"

I reassured her that everything was cool and squinted through the glass in the front door but saw only pixelated shapes. The rain started to drizzle, and I pulled my coat tighter.

"Darcy! What are you doing?" Harry called out.

The kids were beginning to bicker. I had a decision to make.

"Just a minute," I hissed.

Tentatively, I pulled down the door handle. The door swung open into a dark hallway.

Shit. This couldn't be happening.

Stay or go?

"Jonathan! Are you here?"

Silence.

The entire house was in darkness. No sign of life anywhere.

Claustrophobia gnawed on my frayed nerves; my heart was pounding harder, faster.

The house felt different.

Cold.

Empty.

Uninviting.

Sliding my hand along the wall, I found the light switch. I pressed it and light flooded the hall.

Ahead, on the kitchen floor, Jonathan lay in the shadows, unnaturally bent and surrounded by something splashed all over the floor.

Blood?

Please no.

A scream sounded from far away. *Was that me?* I couldn't breathe. Frozen in fear. My eyes darted from side to side, searching for danger, searching for help—I didn't know which.

After what felt like an eternity, I rushed towards him, my footing gave way underneath me.

The floor was slick, and I struggled to remain upright.

"It's alright, Jonathan." I barely recognised my own voice. Manic. "I'm going to get help."

I pounded the light switch by the door.

And regretted it.

Fuck.

My legs buckled.

His face was turned away from me, the back of his head a matted red mess. It didn't seem possible that so much damage had been done.

Dark blood had pooled around him over the whitewashed wooden floor. Seeping through. Not just the floor. The doors, walls and even the ceiling were streaked like some grotesque piece of modern art.

Vomit. I could taste it. Climbing up my throat. I swallowed it back down, bent over and gulped in air. It hurt. Couldn't get enough oxygen into my lungs. Noticed the blackish red liquid on the front and side of my shoes and realised I had slipped on Jonathan's blood. My gag reflex jumped into overdrive and my hand flew back to my mouth.

Can't breathe.

Fuck.

I counted to ten.

Another five.

Gathering what was left of my wits I stumbled to the front door.

"Harry! Ambulance!"

Harry sprang from the car; a look of confusion or horror swam across his face. I wasn't sure which. He talked into the phone, then looked over at me. "What's wrong? They need to know."

"Jonathan's dead. His head! Oh, Harry, his poor head."

Still speaking on the phone, he rushed past me and into the house. Seconds later he was back, hands on his knees, head down.

"Jesus Christ! W-what the hell happened?"

I reached for him.

"Mummy, what's wrong?"

There, standing in the frozen driveway, were my two little babies, shivering in their pyjamas and slippers. Their innocence seemed even more beautiful against the horror that lay in the house.

I hugged Georgie tight against me. "You have to listen to Mummy. Jonathan isn't feeling well. We have to wait until the doctor comes to visit him."

"Can we see him, Mum? We can cheer him up."

Their little heads nodded, and they moved towards the door. I blocked them like a line-backer and ushered them back to the car.

"Not this time, guys." I grabbed Georgie's hands and crouched down. "Georgie, Mummy needs you to wait in the car with Henry for a little bit. Can you be a grown-up girl and do that for me?"

Smiling and clearly proud to be the grown-up, she took Henry's hand. "Come on, Henry. It's cold out here."

She marched him back to the car. Such a small act of kindness in contrast with the brutality that had occurred in Jonathan's kitchen.

On hearing the door slam shut I let my tears fall.

Sirens wailed, lights began to pop on and blinds twitched in the surrounding houses.

Hurry up.

The ambulance arrived. I told Harry to sit with the kids and showed the paramedics into the kitchen.

A radio crackled and one of the paramedics barked, "Faint, but it's there. BP 192 over 124. Hypertensive crisis. Possible stroke. Massive head trauma. Extensive blood loss."

"Is he alive? Oh God, is he?"

"Barely, but yes."

Another green uniform moved me into another living room. I was getting in their way and every second was crucial.

I grabbed his arm. "What hospital are you taking him to?"

"It'll be the university hospital. Sit tight and stay in this room. Don't move."

Dropping my head into my hands, I sobbed. The release of emotions brought an urge to vomit again. I pressed the back of my hand against my mouth. Couldn't hold it down. Some of my dinner landed on the floor and splashed on my shoes. Mixing in with the blood.

I wanted to let a scream rip from my throat.

Grabbing my hair with my hands I pulled hard until it caused me pain.

Swallowing slowly, I released my hair.

It's alright. Breathe, Darcy. Everything's going to be alright.

But it wasn't alright.

Whatever had happened to Jonathan was bad.

But he was still alive, and I held on to that sliver of hope as best I could.

***

Spruce Drive had erupted into chaos.

Lights flashed all around me.

People moved with intent, jobs to do.

Neighbours gathered and cried out to me. Hurling questions into the air.

What was happening?

What did I see?

Where was Jonathan?

Officers moved everyone back. Minimising the turmoil. Radios crackled. Phones were ringing. Notifications buzzed. Dogs barked. Someone was crying.

I turned my head to the right, pretending I didn't see them.

Reece stood on Jonathan's lawn, typing into his tablet whilst trying to shield himself from the aggressive wind.

"So, tell me again, Darcy: what made you come over here?"

My head was splitting, and my body ached like I was consumed with a virus. I rubbed my frozen hands against my arms to generate heat — it didn't work so I pressed my numb hand against my burning forehead.

I stuttered through the whole story again, from the missed phone call to finding Jonathan on the kitchen floor.

"I have the voicemail if you want to listen to it."

I scrolled through my phone. Jonathan's pleasant voice drifted from the speaker and my heart broke.

"You're freezing. We'll have to do this at the station, Darcy, but at least it'll give you a chance to warm up."

"Do you see what I mean?" I didn't move. If I did, I'd throw up again. "Jonathan sounded worried in that voicemail. He must have spoken to someone else, after he'd called me, alerted them, and they came here."

"There's no sign of forced entry..."

Meaning Jonathan had invited the person inside. He'd known his predator.

"Elle died on Thursday, and now Jonathan's been attacked. There must be a link. Do you really think Elle fell, or was she killed?"

He sighed. "We don't have the results of the PM. They'll be ready first thing in the morning. I told you, the whole scene at Elle's concerns me."

I lowered my head and stared at the now frozen grass, which was glowing blue against the backdrop of flashing lights. "I need to do *something*. Shit, I can't stand this." I caught sight of my shoes.

"Reece, I have Jonathan's blood all over these. Please. Take them." I kicked one toe against the back of my other heel, desperate to free myself of the blood-soaked reminders. I lost my balance and fell against the policeman, who grabbed my arm.

"Calm down, Darcy. I'll take them." He turned to bark an order for an evidence bag.

DNA. I'd vomited all over the floor, my DNA would be everywhere. Damn. Everything was spinning out of control. I tasted the stale remnants of bile in my mouth and I started to gag again.

The remainder of my dinner landed on the grass.

Wiping my hand against my mouth, I kept my head bent down. Ashamed and embarrassed at my weakness. Not ready to face the world. I finally balanced myself enough to rip the damn shoes from my body and felt the soles of my feet go numb against the frost tipped grass.

A hand reached out and collected them. Someone mumbled something about taking the rest of my clothes.

The horror of what had happened in that kitchen was too much to comprehend. Jonathan had opened his door to someone he knew and set off a chain of unspeakable events. Hot tears slid from my swollen eyes and fell from my chin. I balled my hands and winced. My skin felt raw.

Alone. I felt so alone.

Selfish, Darcy.

But I wanted someone to reach for *me*, to hold *me* and tell *me* everything was going to be alright.

Selfish, Darcy.

A woman came into view, pulled her hair back and fixed it into a low ponytail. Zipped up a forensic suit and slipped on booties. She nodded to me as she passed by and entered the house. I'd seen plenty of forensic teams on police dramas over the years—been hooked on *Dexter* for eight seasons—but this was real life, and I was smack bang in the middle of it.

Voices continued to swirl around me. The constant strobe of colour from the police cars burned my eyes. Neighbours continued to yell, seeking answers. One dog after another had begun to bark. A baby was crying.

My brain felt ready to explode.

Sergeant Burns ducked under the police tape that had been placed across the door not five minutes earlier, crossed into the garden, and cleared his throat. He murmured something to Reece, who then nodded.

"Come on, Darcy. I'm so sorry but I have to take you to the station to take the remainder of your clothes and take your prints." He held up his hand to ward off any questions, but I didn't have any. I didn't care what they needed to take from me. I was too tired, too sick to my stomach to care much about anything.

"I'll drop you straight home afterwards. It'll give me a chance to speak with your husband. I promise I'll rush you through."

"You can have my clothes, Reece. Burn the damn stuff for all I care! I never want to see any of it again."

Harry had been allowed to leave the scene and take the kids home. Looking at the chaos that was now unfolding all around me I couldn't have been more grateful. It would have scared the life out of my little ones because it had shaken me to my core.

Reece offered me his arm and dished out instructions to his team: forensics team. Tape up the entire perimeter. Contact PF office. Send an officer to the hospital.

Here we go again.

***

The room was freezing cold.

Dark.

Empty.

Faceless.

Shivering, I rubbed pathetically at my arms to generate some heat. It didn't work.

I stared down at my stained fingertips, as if they didn't belong to me anymore.

I'm going to vomit again.

But I didn't. There was nothing left in my stomach to fall on the floor.

I fidgeted in the itchy polyester coveralls they had handed me to protect what was left of my dignity.

How the hell did I end up here? In this hell hole.

Shut up Darcy.

Stop complaining.

Think about Jonathan.

Claustrophobia was setting in, so I sprang from the wobbly chair and paced around the table. Around and around.

Please, Reece.

Let me go home.

I need someone to hold me.

A single tear slid down my cheek.

***

Harry came downstairs as I crossed the threshold of home and pulled my body to his. Not a man to indulge in public displays of affection, his embrace told me he was worried. I sobbed and Harry rubbed my back.

"You're freezing," he said. "Why don't you go upstairs and put something warm on?"

I translated that as code for go and wash off your make-up because you look like a meth head.

I scrubbed at my face until it hurt, then turned to the mirror. Swollen, puffy eyes and cracked lips stared back at me. My complexion looked as fresh and dewy as a decaying corpse. I didn't recognise myself anymore. Could I come back from this?

I shrugged into my bathrobe and dragged myself towards the kids' rooms.

I kissed Georgie's head, instantly calmed by the scent of her coconut and hibiscus shampoo. I yearned to take my kids far, far away from this nightmare.

"Mummy, will Jonathan get better? It wasn't just a tummy bug, was it?" She stared at me, daring me to lie to her. Her smarts didn't play in my favour.

"No, Georgie, it isn't just a tummy bug. Jonathan had a serious accident at home. He hurt his head very badly. He's in the hospital right now and the doctors are going to try their absolute best to make him better."

Tears pooled in her eyes and her bottom lip trembled. I brushed away her warm tears and cuddled her, wishing that I could pack up all her pain and throw it away.

"I know it's hard to understand when bad things happen, especially to good people, but the doctors are going to work super hard to make him better."

She nodded. "That's why I want to be a neetnotoligist."

Her mispronunciation made me smile.

"I can help people get a good sleep while the surgeon makes them better. My job is more important because I have to keep the patients alive." She gave me a gap-toothed smile, and I ruffled her hair. Had she been watching *Grey's Anatomy* while I was in another room? I hoped not.

"Oh Georgie, you'll be the best anaesthesiologist in the world, just you wait and see."

Henry was sprawled in his bed, one foot hanging out, snoring soundly, oblivious to the sorrow all around him. For that I was grateful. I was not, however, grateful for the mess his room was in, but that lecture could wait until the morning.

I blew him a kiss and padded down the stairs and past Pepper, snoring in a heap on his fluffy dog bed the kids and I had picked out for him.

Harry and Reece were in the living room.

"Reece, can I shower now?"

"Sure you can."

Harry sipped at a whisky and had placed what appeared to be a glass of grey goose and lime and a hot cup of coffee on the table for me. I could pick my poison. My social graces were all played out and I needed to take the edge off. I lifted the glass and dropped into the chair.

Reece waved his notebook and patted his tablet. "I just took a short statement from Harry. Sorry to have kept you so long on a night like this but I think…"

His mobile rang, and he left the room.

A minute later he was back, his sandy hair now rumpled.

"I've got to go back to the scene. I'll be in touch but please, if you think of anything, no matter how small, call me."

No sooner had his car pulled away from the house my phone rang. I answered it before it woke the kids woke up. I hated a phone ringing after nine p.m.—it rarely brought good news. This night was no exception.

A staccato voice spat my name. A tone that demanded respect, but none would be forthcoming—not from me, not tonight, not ever.

"Hi, Sarah." Even her name left a bitter taste in my mouth. *Well, well, well.* Why on earth would the mighty Sarah Evans be lowering herself to call me? Maybe she'd run out of champagne and got bored. Maybe she wanted to say how sorry she was for the recent turn of events. *Maybe pigs might fly.*

"Is it true? About Jonathan?"

I nodded even though she couldn't see me.

"Has he been hurt? I'm told the police are everywhere, that there's a forensics team over at his house."

It was just possible to detect genuine concern for Jonathan. A smidgeon. Nothing more.

A lump formed in my throat. "Yes, it's true. He's in a bad way. I can't talk right now."

If she noticed the anguish in my voice, she didn't let on, didn't offer any words of comfort or even roll out a cliched "everything's going to be fine".

Not. One. Damn. Word.

And in that second, I hated her for it.

"I don't often indulge in prayer, but I'll be saying one tonight. Meet me tomorrow morning for coffee," she barked. "I need to speak to you. I mean, first Elle and now Jonathan?"

I closed my eyes, intending to count to ten. I hit four and sighed. "Text me where and when." Even though sharing a coffee with Sarah was the last thing I wanted to do, it might be a good opportunity to wrangle a little background on Elle.

Hours later, as I stared at shadows crawling across the ceiling, I recalled Sarah's stark words: "First Elle and now Jonathan."

Once more I saw the puddle of red, the splattered walls, Jonathan's broken head.

I threw back the duvet, escaping my sweat-soaked prison.

There would be no slumber tonight.

CHAPTER TEN

Monday, 21 October

I AWOKE WITH SUCH A fierce headache that, for a second, I wondered if I'd sunk a bottle of tequila in the middle of the night. No, only plain misery. I staggered to my feet then dropped back onto my bed. Harry and the kids were yelling and moving about downstairs.

Life went on.

I'd slept way past my usual time. Harry must have switched off the alarm, bless him.

Downstairs, I rummaged through the medicine drawer and tossed back my migraine medication.

I'd already decided I'd work from home. If I had to deal with any more problems, I'd have a breakdown. Instead, I'd pick up a few files that required my immediate attention and deal with them at home. For a moment, I savoured the taste of coffee and relaxed.

And then I remembered—Sarah Evans.

Damn it. I turned on some music, my way of giving my headache the middle finger. Simon and Garfunkel drifted into the bathroom as I showered, telling me about rocks and islands. *No pain, no crying.*

Those words would be my armour for today.

Time to hustle.

***

We'd arranged to meet at Roast, a gorgeous little coffee shop on Firmont Road. Martha Reeves and the Vandellas were singing about a heatwave. I peeled off my gloves and looked at the condensation on the windows; the irony wasn't lost on me.

Sarah shrugged off a gorgeous charcoal-grey wool coat and air-kissed me as if we were old friends. I flinched but I wanted information as much as Sarah did.

"I ordered you a skinny latte."

I waited for the inevitable little bitch slap as she looked me up and down.

"Hope that's a good choice. I assumed you'd want skimmed milk; got to watch those calories."

And there it was.

"Thanks, Sarah. At least you're on the coffee this morning and not the booze." I tapped my watch and faked a laugh as I took my seat.

She sat her handbag on the table and my coffee teetered so close to the edge it almost landed in my lap. Message received. Her handbag was more worthy than my personal space. To be fair it had probably cost her more than I'd spent on fashion all year.

On first appearance, Sarah might have been mistaken for a lady of leisure who filled her day with lunches and facial treatments. Late forties, she was no stranger to Botox and fillers, but she'd overdone it—the swollen puff of her cheeks and the blinding shine from her ridiculously smooth forehead gave her away. I suspected her lips had recently met with a needle, too.

"Glad you could make it this morning, Darcy. I admit, I haven't reached out to you as much as I should have. I like to think of myself as the beating heart of our little community and I could have done more to include you so I'm sorry for that."

God she's good. Two beats passed as I considered my response.

There was more to Sarah than pampering sessions. Much more. She'd earned her accountancy degree with ease, gained her ACCA qualification and now specialised in complex taxation issues for numerous clients. A smart cookie indeed.

Truth was, at that very moment I felt like I was participating in a game of chess. With a master. But I would give her a good run for her money. I could play her game all day long.

"No need to apologise, Sarah. We're both busy and time flies, right?"

"How are your kids getting on at Cedarwood Primary? I still don't understand why you didn't enrol them in Firston. It's one of the best schools in the country and it's right on our doorstep. I'm on the Board. If you were struggling, I could have smoothed the path for you."

All the right words, but not one genuine emotion behind any one of them. My cheeks burned at the veiled insinuation that we couldn't have afforded Firston school and that my kids wouldn't have been accepted on their own merits.

Calm down Darcy.

"Harry and I chose well, Sarah. Cedarwood Primary is a lovely school, great teachers, good kids and a nurturing environment. What more can a parent ask for?"

"Still, Firston looks better on any CV. Trust me on that, Darcy. I wouldn't have dreamed of sending Jessica anywhere else."

As her daughter appeared to possess every nasty character flaw I could imagine, I didn't take that as a ringing endorsement.

Of course, I said nothing and let her continue.

"How's work at the firm? I hear Bob is still a nightmare to work for. Did you know he used to be at my mother's firm? Oh, that must have been over twenty years ago now. She couldn't stand him. Never thought he was quite good enough to be a Partner."

And there it was. Another little jab.

Sarah's mother was a renowned judge who for two decades had sat on the bench of countless Court of Session trials in Edinburgh. The woman was a legend, one of the first female Partners in a Glasgow law firm. Sarah might have been many things, but I knew she had a gutful of grit and determination so perhaps she had inherited that from her mother. She was showing plenty of that determination to get on my nerves right now.

"Have to disagree with you, Sarah. Bob's one of the best lawyers I've ever worked with. Remember I worked at Richardson Summer? *The* biggest law firm in the country so I know my way around. He does a good job for your husband Eric's firm doesn't he? I assume that's why they renew Bob's retainer every year."

Her eyes, cold as glacial springs, bore through me.

Round one to me.

"True enough, Darcy and I respect your loyalty."

Lifting my cup, I shifted in my chair, waiting for whatever was coming next.

She stared at me, no doubt working out how best to wrangle some answers out of me.

"Elle Bradshaw. I still can't believe she's gone. Doesn't seem real to me. I'm waiting for her to walk through the door and tell us it was all some sick joke."

"I'll be honest, Sarah, it was a hell of a shock. I was glad Maddie was with me."

"Funny that. I know that Elle had invited you but why was she there?"

How on earth did Sarah know why I had been at Elle's house that morning? The grapevine in Cedarwood never ceased to amaze me.

"I just happened to bump into her. She lives just a few houses down from Elle, as you know. Nothing weird."

But, of course, there was…and even Sarah had picked up on it.

"You've always struck me as someone who tells it like it is, Darcy, so I want you to be honest with me. What did you find at Elle's house?"

"Find? What do you mean find?"

"Don't start with me," she snapped. "Just tell me if you found anything unusual."

"You mean besides the dead body?" I searched her face for a hint as to what she was really asking me. No dice. "Sarah, I don't have a clue what you are asking me. I didn't find anything except Elle. We called an ambulance. They arrived, followed by the police. We each gave a statement and left. The end. I wasn't rifling through her drawers."

Though, of course, Maddie had been.

"What kind of thing did you expect me to find?"

Silence.

"Porn?" I said, just to annoy the hell out of her.

Still nothing. I don't think she'd even blinked.

I threw up my hands. "What the hell is going on here?"

She continued to stare so I stared right back and began to appraise her to wait out the awkwardness.

Her subtle honey-blond hair was never out of style and her ice-blue eyes always shone with just a hint of malice. Though she was always beautifully dressed for whatever the occasion might be, Sarah never quite managed to look *inviting*. The cloud of entitlement surrounding her hardened her edges, draining away any warmth and elegance that she might have once possessed. Depending on who you asked, Sarah was equal parts admired or feared; it was the toss of a coin. The same was said of her husband Eric.

The man was everything I had come to expect since moving to Cedarwood. Successful and charismatic, sure. Did any of that matter? Again, it depended on who you asked. I couldn't have cared less but I was likely an anomaly. When I'd sat in Eric's company, I'd found him to be a lot of fun. He was a generous man who gifted a lot to many charities, one being the local animal shelter, which was close to my own heart.

And this was where I couldn't quite get a handle on Sarah. Sometimes I thought she was two people as she also donated a lot of her own money and more importantly her time to multiple local charities but, rather like Elle, Sarah would lure you into her much-sought-after inner circle, have you spill your deepest, darkest secrets, then stab you in the back the second you let your guard down. And all while smiling and telling you that she'd only done it because she cared.

Up close and personal, that was her MO.

I kept her at arm's length.

She nodded, albeit stiffly. "Good. I believe you. Now tell me this, how did you come to be at both Elle and Jonathan's at the worst possible time?"

I delivered a condensed version of the story. She was the last person I'd confide in. Scratch that. The second last. I'd forgotten about her demon seed—precious Jessica.

"So, Jonathan called you? Wonder what he wanted to speak to you about? You know, Darcy, by going over there you might just have saved his life."

"Thanks, although I hate myself for not answering his call. I might have prevented…well, you know."

"Don't waste your energy on guilt Darcy. You can't change it and it's not your place to take on that burden. Leave that to the bastard who hurt him."

My mouth opened but no words came out. It might have been the sincerest thing she'd ever said to me and I could have hugged her.

"Well, we can't have this. Spent an hour rechecking my doors and windows last night. *Me!* It's all a little too close to home."

Blatantly narcissistic, and not a hint of regret. Back on solid ground.

"I heard you met Cole Bradshaw at Jonathan's yesterday. We couldn't make it."

Liar.

"Well? What was Cole like? I haven't seen him in years, not since he was a kid. Is he like Charles or Elle?"

"Honestly, I'm not sure because I didn't know Charles that well. I only ever met him a couple of times before he passed away. But I'd say Cole is definitely more like Elle."

Sarah stared at her coffee. "You know, I don't think for one minute the police think Elle died of natural causes. Or that it was accidental. I'm sure you've heard they had a forensics team over at her house. No way would they be doing that if she'd had a heart attack or something along those lines. Eric was at the club last night and it was all anyone could talk about. Apparently, the police have been contacting people who had been in touch with Elle over the last few days which means they're going through her phone records. Doesn't that seem suspicious to you?"

My heart rate accelerated. How on earth did Eric Evans know this?

"Look, I don't want to speak out of turn, Sarah, and I certainly don't want to add to the gossip that I'm sure is flying about all over the village, but, let's just say I can understand why the police are taking it seriously before they make a determination."

She droned on about inviting Cole and numerous other unsuspecting victims to a new neighbourhood-watch team she was determined to throw together. A simple ploy that would allow her to obtain information and control how it was dispensed. I was having no part of it. I'd already been guilted into enough of this community nonsense and look where it had landed me—one small step closer to the nearest loony bin.

The wind chimes at the door delivered a cheerful tinkle, and Maddie strode in followed by Olivia Miller.

My gaze landed straight on Olivia. At least ten pounds lighter than when I last saw her several weeks ago, she appeared painfully thin. Her hair had grown out of its usual shoulder length blonde bob, and it added to the gauntness of her face.

She caught my gaze and waved shyly at me. I beckoned to her but when she spotted Sarah a look of fear crawled across her face.

Scraping my chair back, I walked towards her, holding my arms out, and I pulled her in for a hug. I was thankful for my ability to know when another needs to be held. I could see it written all over her face.

"Olivia! How are you? Give me five minutes until I shake off Sarah then I'll come over a catch up. Alright?"

She nodded and then turned to find Maddie.

Sarah twisted in her chair as I sat back down. "Dear Lord, what is she wearing?"

"Sarah." My voice held a warning tone.

Confrontation wasn't my thing, but I despised bullies and Sarah was already getting on my nerves. Any more flapping of her cruel mouth and my skinny latte would be dumped over her perfect hair.

I watched as Maddie pressed a coffee and a pastry towards Olivia. She grabbed the coffee with one hand and pushed the cake away with the other.

Olivia had married well, divorced badly and never moved past the change in her social status. Bob Dylan and Ginsberg might have written about the narcissistic plight of the spoiled masses many years ago, but their stark words played out right in front of me every day.

Sarah rolled her eyes and turned back to me. "I don't know what's happened to her. It's sad. What idiot voted her to be treasurer of the church committee? She needs an abacus to get to ten."

It was obvious that Sarah, like Elle, had rejoiced at Olivia's downfall. After all, it made for great fodder at cocktail hour.

Olivia had seemed to have it all—fancy house, successful husband, lovely daughter, a wardrobe bursting at the seams with designer clothes. Every box was ticked. None of it mattered in the end. One day, out of the clear blue sky, her perfect house of cards had collapsed. Not one solid reason had been offered to her from her husband, just goodbye. Having only met him a few times, I couldn't get a handle on Allen Miller. On first impression he'd been likeable, even affable, but since Olivia's public shaming the hairs at the back of my neck had stood on end.

"Do you think she needs Allen? Her daughter's heartbroken and hasn't uttered a word to her dad in almost a year. Do you honestly believe that the collapse of a family is to be laughed at, gossiped about? Some friend you turned out to be."

"Saffron is fine, Darcy. The girl's in her twenties for goodness sake! She's an adult and she'll get over it."

Saffron was Olivia and Allen's only child, and so unlike either of them that I wondered if she'd been left by the stork. Although she'd just turned twenty-one, Saffron had an old soul with a sunny nature and was as smart as the day was long. Currently, in her third year of biochemistry at the University of Glasgow, she was loving her studies and being seen in the arty west end of the city. She frequented a lot of the old Northern Soul hotspots that Harry and I had back in the day, so we had a love of music bond.

Sarah's eyes narrowed. "Look, is it sad? Of course it is. But don't jump to conclusions Darcy. The way I heard it Allen wasn't the one to blame so remember that before you pick sides. Don't fall on your sword when you don't have to. She can't afford to live here, not since Allen dumped her. I guess she's still holding out hope he'll give her a second chance."

That had stung. It was a not-so-subtle dig at me. She knew, as I'm sure everyone did, that I'd inherited my house. I loved my life in Cedarwood, and I thanked Annabelle every day, but I'd be damned if Sarah knew that, and so I wanted to give her a little verbal slap in the face.

"Sarah, Cedarwood is a beautiful place to live, but honestly? It's just like every other nice village."

And just like that, the mask slipped.

Her head reared back, and her glossed lips turned to a thin slash. "You should be more appreciative, Darcy. You have a nice house that you didn't have to earn, so you've no idea of the real cost."

"Oh, I'm beginning to get an idea, Sarah. Tell me, is it worth it?"

She beamed with a vicious little smile. "Of course it's worth it. Have you seen my house?"

We sat in a childish standoff. To my delight, Sarah was the first to give in.

"What really happened to Jonathan? What did you see?" Her voice had softened a smidge.

I closed my eyes, trying to shield myself from the brutal image of Jonathan on that cold kitchen floor, and spilled. "Some bastard tried to kill Jonathan and they left him in a hell of a state. I'm not sure he'll ever recover."

I couldn't stop the tears, sitting there in the middle of Roast, with Sarah Evans of all people, my heart broke. It broke for Jonathan. It broke for Elle. It broke a little for me. So much for being a rock or an island. I glanced back up at Sarah, who grudgingly patted my hand. Her touch felt cold as ice, and I snatched my hand back.

I dabbed at my eyes and prayed mascara hadn't streaked down my face. "What can you tell me about Elle? You knew her well, didn't you?"

"Elle and I went way back. Honestly? We might have been old sparring partners, but she didn't deserve to end up at the bottom of her stairs. That's all I have to say for now."

She pushed her chair back and stood. "I don't believe in coincidence, Darcy. Never have. Be careful."

On that bombshell, she grew tired of me and moved to another table and greeted a few friends that had come in for coffee and some malicious chatter.

I grabbed another skinny latte and sat down with Maddie and Olivia. Olivia's eyes were scarlet from crying and Maddie was soothing her. I glanced at Maddie and reached for Olivia's bony hand. "Are you alright?"

"Sorry, I'm a mess."

"Olivia, listen to me, Jonathan's still alive and that means there's hope."

A cliché, but I'd meant every word.

Maddie gasped. Olivia's eyes widened.

And it dawned on me. They didn't know. So, what the hell had been going on at the table before I arrived? For a split second, everything was quiet. All I could hear was Marvin Gaye singing softly through the speaker.

"Oh, no! What's happened?" Maddie said. "Is Jonathan alright?"

Exhausted by my burden, I told the story once more.

"But it can't be! Jonathan, attacked? In his home? We were just with him yesterday afternoon. Oh my God." Maddie's hand trembled as she held it against her forehead. She looked at Olivia in the most peculiar way before turning back to me. "I'm going to call Dave right now. He can speak to Jonathan's ward and find out what's going on."

As Maddie rummaged for her phone, a whirlwind burst through the door in the shape of Jessica Evans.

If the mother was a nightmare, the daughter was a doozy.

CHAPTER ELEVEN

J ESSICA EVANS WAS MANY things that I loathed, all wrapped up into one pretty little bundle. She was cruel. She was entitled. She was lazy, and she was spoiled through to her rotten core. What I couldn't decide was whether she was just old-fashioned mean or borderline sociopath. The jury was still out.

I could be an overprotective mother—who isn't? But Sarah was an enabler and from what I'd witnessed she'd managed to dismantle most of her daughter's basic human emotions. All parents beam with pride when their kids do something exceptional or selfless, but Sarah would have basked in her daughter's ability to aim her verbal sniper rifle at an innocent. She'd watch proudly as the girl unleashed her cruel tongue like a sword, disassembling someone's reputation, usually just for fun.

Blood sports.

Like mother like daughter.

And yet Jessica amused me.

The smile died on my lips, though, as her grating voice yelled, "It's murder!"

If anyone hadn't already turned to ogle Jessica's gorgeous charcoal-grey suede thigh-high boots and butter-yellow Italian wool coat, they sure did now.

She flounced across the room, eyes snapping at every table, lips turned up in contempt.

My throat dried—*Jonathan?*

"I bumped into Martha Burns only ten minutes ago and she told me that her creepy son Jim—you know that policeman who's always checking me out—said they have some report back, and it's official. That's two murders now!" Jessica sat back in her chair and looked around as if awaiting applause.

"What the hell are you talking about? Jonathan isn't dead! Shut your mouth!"

A dozen heads swivelled in my direction. A hand clamped over mine, Maddie's, her knuckles turning white. For a split second I could have punched her out too.

Jessica tossed her golden waves over her slim shoulders without having the grace to turn and address me. "I wasn't talking to you, Darcy. This is a private conversation."

Maddie's hand continued to tighten around mine and, slowly, my fury dissipated. Just as well, as I'd been about to make a damn fool of myself. Kicking ass in the village coffee shop was just not the proper thing to do.

Sarah looked at her daughter with pride and turned to me. "You should be grateful for the heads-up. At least my daughter cares enough about our neighbours to find out what's really going on around here. Now we know."

"Oh, shut up, you cow! You don't know what caring is," Olivia said, now on her feet.

I couldn't have been prouder. That little move had taken some courage; no doubt months of being the butt end of Sarah and her cronies' malicious jokes had finally made her finally boil over.

Welcome to the club, Olivia.

"Okay, ladies, please! Let's all settle down," Mel Young yelled over the bedlam.

Mel was the owner and manager of Roast. She swept around with a tray of Scottish shortbread and caramel shortcake. Mid to late thirties, she'd recently cut her hair in an angled bob Vidal Sassoon would have been proud of. The paprika colour looked fantastic against her black-rimmed glasses, and I wouldn't have been surprised if she'd started a beatnik night on the coffee-shop floor

"Let's have a little pick-me-up to go with our coffees."

I'd wondered if she was going to produce a bottle of brandy. Turned out she was referring to the cakes. I was disappointed—a brandy would have taken the edge off. Almost all the shortcakes were promptly pushed to the side by the calorie counters.

"What the hell is that idiot Martha Burns doing, walking around town telling people that Elle was murdered? She'll cost her son his job if word gets back to the station," Maddie hissed.

A piece of caramel shortcake was dropped in front of her, and just as quickly she pushed it away.

She wasn't wrong. It wasn't the first time I'd heard Martha spit gossip over the library counter. And then the reality of what Jessica had said hit home.

Elle had been killed.

In her own home.

And I had found her body.

That sick feeling in my stomach reared its head again. The crushing sensation of anxiety settled on top of my chest like the weight of the world had just been placed there. The instant I'd walked into that house on Friday morning I'd felt it. Rage, evil, take your damn pick. Like a scent spritzed around a room, it had hung in the air.

Olivia's hand was pressed against her mouth. "Darcy, I'm scared. What if...I mean...what if the police think..."

She didn't finish her sentence. Instead, she clamped her mouth shut and stared into oblivion.

"Think what?" I pressed.

"I wish Allen was here. God, I miss him."

Olivia once told me he hadn't always been so cold, but I had my doubts. According to local legend, Allen had dumped her at the first sign that her Botox wasn't lasting longer than two months and she couldn't fit into her size-zero designer jeans anymore. He'd had a prenup tighter than a bass drum and he hadn't given Olivia one penny more than he'd had to. She'd walked away with her wardrobe and a pittance. Her Chanel suits were faded, her Hermes bag a little tattered. She still sat on all the right committees, but she had nothing left to say. I couldn't for the life me of understand why.

"Olivia, what's wrong? You said you feel scared. Is it because of what happened to Elle and Jonathan? Talk to me."

"It's just, I'm not feeling well and, eh…"

Her eyes moved straight to Maddie as if begging her to take over talking. Maddie was typing into her phone, oblivious.

"Can I help?"

I wasn't sure what was happening. Was she upset, frightened, or something else entirely?

I waited.

Nothing.

Olivia continued to stare into oblivion.

I should have got up and left the chaos behind, but I couldn't. The whole shop crackled with the chatter of gossip. Theories were flying around the room like an unsettled spirit.

And then Cole Bradshaw walked in.

If there'd been a tumbleweed handy, it would have drifted by.

He stopped, gazed around and squinted up at the counter. Damned hot and he knew it. Conversations halted. Necks craned. Every woman in the shop had turned to get a good look.

Including me.

A plate of shortbread bound for a pair of septuagenarians wobbled as Mel swept toward him, hand outstretched, her greeting husky, body language inviting. I wanted to hand her a cigarette.

His easy smile widened. "I'd love a flat white, please, and maybe a blueberry muffin. Oh, by the way, I'm Cole Bradshaw. Nice to meet you."

Gasps bounced off the walls as the collective penny dropped. This was Elle's prodigal son.

Chairs scraped around him like a disjointed symphony. Amusement glittered in his eyes.

Mel blinked as if she didn't know what a muffin was, then snapped out of her stupor. "Flat white. Cole, take a seat and I'll be right with you."

She fanned her face theatrically, throwing us a wink as she bustled back to the counter.

Cole asked if he could sit with us. Olivia gestured towards the empty chair beside her and flicked a lock of hair over one shoulder.

"Have you heard, Cole?" Maddie said, eyes brimming with tears.

He paled as she told him about Jonathan's grisly fate, cradling the cup Mel had lovingly placed before him. He hadn't even taken his gloves off. "We were only with him yesterday. What the hell's going on here? And you found him, Darcy? Are you alright?"

"That's not all," I said, and filled him in on what Jessica Evans was already broadcasting all over town.

A range of emotions flashed across his face as he digested the news, anger being the last.

"Why didn't the police call me right away? I don't care how small this damn place is, they should be as professional here as they are in any city. I saw a missed call from that cop earlier, but they should have been on my doorstep immediately. I'm going to call McDonald and tell him what a useless piece of crap he is. How can a person walk into a coffee shop and hear his mum has been murdered? How is that even possible? It's sick."

I flinched as he spat out his fury, but he had every right in the world to cycle through his emotions. I wouldn't have been standing upright if I'd heard that news the way he just did. Finally, he shook his head, composing himself.

"I'm sorry, but why would someone kill her? For what possible reason? It just doesn't make any bloody sense. None of this makes sense. And now Jonathan? What are the doctors saying? Is he going to pull through?"

"He's in a bad way. Cole, regarding your mum, this is just gossip from an idiot who can't keep her nasty mouth shut." I looked across at Jessica. "I don't think the police have made any official kind of statement about your mum's death. I'm sure you'll hear from Reece shortly if there's any truth to it."

A shadow fell over our table and the infamous theme tune to *The Omen* started to play in my head as Jessica Evans walked over and offered Cole her hand and glossy pink pout.

"It's so nice to meet you, Cole."

Her eyes traced over his body as he stood and shook her hand. She shrugged one shoulder, parted her glossed lips and shook her golden hair, which tumbled perfectly around her lovely face.

Even I was mesmerised.

"Did you know our mothers were the best of friends?"

I couldn't help it. I snorted.

"I want you to know that I'm here for you anytime."

She extracted a business card from her Marc Jacobs handbag, which I eyed with envy, and handed it to Cole, her crimson nails brushing his hand ever so slightly. "Call me if there's anything I can do for you." She held his gaze. "And I do mean anything."

With a final toss of her hair, she slipped on her coat and glided out of the coffee shop. Cole watched her every move. She'd hooked him within seconds.

God, she's good.

Sarah marched towards our table, beaming with pride. I rolled my eyes and had a sudden urge to take a shower. She extended a hand, as if expecting Cole to kiss it.

"Lovely to finally meet you, Cole. As Jessica said, your mother and I were old friends for many years." She pressed her hand to her chest. "I'm just heartbroken."

If someone had told me I was watching a theatre production I'd have believed them because Sarah was acting her little socks off. Cole appraised her with a hint of amusement in his eyes and said, "Thank you Mrs..."

"Oh, it's Mrs Sarah Evans but please just call me Sarah. And my daughter is Jessica." She nodded towards the door. "She'll be glad to put you in touch with whomever you need while you're staying at your mum's house. I assume you're staying there."

Cole nodded.

She beamed again, and for a moment looked almost human. "I've been noodling over getting everyone together to chat about a new neighbourhood watch. I'd love to double up and put on a little welcome-home dinner for you tonight. You've been through hell. How about it? Some good food, good drinks, good company?" She shifted, blocking me, dismissing me from the conversation.

Cole continued to smile but shook his head. "I wouldn't dream of imposing. And I doubt I'd make great company right now."

"Not at all! It would be my absolute pleasure. Look, I can't pretend to know how you're feeling but I do know misery is best shared, so let us be your shoulder." Sarah looked at the door, no doubt dreaming of matchmaking Jessica with Cole. "Just say yes and I'll organise the rest."

"Alright, that would be nice, thank you. Truth is, I don't feel like being alone right now. But since I don't know many people in town, could I bring my new friends Darcy, Maddie and..." He looked at Olivia.

"Olivia Miller," Olivia said, blushing.

"And Olivia. Would that be alright with you Sarah?"

He held her gaze and I wanted to hug him. While Sarah sputtered a response, I took a closer look at Cole Bradshaw.

Well now.

Handsome, charming, and street wise enough to spot a smiling cobra a mile off. He might be a work of art, but he was no fool, and this little pantomime was beginning to get remarkably interesting.

CHAPTER TWELVE

I BREATHED IN A GUTFUL of fresh air and kicked at a pile of leaves. The action didn't deliver the usual hit of childish delight. The ugly bombshell that Jessica had dropped rattled around my brain like unwanted shrapnel.

Elle's group of friends had been small and select. Chosen with care and attention. Nothing had been taken from the house, so a robbery would appear highly unlikely.

Personal then.

Someone had known her routine well enough to get inside or to be invited over the threshold. It stood to reason that it was someone within her inner circle, *our* inner circle, not a stranger.

Would Cole inherit everything? Time to catch up with my colleague Katie McAndrew, who'd drafted Elle's will. She'd told me that the original drafting had been one of the most exhausting client meetings she'd ever endured. With countless revisions thereafter.

Ten minutes later I waved to Laura at the gleaming walnut reception desk in our office building. She wiggled her fingers back at me while whispering into the phone—which meant she was gossiping on a personal call. She sat straight and glanced furtively around, on high alert for Bob and any of the other partners.

I bagged up a few files, checked my inbox, responded to the urgent emails, and punched in Katie's extension.

"Darcy! What the hell's going on?" Katie boomed before I could offer her a good morning.

We were gossip buddies, but I held back on the detail, saying I was just headed out, but could I have a condensed version of Elle's will for my ears only? Katie obliged.

There was a sizeable estate—no surprise there. Several donations to different charities, a nice chunk of change bequeathed to the church and some holdings that would be passed to Richard Bradshaw. That did surprise me given there'd been such animosity between them. The substantial remainder would go to Cole. No revelations or leads there. I closed my eyes and leaned back in my chair, thinking.

"Have you heard how Jonathan is?"

I jerked upright. Laura sat across from me.

Tucking her long blonde hair behind her ears and adjusting her tortoiseshell framed glasses she stared at me through long lashes that framed huge, perpetually surprised blue eyes. Snarky with no filter, Laura supplied me with the latest office and village gossip. Consequently, she was great fun to be around. She'd also just enrolled part time at the University of Glasgow to obtain her law degree so between her job and her studies she was a hell of a hard worker.

After she digested my news, Laura released a small squeal and rolled her eyes.

"Have you met Cole Bradshaw yet? Oh. My. God! He's so hot. Even though, like, he must be nearly thirty, I'd go there, if you know what I mean."

I filled her in on the impending dinner from hell. "You should have seen Sarah's face when he invited Maddie, Olivia and me. Her head almost exploded. Priceless."

"So lucky! Wish I was going out to dinner with him." She batted her lashes. "I wouldn't get through starters." A low growl came from the back of her throat.

"Christ, Laura, it's not a date." I held up my wedding-ring finger. "Then there's the fact that it's at Satan's lair."

Laura leaned back and frowned. "I'll just bet he's a player though. Can tell a mile off. I was out for lunch over at The Farmhouse yesterday with my big sister, Meg, and her pal Carly. Did I tell you about this guy Carly hooked up with? Met him on some despo dating site. Looked like a hot serial killer. Dexter vibes, you know? Like, nobody has that many profiles. Of course, the date was a disaster. She uses too many filters on Insta."

I opened my mouth to speak but she barrelled onwards.

"Anyway, Meg and Carly used to go to school with Cole, for like five minutes, a gazillion years ago before he got packed off to that posh boarding school. She wasn't even sure if it was him because he's smoking hot now, but Carly said it was, and you know Carly, she's always got to be right."

"I think he's going to be breaking a few hearts around here before Christmas. Anyway Laura, I'm off home. I'm just...well I'm done in, so if anything comes up just give me a buzz."

"Do you think they'll find him Darcy?"

"Who?"

"The killer. Whoever killed Elle and hurt Jonathan. It's got to be someone close by, right?"

***

Dumping fresh coriander into a large pot of vegetarian chilli, I wiped my hands when the doorbell chimed.

Reece McDonald was waiting on my doorstep. Typical. I was a hot mess—leggings, oversized t-shirt smudged with tomato puree, my auburn hair in a messy top knot, and not a lick of make-up. Did I even have a bra on? Yep. Thank God for that.

"I'm cooking," I said, ushering him into the kitchen with my cheeks burning from the embarrassment I felt for how I looked. "Join me while I finish off. I'll pop the kettle on...Is it true?" The question fell from my lips before I had to chance to stop talking.

"Is what true?"

"Was Elle really killed?"

Reece blew out a long, exhausted sigh as if he'd pulled an all-night shift and I felt crappy about my abruptness.

"You know I can't go into specific details. Nevertheless, based on the findings in the PM report, we've concluded that Mrs Bradshaw's death wasn't accidental or from natural causes. She was murdered."

"How so?" I reached for a chair to steady myself.

"This remains in strict confidence, and I'm only telling you because Cole Bradshaw has already been informed." He searched my face for a reaction. "The position of the bruising on her neck suggests Elle was grabbed with extreme force and shaken so vigorously that her neck was broken. She'd also been struck on her face. In other words, it wasn't the fall that killed her. She also suffered swelling to her brain, multiple blunt-force trauma to her skull likely sustained during the fall and that resulted in a large amount of blood loss. That's the direction of the investigation now."

I gawped at him, my vision blurred. All I could hear was the bubble of vegetables in the pot.

Reece cleared his throat, breaking the spell. "How did you know?"

"I heard some gossip in Roast this morning."

As much as I didn't like Martha or her son, I wasn't about to dump them in a shitload of trouble. Not that Reece wasn't already aware of his colleague's unprofessionalism; his embarrassment was written all over his face.

"Thought so. Cole looked ready to punch me out when I landed on his doorstep an hour ago. Well, it appears that I'll have to tighten up our security protocols at the station. Small villages, eh?"

We raked over my statements one more time, then Reece stood and thanked me for the coffee.

"Jonathan's attack…It must be connected Reece. There's no possible way that this quiet village can have two horrific incidents like this within days of each other. Not a chance. Tell me I'm not losing my mind?"

"I agree, Darcy. We're looking into every connection possible. I'm aware that Elle and Jonathan were friends and that they shared a lot of common acquaintances. People you know. Even people you trust."

The statement hung in the air between us.

"And."

"And, well, as you say there must be a connection. That's exactly where my focus is right now. If you hear anything, anything at all, that might prove useful then please call me. Even if you think it's irrelevant."

"It feels like a blanket of something rotten, evil, has fallen over this town. I can't put my finger on it. It's just, I don't know, skeletons where you least expect them. I'm beginning to wonder how well I really know anybody around here."

"You sound like a cop." He released a sharp sound of amusement. "I'm not being an alarmist, but we don't know what the motive for both incidents were yet. And until we do everyone should be cautious. I'm serious. Take every precaution you can. Be vigilant."

"Honestly? I don't even want to let the kids outside to play in the garden right now. I feel, I don't know, anxious…on edge. I'll never get over finding Jonathan the way I did. I have no idea how you guys can do the job you do. How you handle it." I was twisting and rubbing the skin on my hands furiously. Feeling the familiar burn, I broke them apart and sucked in some air. *Breathe.* Old habits I'd managed to shake were beginning to creep back in.

And I didn't like it one bit.

"Darcy, some things stay with you forever. I wish they didn't, but I can't lie. You just have to find room for them and put them in the right place." He tapped the side of his head.

Nodding, I leaned against the door as he stepped out into the garden. "Yeah, I know the drill."

He stared at me as if he could see into my deepest, darkest place. I wondered what the look on his face represented. Empathy? Perhaps.

"If it's possible, could I get some of Jonathan's stuff from his house to take to the hospital. Just whenever you've, eh, well, finished doing what you need to do. I think it would be nice for him to have his own pyjamas. Even if he doesn't know." My lip trembled. This time I just let my tears slide down my cheeks. I was too tired to fight them. "Is that stupid? It sounds stupid. I'm stupid. It's just, well, I wouldn't have wanted my mum in hospital without her own things. It makes it just a little more bearable. Maybe the feel of them, the smell of them will give him some fight, you know?"

"As it happens, I know exactly what you mean. And it's not stupid, Darcy. Tell you what, call me in the morning and if we're finished you can have five minutes to lift a few items of clothing. Alright?"

I waved him goodbye and sank into a chair at the kitchen table. Pepper padded into the room and plunked down at my feet. I patted his big, solid head and wondered what I'd do with him long term. "Don't worry, Pepper. Everything's going to be alright, I promise. I won't let you down."

Elle's perfect life had been a façade beneath which had lain an ugly mess. She'd been sleeping with her good friend's husband, and if Cat had known all along, she must have hated Elle for it. Being the laughingstock of the town could be a very lonely place.

Bill Henderson had been her lover. Had he been her enemy too?

Her relationship with Richard had been toxic. Had it spilled over into hate?

Sarah Evans, Jessica Evans, Olivia Miller. Three more people who'd encircled Elle's world, each of whom had been burned in some way or another.

And then there was Cole. Everyone was smitten with the guy but what did we really know about him? Then again, he'd been in London when Elle was killed. Confirmed alibi. But still…something about him had set my radar off. Just a smidge too perfect for my liking.

Perfection—I didn't trust it.

I'd seen what perfection looks like to the outside world. And I'd seen what its rotten core looked like when you peeled back the pretty layers behind closed doors.

And my dear, old friend Maddie. *What piece of the jigsaw are you?*

But my biggest obstacle was the brutal attack on Jonathan. Why? Everybody loved Jonathan. What on earth could have been the catalyst for such a brutal attack? I recalled his message, replayed his voice in my head. He'd sounded scared, anxious. Did Jonathan know something about Elle's death? No, that didn't feel right. Had he suspected something? Yes. It seemed the most obvious conclusion. Had he confronted that person? It was the type of thing Jonathan would do; offer to help a troubled soul without realising he was putting his own life at risk. One little question had crawled into my brain and refused to leave—why call me? Of all people, why did Jonathan call me? Sure, we were friends, but I couldn't imagine that I would be the person at the top of his list to call to discuss an urgent or personal matter. It didn't make any sense.

Why couldn't I mind my own damned business? Because someone had cruelly served Elle and Jonathan an injustice. I couldn't let that go. My childhood had taught me dark things can happen behind closed doors. I wanted, no I needed to open the door and let the light shine in.

Craving a hit of normal, I passed the next half hour chatting on the phone with my brother, Adam, about the trials and tribulations parenting his teen kids, James and Emily. The stories he regularly fed me were the stuff of nightmares, and I was beginning to wonder if he was exaggerating just to mess with me.

By the time the call had ended, I felt almost human. That feeling evaporated as soon as I began to rummage for something to wear to Sarah's for what was sure to be the evening from hell.

Two hours later my bedroom looked like a frat house.

Clothes, shoes, and accessories strewn everywhere. I was pissed at myself for giving a damn about my appearance. This was, after all, a dinner party I didn't want to go to, hosted by someone I didn't care for. And yet my little bubble of self-worth had popped and fizzled and suddenly I hated every piece of clothing I owned. It didn't matter how

I angled the mirror; I looked like crap. My hair hung limp and my make-up looked like it had been applied by Gene Simmons.

I told myself to get a grip, scrubbed my face clean and poured myself a large drink. The tinkle of ice cubes against the glass pleased me. By the end of this week, I might be checking into the nearest AA meeting.

With the second application, my highlighter and bronzer didn't appear to have been mixed up with crayons from the kids crafting box. Instead of trying to straighten my hair, I waved it slightly. I crammed myself into a pair of skinny jeans—*skinny? Who the hell was I kidding?*—and finished off with a black, sleeveless shell top and a silver bracelet. Casual but dressy, and it had only taken me several hours.

I was ready to enter Dante's circle of hell.

CHAPTER THIRTEEN

OLIVIA SLUMPED AGAINST THE rain-spattered car window.
"You look lovely," I said.

And she did. The black Carolina Herrera shift dress was faded but still had enough going for it to leave me feeling woefully underdressed.

She didn't utter a word.

I eventually ran out of inane conversation and thought back to last year. One memorable night at the Cedarwood Country and Golf Club, Elle had had a few too many gin and tonics and had taken Olivia down like a lioness stalking a gazelle. It had been quick and merciless, and meant Olivia was no longer part of the pack because she couldn't afford to be.

I'd held Olivia's hand in the bathroom while she sobbed. I'd uttered empty platitudes about being better off without him, but her red-rimmed eyes had been empty; she wasn't buying it. Maddie had supplied the tissues and a large glass of sparkling wine, and Olivia had downed it like a sorority pledge at spring break.

Of course, her dearest friends had fallen away from her quicker than if she'd announced she'd just returned from a leper colony.

I was relieved when we turned into Oakwood Grove and approached Sarah's elegant six-bedroom house, with its gleaming white sandstone dotted with dormer windows and topped with a black slate roof

Harry pulled into the circular driveway, and Olivia gasped.

"What's wrong?" I asked.

"What's he doing here?" she said as if she'd just spotted Jason Vorhees in his obligatory hockey mask.

She pointed a trembling finger towards a white BMW. "Allen."

It seemed Sarah hadn't tired of using Olivia as her emotional punch bag, why else would she have invited the man Olivia was still very much in love with and longed for?

"Do you want us to take you home? Harry, turn the car around right now. I'm not putting up with this."

"No!" Olivia said. One word, but she had delivered it in such a steely tone it stopped me in my tracks. "No. If that cow wants a showdown, I'm going to let her have it. I'm so tired of all this, Darcy." She sighed and lowered her head. "If I hadn't been so pathetic, I'd never have allowed to get myself into this mess in the first place."

Before we could escape, the glossy, black front door opened, and Sarah presented herself like the goddess of the underworld. She reached out to embrace us, her perfect smile like a mask. The hypocrisy made me want to run for the hills.

"So glad you could all make it," she said.

She wore a deep plunge charcoal shift dress and five-inch pale-pink heels with a distinctive red sole that screamed, *look how much I paid for my gorgeous shoes.* A shimmering diamond tennis bracelet adorned her slim, bronzed wrist. One simple but stunning accessory was all this chick needed. How did I know these things? Because I watched *The Real Housewives of*...well, everywhere.

Sarah leant towards Olivia and whispered loud enough for the next-door neighbour to hear, "Oh, Olivia, don't hate me! I bumped into Allen, and before I knew it, he'd invited himself for dinner. I didn't have the heart to say no." Her eyes glittered wickedly. "I'm afraid he's brought Gabby with him—you know, his latest girlfriend."

Itching to punch her lights out right there, I said, "This is low... even for you." I took Olivia's hand and led her towards the door. "Let's go and have dinner somewhere else."

"It's fine," she whispered. Her lips formed a shark-like smile, and she squared her bony shoulders. "Once you've hit rock bottom, you've nowhere else to go. It's time to start climbing back up. I've got this."

And with that she swept into the living room.

The interior designer had it bang on the money. A palette of bright white, hazel and bronze presented clean, soft lines. As much as I hated to admit it, Sarah had beautiful taste, in décor at least.

Allen and Jessica were talking with a tiny, slim woman with shining blue-black hair cascading down her back. The woman looked at us. She couldn't have been more than twenty-three. Allen Miller had to be somewhere in his early fifties. They say size matters, and from what I'd heard, Allen's wallet was big.

Harry coughed, barely masking a snort of laughter.

Olivia shuddered. It was a micro movement, but it was there. But then, as if possessed, she glided towards her ex-husband.

"Allen Miller! You've put on weight! Have you stopped going to the gym? Doctor Hall isn't going to be happy when he sees this." And right there, in front of everyone, she slapped his belly.

Jessica's eyes bugged as if a stripper had started to pole dance in her mother's living room. Elsewhere, this wouldn't have even registered a one on the bizarre-night-out Richter scale; Glasgow is a wonderfully intense city but, here in Cedarwood, this bordered on the socially outrageous. I was positively gleeful.

Olivia grazed a stupefied Gabby's hand with three fingertips. "Hi, sweetie. Lovely to meet you. I'm Olivia, but I'm sure Allen or Sarah's told you all about me. I'm usually the hot topic of conversation." Then she cupped her mouth with her hand. "A little tip for you, Allen likes to eat after, well you know. He's not as young as he used to be and needs to keep his strength up. It's a shame because he had a lot of stamina when he was younger."

With that bombshell, she threw a malicious grin to Sarah, who was standing open mouthed and openly seething. Olivia snatched up a glass of champagne. "Cheers, everyone!"

At least half the contents of the flute glass disappeared.

Allen looked like he was about to pop a vertebra, Gabby appeared stunned, and Jessica scowled.

"Beautiful room, Sarah," I said to defuse the situation. "I love what your designer's done."

I had no bloody idea what the designer had done but it sounded right, and I knew she'd engaged the services of an interior designer because she'd told me so…often.

"Thank you, Darcy," she snapped, her eyes still on Olivia.

Olivia banged her glass down on the tray and lifted another glass, then settled herself on the sofa, one long leg crossed over the other. This girl was on a roll. Whilst I would be her cheerleader, I prayed she wouldn't get her heart broken all over again.

A wolfish smile spread over Allen's face. "Well, Liv, it's been a minute. You're looking good!"

He moved towards Olivia, the leer evolving into a genuinely happy smile. I could see it in his eyes. Softness. Perhaps it was a glimpse of the new Olivia that had done it, or maybe he could see the old Olivia—the person she'd been before he'd tossed her away.

"Allen!" Gabby squeaked, now standing alone like a plotted plant.

Sarah's hideous mind game had backfired. She threw the champagne tray onto the table and stormed from the room, muttering about canapés.

A breathy whisper snapped me out of my trance. "Surprised to see you here."

Not as surprised as I was to see Bill Henderson. I'd assumed Cat would have locked him in their basement.

I looked him over him for obvious signs of violence. Unfortunately, there were none. The little glimmer of smugness in his eyes told me he thought I was checking him out.

Dear God, help me.

"How you are?" I said, out of politeness rather than concern, and I followed his gaze, which had landed right on the abandoned Gabby. She wouldn't be lonely for long.

"All good. Catch up later." he said and made a beeline for the petite woman.

Cat was chatting with Jessica in the corner. She gave me a knowing look and a small smile. Her shining eyes dimmed a little as her husband began chatting it up with Gabby. I wanted to shake her and tell her she was worth so much more, but of course I didn't. I pretended I hadn't seen the pain in her eyes.

Shame on me.

Intertwining both of my hands I began the fierce rubbing again, hoping for the familiar burn to chase off the feeling of anxiety that was approaching.

Voices drifted in from the hallway. Gabby's eyes widened. Her tongue flicked over her glossed lips. I knew Cole Bradshaw had entered the room before I'd even set eyes on him.

Once again, his embrace of the ladies lingered just a little too long. Flirting seemed to be in his DNA, and I wondered what branch of the family tree he'd acquired that from. His mother no doubt. He caught a glimpse of himself in the bleached-wood mirror and smiled, liking what he saw. Yep, I'd bet he thought every song was about him.

Bill Henderson checked out the competition in his peripheral vision. His Adam's apple bobbed as he swallowed.

Maddie and Dave arrived and the social merry-go-around began all over again. Dave sidled over to Harry, while Maddie and Olivia exchanged a glance, and I itched to scratch beneath the surface of the silent narrative floating between them.

I stood quietly, feeling alone in the room full of people. *What am I doing here?* The question turned around and around in my head until I felt dizzy. The room was filled with longing looks, furtive glances, coded body language. I could almost hear the unspoken words. All I wanted was to go home to my kids, play Monopoly, drink hot chocolate and chatter to my adopted animals.

I didn't belong here.

I didn't fit in here.

I wasn't part of the pack.

I never would be.

Tears itched at my eyes. Grown woman or not, in that second, I missed my mum and I wanted her to hug me and tell me everything was going to be alright. Damn it all to hell, why did she have to fall ill? Why did she have to leave me? Grief had gotten hold of me again.

Allen's mouth moved but I hadn't heard a word.

"Sorry, I was a million miles away there, Allen. What did you say?"

His voice was soft, any trace of arrogant bluster he might have once possessed was gone. "Olivia told me it was you who found Jonathan. Christ, Darcy, it's unthinkable. Jonathan would give you the shirt off his back. What the fuck?" He drained his glass. "Sorry, I'm upset."

I appreciated his honesty so much that I wanted to hug him.

He grabbed my hand. "He was close with Elle, so it can't be random, can it? Hell of a thing you've been through, and I take my hat off to you for even being able to leave the house, let alone sit through tonight's bullshit."

My eyes widened and I wondered if he caught my look of surprise. Allen seemed like a completely different person. I knew his concern was genuine; his smile was real and the look of anguish in eyes hinted at real pain.

He continued, "I don't know why I'm here just as much as I bet you don't either. I'm too old for this crap, Darcy, and I've lost the one thing that mattered to me the most."

"Tell her, Allen."

He smiled but still managed to look a little lost. "It's never too late to make amends, is it? Especially now. After, well, after everything that's happened. Makes you re-evaluate, doesn't it? Olivia looks thin, too thin. She's not looking after herself. My fault, Darcy. God knows, I've made a mess of things." He looked around for another whisky.

This was the man Olivia had told me about. The man she had sworn had existed all along. The one she'd fallen in love with. I was so grateful to finally meet him, but his words hit me like a punch to the gut. Unshed tears that were already gathering prickled and burned. I couldn't stop them.

Allen didn't flinch. "Better to let them fall. Let me get you a tissue."

"Thanks, but I've got one in my bag. I just need a second."

He patted my hand, and it delivered the comfort he'd intended. From the corner of my eye, I saw Olivia watch our exchange with such a look of longing that, in that very moment I wanted nothing more for them to patch things up if that would make her happy.

"You alright? You look upset," Harry said.

"I don't think I can do this, Harry. I want to go home."

But Sarah was back with another round of cocktails, so I swallowed my misery and grief and slipped the mask in place. If everyone else here could, so could I.

I picked up what appeared to be a Cosmopolitan, sidled over to Cat and touched her arm. "Did you get in touch with Reece McDonald?"

"Who? Oh, the cop. I told him Sandy Olsen's a nutcase with too much time on her hands. I walked past Elle's house on Thursday night…well, alright, I went into her garden. Had this crazy idea about asking her if she'd been texting Bill about anything other than training at the gym, but I changed my mind. Hand to God." Her voice crawled up an octave. "Detective McDonald, Reece, whatever his name is, grilled me for an hour. I told him a hundred times I didn't go in her house on Thursday, didn't speak to her, didn't see her. This is a nightmare. He's looking for Bill, too, by the way. God knows why."

If Carla was on the money, I had a good idea.

"As far as I know," Cat said, "Bill hasn't returned his call. I'd better sort that out before the stormtroopers arrive and huckle us off. I bet I can lay the blame for this at Sarah's door. Going around town telling everyone Bill had an affair with Elle. What on earth am I doing here making nice?"

She began furiously turning her wedding band and delivered a tinkling laugh that was devoid of mirth and sounded hollow to my ear.

"I'm wondering the same thing, Cat."

Feeling a tap on my shoulder, I turned.

"Reece McDonald landed on my doorstep earlier," Cole said. "He confirmed it. The police believe my mum was killed on Thursday night. Her neck was broken, not from the fall. I just can't get my head around it. It can't be true"

"Cole, I'm so sorry but they're right. I found your mum and, well, it appeared even to me that someone else had been in the house."

"How so?"

I told him about the storm that night and the mess left behind.

"Your mum would never have allowed it; you know what she was like. A surgeon could have worked in her hallway it was so clean. And if she fell and someone was there, why didn't they get help?"

"Maybe she fell minutes after they left. I don't want to believe someone could have hurt her. To tell you the truth it makes me uneasy about staying at the house. I'm jumping at every sound and it's giving me the creeps. Thank God I was in London when the police called on Friday morning. I know that cop Reece spoke to my friend whom I'd spent the night with. They called her this afternoon, obviously checking up on me. I guess I can't take it personally, but it stung. I might have been distant from my mum for the longest time, but I could never have hurt her. The police better get to the son of a bitch that did this before I do because I'll not be responsible for my actions."

I offered as much sympathy as I thought he could bear. Then someone nearby mentioned Jonathan.

"I spoke to him after lunch on Sunday," Cole said.

This was news, and I wondered why he hadn't mentioned it earlier.

"It was such a trivial conversation that I forgot about it until the police brought it up. They must have combed through his phone records."

Maddie fidgeted and Olivia gulped at her drink.

So, the gossip Eric had heard was on the money.

"What did you talk about?" I asked. "Did he sound normal?"

Harry found something of great interest in the curtains, obviously affronted at my nosiness.

Cole frowned. "He called to discuss my mum's funeral. Gave me some good advice about my next steps. He sounded fine. There was no hint that anything was wrong."

A trivial conversation? I couldn't imagine describing the discussion of my mum's funeral in such a way.

"He simply told me to take my time with my decision making," Cole said. "I was trying to work out whether to stay here or to go back to London. He said not to act on grief. Which reminds me, I need to talk to a lawyer in your office called Katie. Is that one of the partners, Darcy?"

I nodded. "Just call and they'll arrange an appointment. I'll give you my number, too, in case you have any problems."

"So, tell me," Sarah said, "who's in charge of the harvest food-bank drive? Without Jonathan is there even a point?"

"Jackie McPherson's a good bet," I said. "She runs her own business and she's super organised. It'll be a walk in the park for her."

Sarah wrinkled her nose. "Jackie McPherson couldn't run a piss up in a brewery. She's been in love with Jonathan for years. Following him about like a schoolgirl. She really believed she had a chance after Sally passed and Doug left her. I mean, can you imagine *her* as the minister's wife? All those years of pent-up frustration, well, it makes you wonder, doesn't it?"

What the hell?

I counted to five before I spoke. "Are you actually serious right now, Sarah? Jackie has never been interested in Jonathan, not in that way! That's the most ridiculous thing you've said all night. And she divorced Doug!"

Sarah shrugged, completely unfazed by my rebuttal.

"Who's Jackie McPherson?" Cole said.

Jessica sniggered. "Just a nobody."

I wanted to hurl a string of expletives at her—I have an arsenal of colourful language at my fingertips, which since having the kids I didn't get to indulge in as often as I'd like.

"My eight-year-old has more social awareness than you, Jessica. And better manners." I glared at her, still reeling from her cruelness.

"Jackie's a great choice," Olivia said. "Loves to be busy, it's probably the only reason she gives her spare time to helping out at the church."

Maddie nodded. "Let's speak to her about it so things don't slide. There are too many families out there depending on us."

Sarah sniffed. "Well, look at you, Maddie Clement—helping the needy. Tending to the less fortunate. Funny, I don't recall seeing you at any of the charity events I've hosted over the years. Given all your free time it might be something you could consider. Give back, you know?"

Dave stiffened, but Maddie shrugged. "I make my own decisions about how I spend my free time, Sarah, thank you."

Sarah surprised me. Altruistic? Perhaps. A jibe at Maddie? Definitely.

"Do you miss the States? Any plans to return there?" A saccharine smile, as fake as her wrinkle-free brow, spread across Sarah's face.

"Oh, I do miss it, but I love it here. Even with your ridiculous accents. I mean, Dave, what did you tell me the other day? How 'this tit came in, still steamin' and reeking of bevvy'. Now what does that even mean? You guys speak in a foreign language."

We all laughed, except Sarah.

Dave finished his story at the dinner table. "I swear to God, the guy was still three quarters drunk. Couldn't even stand let alone get on the examination table. The nurse and I had to practically lift him onto it. The alcohol was streaming out of every pore, and I think my eyes were watering. I felt drunk by the time he left my office. Never a dull moment."

"I don't know how you can stand it," Jessica said, and shuddered. "Thank God I can afford private health care."

Dave shook his head. "It's the best health care system in the world. What could be better than a system designed to give everyone, and I mean everyone, free treatment at the point of delivery?"

She continued to season her starter.

"Regardless of class, wealth, race, religion or status. A system of equality must surely be better, no?" He folded his hands and stared at her.

Sarah tossed her napkin on the table. "Oh, get off your soap box, Dave. You run a private practice as well so don't kid yourself with that liberal nonsense. As I said to Maddie, it would be nice if she spent some of her time helping and getting her hands dirty rather than just talking about charity work. So, you can pipe down."

"Let's talk more after you get your medical degree—public-health economics is not your forte, it would seem," he snapped, and downed half his drink.

"Please don't jump to conclusions Sarah. You might just embarrass yourself," Maddie added quietly.

I fiddled with my linen napkin, watching Sarah scan the table looking for a new victim. She found one.

"I love your dress, Olivia. Isn't that the one you wore a few years ago at the club's Christmas party?"

Old Olivia would have cringed. Old Olivia would have sunk into silence. Not anymore.

"Thank you, Sarah. I wouldn't say it's one of my more memorable outfits, but it must be nicer than I thought for you to have remembered it."

"You always did have good taste," Allen said, a hint of melancholy in his voice.

"Not in everything, Allen."

"Touché," he said, and raised his glass.

Gabby glared at him, then resumed batting her eyes at Cole.

Bill stared at Gabby like a Doberman eying a slab of meat.

I had an urge to run a hot shower and scrub myself clean.

CHAPTER FOURTEEN

JESSICA RAMBLED ON ABOUT her social-media activities while Cole stared at her with an expression of...something. Disinterest? Boredom? Maybe I just didn't recognise lust anymore, although I doubted that. I was fantasising about slapping some duct tape over her mouth when Cole stopped the torture.

"Want to join me for a coffee sometime, Jess? Be nice to have the chance to get to know each other a little better."

"Sure, that would be good."

She must have it bad, I thought. She hated the name Jess—no one called her that. Leaning forward, she offered a glimpse of her impressive cleavage. *Agent Provocateur* would be my best guess although I couldn't be sure. I'd long ago opted for boring and comfortable. But after receiving an eyeful of her hot pink lace maybe I'd have to rethink that.

My mind meandered to my drawers stuffed of lingerie that I didn't often wear anymore, which was a shame. Regardless of whether it was a jeans and t-shirt day I'd always worn something silky and pretty underneath. I never wore it for Harry or any other man I might I have dated in my past; I wore it for myself. It made me feel good. So why had I given that up? Why had I deprived myself? I guess like most women once the kids had come along, I'd forgotten all about myself and the silly little pleasures that I had once indulged in.

Still, the peepshow Jessica had just given me had me rethinking that.

"Cole, do you follow football?" Harry asked. "Scotland's playing in the UEFA qualifiers tomorrow night, and it's apparently

Bake-Off-and-booze night. Why don't you come over to Dave's with me? Have a few beers?"

Cole hesitated.

"Come on," Dave said. "It will do you good. And if nothing else it'll be a laugh. Scotland will get gubbed anyway."

"Gubbed?" Maddie said.

"Beaten, get their arses kicked!"

"Bake-Off-and-booze night?" Olivia said.

I laughed. "More like an excuse to get together with Maddie and Gia and have a few drinks. Usually, the *Bake Off* is on in the background, or *The Pioneer Woman*, or *Barefoot Contessa*, or a cooking show of some description. Not that we get much of a chance to watch it, so I suppose it's about the booze. Maddie thinks adding in a baking show gives us an excuse for a cocktail on a Tuesday night. You should come over, Olivia."

Jessica smirked and played with her hair. "Can't wait for middle age, Darcy, sounds like a riot."

"You're almost there, *Jess*."

Cole ignored our childish exchange, and said the guys could count him in. "I was thinking about visiting Jonathan. Since you work at the hospital, Dave, do you think it would be alright?"

Dave nodded. "Don't see why not but let me check with his team first. He's in neurology intensive care and sometimes visiting is restricted. He had surgery last night to reduce the swelling on his brain and stop the bleeding. Now he's in a medically induced coma. They won't know the full prognosis until they bring him out."

Everyone was silent. Pressure began to build in my chest, and I found it difficult to breathe.

Jonathan's damaged head.

The blood.

Pooling and seeping.

Sprayed and dripping.

I need to get the hell out of here.

Sarah gulped champagne. "You know, a strange thing happened." She glanced over at Cole, pausing for dramatic effect.

"Go on Sarah," I said.

"Well, you all know how athletic Jessica is—I mean the girl runs every day; that's why she has that amazing figure. So, she passed Jonathan's house on Sunday afternoon and saw Richard's car parked outside."

"Richard was at lunch with us on Sunday," Maddie said.

"No, this was much later in the afternoon, way after you'd all left."

She leant back against her chair, pleased with herself for delivering a ticking time bomb.

My mind went into overdrive. Richard had spent almost two hours with Jonathan. Why go back?

"Sorry, Cole," Sarah said. "I don't mean to insinuate anything, but there it is."

"No need to apologise. I barely know my uncle Richard, but I'm not entirely sure what you're inferring. You think he went back to Jonathan's and hurt him? Why? It's not possible. What did the police say?"

Sarah flushed. "Ah. Jessica hasn't contacted the police yet."

"What?" I said, "Come on, Jessica. What are you playing at? You should have told the police the second you heard about Jonathan."

"Oh, shut up, Darcy! You really do go on and on. Nobody cares. Unlike you, I have a life."

"Not too busy to float around the coffee shop this morning, dropping bombshells, or to sit here eating dinner. You'd better call them, or I will."

"Sorry I'm late!" a voice boomed from the hallway. Eric, Sarah's husband had arrived.

He entered the room with Richard Bradshaw, followed by a whisky-filled breeze. A pin could have dropped, and I'd have heard it. Richard might have been the topic of our conversation, but as both men seemed to be at least three sheets to the wind it was unlikely either noticed the atmosphere.

"I didn't set you a place because you didn't tell me you'd be home," Sarah said icily.

"I'll rustle something up from the kitchen. Smells good in here and I'm starving." Eric saluted his wife and gave us a lopsided smile. I felt a surge of sympathy for him. "Apologies for the late intrusion," he slurred, "but Richard and I got caught up at the club."

"At the bar more like," Sarah said with a glare.

I wanted to crawl under the table.

Eric ignored her and introduced himself to Cole. "You look just like your uncle! Shame." He slapped Cole on the back as he laughed at his own joke and clapped his hands together. "Anyone need a top-up? Richard, have a seat and I'll see what I can rustle up."

Seconds later he called out from the kitchen, "Sarah, why are there fifty containers from Nick's littered all over the place?"

Oh, the joy! Nicks was the best Italian in town. She hadn't lifted a finger. I knew it!

Plates rattled, cupboard doors slammed, a microwave pinged, and Sarah's face bloomed a magnificent shade of purple.

"Please excuse my husband. He's clearly enjoyed himself a little too much at the bar." She cleared her throat and sat ramrod straight, as if about to deliver the Gettysburg Address. "By the way, the police have checked all the security footage on Spruce Drive and found nothing. Zip. Most of the cameras are aimed at the houses and driveways, not the road, and Jonathan doesn't have any security cameras."

"How do you know?" I asked.

She shook her head and said in a pitying voice, "I have many friends—I hear things."

Damn it! Bloody Martha and her coven had been at it again.

Bill cleared his throat. "Any leads on what happened to Elle?"

"I'm still not convinced the police are correct," Cole said. "My mother lived here her whole life; this is a safe place. I know she could be difficult, but I just can't believe anyone would have killed her, it seems impossible."

Jessica placed her hand on top of Cole's and squeezed.

Sarah sighed. "I think our little police force are out of their comfort zone. They don't seem to be doing much to solve this if you ask me. They seem way over their heads. No leads, no ideas, nothing. It's like a nightmare has descended on our village. Murder? Here? Which leads to me to my next point. Neighbourhood watch. Thought's, people?"

Anxiety finally got the better of me, and the chicken dish placed before me was the sign from above I'd been waiting for. I threw my napkin on the table and stood.

"I'm sorry but I don't feel well. I...I keep thinking about last night and...I need to go home." I titled my head in Harry's direction.

"Oh, don't be silly, Darcy. You need company after the shock you've had. Please, sit down and stay."

I wavered. Sarah's request sounded genuine, and I was touched by the unexpected sentiment, but I nodded towards the plate. "Besides, I'm vegetarian. I really am sorry, I thought I'd told you."

Harry jumped up and placed his hand on the small of my back. Tension fell away from my shoulders as I felt his touch.

"Jessica," I said, "call Reece McDonald. This isn't a game. It's sick and it's twisted. Tell them what you saw." I cut my eyes to Richard. "It's obvious that someone in this village, someone close to home, either knows what happened or had a hand in all of it. I'm going to do everything I can to help the police get to the bottom of it. That you can take to the bank."

I'd lit the match.

Time would tell if it would burn.

***

I was quiet on the drive home, pondering where the answers to this dark conundrum lay. There had to be a connection, something deeper that had taken one person's life and attempted to end another's.

The monster must have left a smattering of breadcrumbs somewhere. I'd follow them into the forest and pray I could find my way back.

"Jonathan doesn't have any family. Both his parents are dead, and he's an only child, right?"

"I think so," Harry said. "Why?"

"Just that it would be nice to take a few things to take to the hospital, water his plants, that sort of thing. I'm wondering who else has keys to his house."

Snooping was part of my plan but elected not to say so what with Harry already glaring at me.

"Stay out of this Darcy. What the hell was that all about back there? You've got me worried out of my mind. What if someone sitting at that table is involved? Did you ever think about that? We have two kids and I need you in one piece. Just let the police do their job."

"What? I'm sorry, Harry, but I had to say something."

"I know you inside and out. I know you want to save the world, but you've no skin in this game. Listen to me. There's a psycho out there and I don't want you on their radar."

But, of course, it was already too late.

CHAPTER FIFTEEN

Tuesday, 22 October

MISTAKES HAD BEEN MADE and the plan had started to fall apart. The police knew Elle had been killed, and then there was Jonathan. How the hell had he survived? The beating had been brutal, and yet...

What if he woke up? What if he remembered? He simply couldn't be allowed to live.

No. More. Mistakes.

Now it was time to pay Darcy Sinclair a visit.

First, a little warning. And if she didn't pay attention, then the delivery of an excruciating punishment.

How exquisite that would be.

The hunter zipped up the black jacket, pulled on gloves.

Keep digging, Darcy. Keep digging.

***

As I waved Harry and the kids off to school, Indy's little brown head appeared around the corner of the house. I filled her bowl and petted her as she tore into the kibble. Animals could soothe me quicker than a pill any day of the week.

Stretching and then rolling my neck, I breathed in the morning air and kicked at the leafy carpet of red, gold and bronze. The mist-laden hills were breath-taking and drinking them in eased the tension between my shoulder blades. Just below my sightline, the ice-cold loch would be lapping against the wind.

I made sure not to take the natural beauty of our little village for granted. I'd not had that luxury growing up on a housing estate, though Glasgow has an abundance of green spaces if you know where to look. I missed the city, but it wasn't a long drive and I visited often, especially the Kelvingrove Art Gallery and Museum, which looked like something out of the pages of a fairy tale. My mum had taken me and my brother when we were little, and my own kids loved it.

My gaze landed on my own little oasis—red sandstone, peaked slate roof and gleaming bay windows that let in swaths of natural light. A bit of a minimalist at heart, I'd gone for a neutral interior décor, with splashes of red, bronze and chocolate inspired by my favourite season.

A flash of black darted through the dense thicket of trees in the garden.

What the...

Chest hammering, I squinted. Was someone watching me? The figure tucked behind one of the trunks and stood so still it might have been a sculpture. I couldn't make out the face, the height, anything, but the threat hanging in the air was so heavy I could almost smell it.

I inched forward.

Opened my mouth.

No sound came out.

Wait.

I patted my pocket. No phone. *Shit.*

Fear gripped me and I froze.

Move.

I bolted for the door, landed inside to safety, fumbled with the keys and locked the door behind me. What the hell had I been thinking? I'd seen *Halloween*, *Friday the 13th* and every slasher film known to man. I knew better than to approach a space in which danger lurked.

Nausea hit me in waves, and I slumped against the door, breathing deep, trying to calm my scrambled nerves. *What the hell?* Who in their right mind would be creeping around my garden in the early morning? It didn't make sense. *I* wasn't making sense. Maybe someone had simply lost their dog as was looking around our garden, or...

Oh. My. God.

Had he come for me? Or she?

I couldn't be sure.

It was an ordinary October day. A mundane Tuesday morning.

Could bad things happen on days like this? Of course they could! That's when you're most vulnerable.

The phone rang, and I nearly lost my breakfast. Fumbling one last time with the lock I grabbed the receiver.

"Darcy!" Jackie McPherson began to sob. "I can't believe what's happened to Jonathan."

I made soothing sounds as Jackie babbled, my eyes still on the door. I didn't have the strength left to navigate Jackie through her grief.

She drew a breath, and I was all out of niceties.

"Do you have a spare set of keys to Jonathan's house?"

"Sure. Why?"

"I want to water his plants, empty the fridge, that sort of thing. If Reece approves it of course."

A moan escaped her. "Why didn't I think of that?"

"This is a hell of a thing Jackie," I said softly. "Don't worry, I'll take care of it all."

"Thank you, Darcy. I'll pop over shortly and drop the keys off."

As I hung up, Pepper flew at the door and growled, his hackles raised. I whipped my head around. Hot sharp pain sliced through my neck. I gripped the phone—my palms slick—and crept along the hallway and into the kitchen. Pepper was still at the door, barking and jumping. I pressed the call button twice, intending to connect to the police, then hung up and skulked, instead, to the kitchen window.

Leaves swirled, squirrels ran up and down the trees. Nothing out of the ordinary. I allowed an exhale of air to blow through my nostrils.

What the hell was happening?

Pepper trotted back into the kitchen and pressed his cold nose into my hand. I buried my face into his fur, soaking it with my tears.

Get a grip Darcy.

Be the girl you used to be. Remember her?

She wasn't afraid.

I was calm enough to go to the front door.

Inching it open, I pressed my full weight against it so I could slam it shut if a threat presented itself. With Pepper at my side, and still clutching the phone, I stepped out and scanned the front garden, concentrating on the little thicket.

Nothing.

My phone vibrated.

I glanced at the screen—a text from a number I didn't recognise. Hands trembling, I clicked on the message.

Nosy bitches get put to sleep.

This time I didn't falter.

I called Reece McDonald.

***

Thirty minutes later, an officer promised to return my phone that afternoon. If possible. *And everything would be fine.* Since he looked about twelve, his reassuring platitudes didn't exactly instil me with confidence.

I paced, nervous about the warning message, but damned angry at myself too. I'd been reckless; blabbering to anyone who'd listen about my ridiculous intention to find answers. In the cold light of day, I'd sounded like a fool last night. Why was I getting involved in any of this? I've always considered myself to a be a relatively smart woman, headstrong at times, emotionally charged at other times, but I'd never considered myself to be overtly foolish, but I'd been making some very questionable choices these last few days. Why? None of my business, right? But it was. Because two people had been brutalised, and I felt compelled to get to the bottom of it.

A therapist would have a field day with my psyche, but I already knew where my compulsion to right wrongs had been born. All I had to do was to look to my past. I couldn't fix things when I was a little girl, but I was bigger now...stronger.

The fight was evened out, and I didn't like to back down from a fight. Especially when I had right on my side.

Still, I hadn't felt this vulnerable—like I wanted to crawl out of my skin—since I was a kid. I was no Marvel Avenger and my Krav Maga skills were a tad rusty.

And yet...

I remembered the girl I used to be. Angry from seeing the underdog get kicked again and again. Shoulders that squared in the face of danger or ridicule. The girl with fiery red hair who could dance to dawn and still make it through every hour of the workday. The girl who had more dates than she could count. The girl who spoke her mind at every opportunity. What had happened to her? Where did she go? She had faded away into oblivion leaving behind the overly cautious, hyper vigilant mess I was today.

Well, to hell with that. No more.

I straightened my spine and drew a deep breath.

Starting now.

Think, Darcy.

Question was, was that message and my uninvited visitor connected to what I'd said at Sarah's? If so, then the rage that had visited my doorstep belonged to someone sitting at her dining-room table. Or, and it was a strong possibility, was someone messing with me just for perverse fun? It was probably the kind of sick joke Jessica would get a kick out of.

Every creak and groan that emanated in the house had me on edge. A sick montage of images from *Halloween* and the *Texas Chain Saw Massacre* tortured my jumpy brain.

Yet I tried to laugh and shake it off. The new and improved me.

Yeah, right.

It was a relief when Jackie landed on the doorstep.

"Are you alright Darcy? You look ill!" Jackie pressed the back of her hand to my forehead the way I did with my kids. The way my mum used to when I was sick.

"Not ill Jackie, just sick to my stomach. I'm jittery as hell."

"Sit down and let me make you a coffee or a nice cup of tea. How does that sound?"

I watched her bustle around my kitchen somehow knowing exactly where to find everything. A natural caregiver.

Jackie's tiny frame and girlish aura made her appear years younger than her thirty-plus years; She had a heart-shaped face, glowing peachy skin, cupid's bow lips and deep-brown eyes.

"So, I hear I was the talk of the town at Sarah's house last night." She leaned against the counter and tilted her head. "Cat called me this morning, which was surprising since we're not really friends. I got the feeling Cat's trying to assemble as many allies as she can right now. Makes me wonder why."

She held my gaze. "Is it true? Did Sarah accuse me of being in love with Jonathan?"

Heat burned from my cheeks so fast I felt I *was* running a fever. Shame did it to me every time.

Had I spoke up on enough on Jackie's behalf last night?

"Jackie, not one person there last night believed a word of it. Sarah vomits nastiness when she has an audience. Nobody pays attention to her."

"You know when Doug and I separated, I didn't want to get out of bed for the longest time. Divorcing him was the hardest thing I've ever done, but I knew we'd drifted too far apart to fix it." She fiddled with the teaspoon until it clattered to the ground.

"Jackie, you don't have to explain anything to me."

"You're my friend, Darcy. I want to you to know that it just isn't true! Sarah's really lost her mind if she's making up stories that ridiculous. And honestly, I only started out helping at places like the church and at the McCullens Riding School because I had too much time on my hands, and I couldn't stand to wallow in my self-pity anymore. It was sink or swim time for me, so I swam. Buying into *Bella Rosa* was the best decision I ever made, hands down." She continued to fiddle with the teaspoon until I wanted to liberate it from her hands. "I could have told Jonathan I was too busy to keep on donating my time, but he was having such a hard time with Sally's illness and then her death that I just didn't have the heart. Anyway, I enjoy it so why quit? But if that's what people think then maybe I should just walk away from it."

Reaching for her hand, I ushered her into a chair. "Jackie, listen to me, no one thinks that. I've no idea why Sarah said it, or why she says any of the things she does. Look, maybe she's not a happy person but don't let her steal away your happiness, what *you* enjoy doing. When did it become a crime to help people? Just ignore her."

"Don't sweat it, Darcy. Truth be told, I'm in a funk anyway. Did I tell you that Doug is about to become a dad?"

Her brown eyes filled with tears as she turned her head away from me to stare out of the window.

I didn't say a word but simply wrapped my arms around her, letting her sob. I knew Jackie had tried to get pregnant during her marriage with nothing but negative results and a lot of heartache so that news must have stung like hell.

We sat like that for a few minutes. Two women connecting in their own grief. Whatever that may have been.

Jackie finally sat back and wiped at her eyeliner which had started to smear. "I must look a sight. I'm happy for him Darcy. For Doug and his girlfriend, but it was like a punch to the gut. He called to tell me. I was so damned angry, I thought he was trying to hurt me. He wasn't. He just didn't want me hearing it from someone else."

"Well, you can put it to bed Jackie. You've digested it, now don't dwell on it. Gone."

After a few lingering sniffles she nodded. "You're right. I'm done."

"Listen to me Jackie. You're a beautiful person. You'll find your happiness."

She squeezed my hand, stood up and stretched. "Enough about my minuscule problems. Whatever is going on around here has me scared shitless. I can't sleep, I'm hearing noises in the house every second and I think there's an intruder in the house."

"You're not the only one Jackie. I'm a hot mess at the best of times. This is the worst of times."

"Jonathan must be the nicest guy anyone could meet, so why on earth would anyone hurt him? In such a violent way? I'm seriously thinking about getting a dog. Like this chap right here." She bent down to pet Pepper and his tongue lolled out. "I've hated being alone in the house since Doug left anyway, I've watched too much true crime on TV."

"I feel someone close to home is connected to this, Jackie. I'm not trying to scare anyone, but I feel it in my bones. It just can't be a coincidence."

"Oh, it's no coincidence. So, look, I'm going to have a rummage around Jonathan's desk, just see if anything weird pops up. I know the police have been there, but I know him, they don't. If I find anything I'll let you know, right?"

She pressed the keys into my hand, and a thought popped into my head.

"Maddie's popping over tonight for a few drinks and a catch-up. Fancy joining us?"

I was delighted when she accepted, sensing Jackie needed a friend. And in that moment so did I.

"And thank you for going over to Jonathan's," she said. "I'm just not ready to face…where it…well, you understand."

Did I ever.

***

An hour later and spitting mad, I stared into the beady, black eyes of Sergeant Jim Burns. What the hell had Reece been thinking, sending him to babysit me?

Reece could have sent anyone else on the face of the planet and I would have been grateful for their company. In fact, I would have breathed an awful lot easier, particularly after the six grim words that had been delivered to me via text message several hours earlier.

Where was the baby-faced officer who had left with my phone several hours earlier when I needed him?

"Regardless of what Reece-bloody-McDonald might have agreed with you, I'm giving you two minutes. I haven't got all day so in and straight back out." The officer appeared happy to have the upper hand this time around.

I didn't let my eyes leave his face once.

Prick.

Jim gnawed at my frayed nerves, and he made me uneasy. Deep in my gut, I could sense that this guy couldn't tolerate my presence and I wasn't sure why.

So, I squared my shoulders.

I couldn't even recall ever formally meeting him prior to being at Elle's house on Friday morning. Still, I grudgingly admitted to myself that I needed an ally, someone to watch over me whilst entering Jonathan's house and so, I offered him a heartfelt and genuine smile to see if we could get our newfound relationship back on track. After all, beggars couldn't be choosers, and I was running out of options.

I decided to try and make nice with the man standing in front of me.

He snatched Jonathan's keys from my hand, rattled them in my face and said, "I think I'll open the door, Mrs Sinclair."

What followed was a veritable production. He slipped inside, perused the bottom floor like he was auditioning for an episode of *Miami Vice*. However, his stretched neon vest didn't quite compare to Don Johnston's gleaming white suit. If I hadn't been so anxious, I might have belly laughed.

"May I enter now, Sergeant?" I snapped.

He beckoned me in, as if one might their dog.

Count to ten, Darcy.

Closing Jonathan's door behind me, I froze.

The house's welcoming ambience had evaporated, replaced by a cold silence.

Sunday night.

The blood.

The trajectory of the crimson spray.

The drenched floor.

His head.

My shoes.

I leant against the door and swallowed a lump of grief, clutching the bag I'd brought to fill with Jonathan's pyjamas and toiletries. Wanting to move. Not wanting to move. *Fool.* I dragged myself along the hallway and into the living room. Pictures of Jonathan and Sally were everywhere, in happier times, before Sally had fallen ill. It was easy to see how much love they'd shared.

"Come on, Ms Sinclair," Jim boomed. "Haven't got all day. I said you have two minutes."

My earlier attempt at warming to the policeman dissipated and a vision of punching Jim square in the face cheered me as I climbed the creaking stairs.

I skittered around the bedroom and picked up bits and pieces Jonathan might need. A large calendar showcased a stunning white husky. I smiled a little; Henry had a similar one in his bedroom.

Today's date, 22 October, was circled in red and an appointment had been scrawled in the square: *Meeting with Olivia M.*

Wait…what?

Jim thundered up the stairs. "Mrs Sinclair, hurry it along."

Ignoring him, I slid open the drawer of a small desk in the corner and flicked through a sheaf of papers stacked neatly inside. One sheet caught my eye – a faded photocopy of a spreadsheet. Question marks had been scribbled next to some of the numbers. A sticky note was stuck to the spreadsheet that read: *As discussed, Elle.*

And there it was, clear as day.

"Mrs Sinclair!"

"I'm coming!"

I slipped Harry's old phone from my pocket and snapped a photo of the spreadsheet, then returned the sheet and closed the drawer.

My cheeks flamed and the phone felt like it was burning a hole in my pocket as I left the room. Figures weren't my strong point by any stretch, but I knew an accounting sheet when I saw one.

Questionable numbers? Perhaps?

Had Jonathan suspected Olivia Miller of wrongdoing and been planning to confront her? Surely the trail of breadcrumbs couldn't be that simple. Reece would have spotted it a mile off.

I was getting desperate now if I was reaching that far.

The front door was wide open. No sign of Jim. I glanced at Jonathan's office. Did I have time to get inside?

Voices drifted in from the garden. I'd never make it to Jonathan's office for a look before Jim came and dragged me out.

Time to get out of Dodge.

CHAPTER SIXTEEN

"JIM BURNS," JESSICA PLACED her hand on the sergeant's arm, "don't you ever get scared going over these terrible crime scenes? I guess you must have gone through years of training. Oh, I wish I could be that brave. So, what's the latest?"

I thought I might barf. The theme tune of *The Omen* played once more in my head. The policeman's face split into a leering grin.

Before Jim could vomit anymore information he shouldn't, I made my presence known.

"Hey, Jess!" I waggled my fingers just to annoy her.

Her ice-cold eyes shone with malice as I walked out the front door. I couldn't help congratulate myself for pissing her off so quickly.

She looked up at the house and snapped, "What were you doing in there?"

"None of your business! But if you must know I was collecting a few things to take to the hospital. Sergeant Burns here was kind enough to come with me." I waited for Jim to back me up.

Not one word.

She moved in front of me, blocking my way. "Why are you everywhere I turn?"

I looked away.

"Didn't you hear me?" She pushed right up against me.

Trying my hardest to count to ten, I hit two. I balled my hands into fists and tried to push past her. "Move out of my way."

Jessica grabbed my arm and sneered. "Some nerve you had last night, speaking to me the way you did. In my own house. I won't forget it, Darcy. I don't know who the hell you think you are, but you should be careful. Stick to cooking or whatever the hell it is you do for fun and stop being so nosy."

Shaking my arm free of her grip, I leant forward, my face up close to hers, and smiled. "Don't underestimate me, *Jess*. I meant every word I said last night. I have two kids to protect. One person is dead, another is fighting for his life. And I've witnessed the aftermath."

Nothing.

She didn't blink.

"Jonathan is my friend, so I'm invested in getting to the bottom of this. Now get the hell out of my way!"

A second or two passed, and I watched her turn and totter the other way on her four-inch heels, Jim waddling behind her.

I rounded the corner, stopped and took a deep breath. What was wrong with me? I loved the film *Goodfellas*, but I was no Robert De Niro.

More important, why had she been so angry that I'd been in Jonathan's house?

***

Harry used the drive to the hospital to lecture me about getting involved. "What did I say last night Darcy? What the hell is going on?"

In a huff, I stewed for the rest of the journey as Harry lapsed into silence. I could feel his anger circulate around the inside of the car. I felt claustrophobic and couldn't wait to escape.

By the time we pulled into a parking space, I was fuming. Harry's message had been received loud and clear and whether it was his intention, I was ashamed of myself for putting our little family in harm's way.

In the ICU, a nurse leaned against a medicine trolley, exhaustion etched into her expression. Limp wisps of hair had escaped her ponytail. Dave was talking to a tall man with dark-brown hair and stubble on his chin. The man looked down at a chart and frowned.

"Just can't get the pressure down. The surgery could have gone better, and post-op steroids aren't cutting it."

I cleared my throat. Dave looked up and slapped Harry on the back. "This is Andy Thomas, neurologist extraordinaire. He's just giving me an update on Jonathan's condition, as a friend."

We shook hands. Andy glanced at Dave, who nodded.

"Ordinarily we wouldn't discuss a patient with anyone other than family, but I understand Jonathan doesn't have anyone. Must have been a hell of a shock finding him that way. I'll step away for a minute. Let you talk amongst yourselves."

Plausible deniability.

He squinted at the chart and went over to a desk.

My eyelids itched, the familiar tears gathering.

"Jonathan's not doing good," Dave said, and I wanted to cover my ears. "The brain swelling isn't coming down as fast as Andy would like. The longer that continues, the more serious the consequences could be. His arm was broken during the attack and a pin has been inserted. It looks like he tried to defend himself."

I swallowed back bile. Harry placed his arm around me. Our anger at each other had dissipated the second we walked into the ICU. Fear and horror will do that.

Dave gave me a moment, then said, "Andy's increasing the medication. There'll be an MRI in the next half hour. Depending on what shows up, further surgery might be necessary. Trust me, he's getting the best care possible."

Andy came forward and the tears I'd tried to hold in check ran down my face. I took the neurologist's hand and thanked him. Something, the thread of a memory, tugged at the back of my mind.

And then it was gone.

We went into Jonathan's room and the scene before me hit me like a sucker punch.

Tubes snaked over Jonathan's body. The machines keeping him alive beeped and buzzed and whooshed. His head and arm were heavily bandaged, his face swollen and devoid of expression. He looked less like our friend and more like he was ready to leave this world.

Sinking into a chair next to his bed, I touched his hand and whispered that we were here, that everyone was sending him their love.

Harry didn't seem to know what to do with himself.

I sucked in a sob and squeezed Jonathan's hand. "We need you tell us who hurt you."

Nurses bustled in and gently ushered us out. It was time to prep Jonathan for the MRI.

On the way home I stared out at the falling rain and remained quiet.

We tucked into veggie risotto with fresh asparagus for dinner. Pumpkin and cinnamon candles flickered, making the room cosy and warm. The kids' presence kept the conversation light.

It was just what I needed to soothe my frayed nerves.

"I'm not leaving you on your own, Darcy. I won't go to Dave's house, I'll stay. I can watch the highlights of the game later if you have the girls coming round. Or I can watch it upstairs." He offered a smile. "I'd rather watch it live, to be honest."

"Don't be silly, Harry. I'll be fine." I glanced at Isla who had arrived minutes before. "Isla's coming with me just now whilst I walk Pepper. See! I won't be alone. As soon as I'm back, you head over to Dave's as planned. Maddie and the others will be here anyway. I won't be on my own. Promise."

And there it was. The ripple effect caused by my questionable decision making. Plain as day. My husband didn't want to leave me on my own. *I* had caused that.

Embarrassed and defeated, I slipped on Pepper's leash and plunged into the cold night. I took a deep inhale and watched as my breath swirled before me on my exhale.

"Spill it, Darcy. What the hell is going on? Why is Harry clucking around you like a mother hen? Not his usual style."

"Isla, I don't even know where to start. This has been the day from hell." I recounted my tale of woe. My narration was flat. It didn't sound like me at all.

"Nosy bitches! What the actual hell, Darcy? What did Reece McDonald say?"

"I haven't spoken with Reece yet. I handed over my phone to some policeman, Isla, I'll get it back tomorrow, hopefully. Other than that, I haven't a clue. You know, I did wonder if Jessica was trying to mess with me. Kind of sounds like something that she would get a kick out of. She didn't take too kindly to me giving her a hard time last night in front of an audience. I mean, lord knows I cannot stand her, but I've never upset her or done anything to hurt her. Why go after me? Other than to scare me for a sick thrill. But then again, it's probably nothing to do with her and as usual I'm way off the mark."

"Well, if it isn't her Darcy then I hate to say it…" She didn't need to finish the sentence. Even though I was bundled up, a chill crawled through my clothes and prickled my skin.

My frosty breath twirled in front of me as we hurried along the dark roads bathed in the glow from lit-up windows and doorstep pumpkins. A light fog began to descend, and I couldn't have been more grateful for Isla's presence. Harry was right all along—I had no business being out on my own. The empty streets were beginning to give me the creeps.

Then I realised where Pepper had brought us.

Mapleway Road.

He'd found his way home.

Gently tugging on his lead, the dog ignored me as he planted his rump on the cold concrete and refused to budge. I bent and cuddled him. "Come on, Pepper. Time to go back. Good boy."

"Bless him, Darcy. He knew exactly where he wanted to go." Isla ruffled his head then turned towards Elle's house as voices drifted from the garden, the sound of heels clacking on the ground. I stumbled as Pepper flew into a standing position, almost knocking me over.

It took me a few beats to place the woman who was walking out of the garden of Elle Bradshaw's house on the arm of Cole. *Gabby.* The black-haired beauty who had appeared in Sarah's living room with Allen Miller.

Well, well, well.

If Cole was embarrassed by his perceived indiscretion he sure as damn didn't show it. Rather he waved as if greeting old friends.

"Hey ladies. What are you doing loitering out here? Darcy, you remember Gabby?"

I did. I also remembered that he was supposed to be taking *Jess* out for coffee. Ah, the joys of being in your twenties and carefree.

"Hi Gabby. It's nice to see you again."

Gabby stared at me. I stared back. This time I didn't see her pretty face. I saw flushed cheeks, black mascara etched under her red rimmed eyes. Was it remnants of make-up left over from a romantic encounter? Was it traces left behind after a screaming argument? Or an encounter that somehow had erupted a volcanic explosion of emotion? She pulled her coat tighter to her body and moved her gaze to Cole.

I didn't like it. Not one bit. Her whole vibe told me to push a little. "Are you alright, Gabby?"

She moved her hand to the back of her head, patting it. Bedhead. The shining penny dropped. Likely there had indeed been a volcanic explosion of sorts, but I pressed her again just to make sure.

"Gabby, did you enjoy the dinner party last night?" What the hell did I say that for? The dinner party that she had attended with Allen.

"Oh, I did thanks. Cole and I got to chatting and, eh..." Her eyes hadn't left Cole's face since I spoke. I could have struck up a conversation with the evergreen six feet away from me and I doubt she would have noticed.

Peering at her as was difficult in the darkness, even with the sliver of light provided by the dull glow of the streetlamp. She didn't seem to be under any duress. Still. Her expression bothered me. I waited but got nothing.

"Cole, this is Isla, my friend and neighbour. And this is Pepper, your mum's dog. I took him from the house the day I found your mum. I, eh, well I hope you don't mind but I didn't want him to be taken to the SSPCA, which is where the officer, you know, Jim Burns? Well he was ready to send Pepper straight to the shelter. I should have asked if you want to take him back." I smacked my hand across my forehead. "I'm so sorry. Do you want me to pack up his things and bring him round tomorrow?"

Inside, my gut was churning. The kids would be devastated. *I* would be devastated. Pepper had filled a little of the emptiness I'd been carrying, and I didn't want him to leave.

Cole didn't look once at the dog, and it rubbed me the wrong way. Whether Cole took my silence as his cue I wasn't sure, but he rushed to assure me that being a carefree bachelor was not conducive to having a canine sidekick.

"Harry and I are happy to keep him, Cole. He'll be safe with us. Truth is, we love having him and the kids adore him." If he cared, it wasn't obvious. He seemed to be edging towards the road.

Isla had been unusually quiet. I turned to invite her into the dwindling conversation, but she was shifting her gaze rapidly between Cole and Gabby, so I kept my mouth shut. Isla was a smart cookie, and I wanted her take on my new friend later. Let her take in the sights.

"I'm off to Dave's for the football. Is Harry coming along? I need to take the edge off with a few beers, you know what I mean? It's been a hell of a couple of days."

"He'll be along just as soon as I get home and relieve him of kid duty."

"Cole," Isla finally spoke, "please accept my condolences on your mum's passing. I knew her for years. In fact, I was a guest at your parents' wedding. I'm truly sorry for everything that's unfolded. It's scarcely believable."

"Thanks Isla." A laboured sigh was released, and it was apparent that we had handed him a reminder of the ugly situation. It made me feel like crap.

"It's a cliché, Cole, but it does get easier. With time. A lot of time. Of course, you are dealing with a whole different set of emotions given what's happened. I'm a stranger to you but I know a lot about grief. So does Darcy. If you ever need to talk, please reach out to us. Sorry if I'm overstepping, it's just my way."

Cole's shoulders relaxed. "I appreciate that more than you know, Isla. Thank you. And I might just take you up on that offer. I'm honestly not sure what the hell I'm feeling."

"Of course you don't. This is the worst of situations. Go get a beer with the guys. Let off a little steam." Isla clapped her hands together. "It's freezing out here, Darcy let's get this pup home. Cole, it's been lovely to meet you. And you, Gabby."

"Night ladies." Gabby finally opened her mouth just as we turned to depart. Her arm gripped Cole's as they continued down Mapleway Road.

"Darcy! Isla!" The silence of the night was interrupted by the shriek of my name being called. My heart sank. Sandy Olsen. Damn. We'd almost made it.

I liked Sandy, but the woman could talk. And talk. Every time she cornered me, she drilled me for every titbit of gossip I might be willing to share on anyone and everyone within a ten-mile radius. I wouldn't have been surprised if someone had told me she had trained with the CIA on interrogation tactics.

Then again, wasn't Sandy the very person who had alerted Jim to the possibility that Cat had been loitering around Elle's property on Thursday night?

For once it seemed that I was in the right place at the right time.

"Keep moving," Isla hissed.

"Darcy. Wait up."

"We're caught, Isla. Let's make it quick."

"I thought you hadn't heard me. Was that Cole you were chatting with? Looks like he got lucky last night. Who was that he was with? Is that his girlfriend? I know her face from somewhere. Where's he going?"

I didn't know which question to answer first, so I simply smiled and asked if she was well.

"Are you kidding? I'm a wreck. It's a shitshow around here. What with a murder right across the street and now Jonathan Mitchell, of all people, attacked, beaten to a pulp! In his own home. Never thought I'd see the day. Not here, not in Cedarwood."

My lips parted to speak but I wasn't quick enough.

"Thursday night is my usual margaritas with the girl's night. We usually start off at Nicks for pasta or pizza then pop over to The Fir Tree for drinks. I cancelled because of the weather. Had I been out, I might have seen something over at Elle's when I came home. I can't believe she was killed, right there, in that gorgeous house, whilst I was sitting on my sofa watching Netflix. Across the street! It's the stuff of nightmares!" Sandy's voice had inched up a few decibels and I was sure that everyone on Mapleway Road would soon learn what show she had been binge watching. But she wasn't wrong. It was the stuff of nightmares.

"Was it you that saw Cat going to Elle's house on Thursday night?" I asked, although I already knew the answer. I just wanted to move things along.

"Yes. I had my French poodles out for a quick walk around nine that night when I saw Cat marching through the rain, straight to Elle's garden. I just assumed she was going to pop in for a drink or something. She didn't even have her hood up or an umbrella or anything and it was torrential. Just marched right on past me as if she didn't hear me yelling at her from across the road. I told the police when they canvassed the street. I know Cat is pissed at me for that but telling the police was the right thing to do. Let the police sort it out. It's Bill she should be mad at, not me! The things I could tell you about that man! I don't know how Cat puts up with him. Hand to God, I'd have killed him years ago."

Isla beat me to the punch. "Did you see Cat go into the house or was she walking up to the front door when you turned away?"

Sandy chewed her bottom lip for a few beats. "Like I told the police, I didn't see her actually go into the house. She started up the garden, walking fast, but then kind of lingered. I didn't see any more than that because Poppy started to whine in the cold, and I turned back home."

That version matched what Cat had told me on Saturday.

"Did you see that photo Jessica Evans posted on Instagram on Monday night?"

"Eh no. I don't follow Jessica on Instagram." I shivered but not from the cold.

"It was a gorgeous selfie of her, obviously, but she'd strategically placed herself to get Cole in the shot. I thought maybe they were hooking up but now I wonder if he even knew he was in the shot if he's got that brunette on his arm tonight. Mind you, if he's anything like his uncle Richard he'll have bedded half the village by the end of the week." As her laugh tinkled into the now freezing air, I could feel Pepper tugging against his leash, restless to move.

"Well Sandy I have to get this boy home and see to the kids. It was lovely catching up."

Sandy bent to pet Pepper. "I'm so glad you've got him Darcy. You're a good soul taking him in like that. Anytime you need a walking buddy give me a buzz. My poodles love to walk and I could do with good company on my excursions. You know me, I love to gab."

Did I ever but I was touched by her invitation, nonetheless. "Thanks Sandy. I'll do that."

"Well, well, wasn't that an interesting wander?" Isla turned up the collar on her coat as I gazed at the frost forming on the ground creating pretty diamond-like sparkles each time light from the street-lamps hit it.

"I met Gabby last night at Sarah's house. She arrived on the arm of Allen Miller."

"No!" Isla let loose a belly laugh. "Allen? He's older than me, for God's sake. Is he kidding? But at least I finally clamped eyes on the prodigal son. Mind you I didn't expect to meet him with a local hottie on his arm days after his mum was found dead. Still. With that face I guess he doesn't sleep alone often."

Deep in thought I didn't reply.

"Are you alright?" Isla asked, eyebrows raised.

"I'm just spooked Isla." My voice sounded wispy, feeble, and I hated myself for it.

"The text message you received? Darcy, I would be jumping out of my skin if I were you."

"It's too weird. Too convenient. I flap my big mouth at Sarah's dinner party last night and the next morning the shit hits the fan? I can't help but think it must have come from someone at that get together at Sarah's house? But why? Why me? I don't know anything; lord knows I wish I did."

"Well, perhaps you've rattled a cage. Or perhaps it's just Jessica being a spiteful witch. But I don't like it either way, Darcy. Not at all. Now I'm not leaving until Maddie gets here so go call her and tell her to hustle."

"I'll text her now." I'd let Isla escape before I sent her over the deep end. She sure as hell hadn't signed on to be my babysitter.

It had to have been someone sitting at that dinner table last night. A sensible enough observation, but one that only led to more questions.

I pondered on that as we neared Cedar Way and I could see my house lit up, calling me home. Halloween was less than two weeks away. Carving pumpkins and long chilly walks would be followed by sparklers and fireworks. Then we'd be decorating the Christmas tree, wrapping presents and writing letters to Santa. I loved it all—the anticipation, the preparation—almost more than the days themselves.

I let out a sigh of relief.

Home.

Safe.

CHAPTER SEVENTEEN

TRUE TO HER WORD, Maddie arrived quarter of an hour later carrying a chilled bottle of Prosecco and a tray of nibbles.

As I waved her in, the phone rang. Gia. She couldn't make it tonight due to a work fiasco. Her words, not mine. I bit back a grin at the melodrama that seemed to unfold in Gia's office. HBO couldn't write it.

Maddie's arrival had proven too much for Georgie and Henry, and a round of squeals and giggles followed, turning my home into a backdrop from *One Flew Over the Cuckoo's Nest*.

The doorbell chimed, and Pepper flew by me, barking his head off.

Olivia stood on the doorstep, clutching a bottle bag.

I pulled her in for hug, feeling her thin frame. "Come in. It's freezing."

She unwrapped her scarf and smiled. "I hope it's okay. I thought about what you said at dinner last night and decided it sounded like fun."

"You're more than welcome." I led her through to the living room.

She and Maddie locked eyes and I sensed a little shift in the air.

I introduced the kids to Olivia and shooed them upstairs. "Guys, take Pepper with you."

Pepper was becoming the best buffer I could have hoped for.

Now for the women sitting in my living room—I was all out of social niceties. *Time to shake out some answers.*

Before I could open my mouth, Olivia said, "Darcy, I'm not sure where to start. Well, it's better if I—"

And again, the doorbell rang, and Pepper was back down the stairs and flying towards the door.

Oh for—

I should have taken it as a sign. Cat Henderson shook a bottle of champagne at me.

"Hey, Darcy. Here I am!"

Yes, here she was. *What the hell?*

She swept past me, leaving the scent of Tom Ford in her wake. Pepper approached her with caution, telling me to keep an eye on this chick. She shrugged off a gorgeous winter-white coat and handed it to me with a smile.

"I assumed the invitation for some girl time extended to me, so I thought I'd drop in. Didn't want to disappoint you."

Was I high last night? Did I hand out invitations to every passer-by? If Sarah appeared, I'd snatch up my passport and make for the airport. As soon as Cat entered the living room behind me, an artic chill descended. Maddie's eyes opened so wide she might have been tasered and Olivia's roamed for an escape. What was I missing?

"Cat, can I pour you a glass?"

Because I'm about to sink a bottle, I thought to myself.

"Make it a large one."

Of course I would.

Two glasses were emptied in record time, and I hightailed it to the kitchen for some respite. I sensed a presence behind me and whirled around.

"Olivia! You scared the hell out of me!"

She welled up and I wanted to stuff the words back down my throat. I reached for her, and she fell into my arms.

"What's wrong?" I asked.

"I can't look at her. I can't do this." She dissolved into wracking sobs.

"Darcy! I'm a little thirsty in here," Cat screeched.

I settled Olivia into a chair, fixed the liquor-free ladies in the living room and returned to the kitchen, now on my knees in front of Olivia.

Gently, like reaching for a scared rabbit, I took her hands in mine. "Whatever it is, we can fix it."

She shook her head. "I can't fix this mess, Darcy, I can't. Jesus, what have I done? She must know." She grabbed my wrists so tight I bit back a yelp. "That's why she's here."

"Who? Cat?"

Some of the fog in my brain began to part, and I had a sinking feeling I knew just where this sad little story was heading.

She nodded and gawked at me, now backed into a corner. And she knew it.

With as much empathy as I could muster, I said, "Is it Bill?"

The raw shame that flashed over her face made my heart sink.

"Oh, Olivia. When?"

"Two weeks ago. I promise, it was just that one time. I keep seeing Cat around town, and I want to crawl right out of my skin. I've never done anything like that before Darcy. You have to believe me."

I wanted to wrap my hands around Bill Henderson's throat.

"I can't go back out there. What if she knows? I need to get this off my chest. I can't breathe."

"We can't talk here," I said, my tone sharp to snap her out of her building hysteria. "Cat's in the next room. Please! Let's not break her heart in front of an audience."

Though I was ready to bet that Cat Henderson's heart had been broken a long time ago.

And then Olivia whispered four words that stopped me cold.

"Elle Bradshaw found out."

"Are you hogging all the booze in here?"

Cat was one high-heeled foot away from entering my kitchen when, by divine intervention, the doorbell sounded.

"Could you get that for me, Cat?"

Time stood still as heels click-clacked away and her voice mingled with Jackie's until it was only white noise.

I was looking at Olivia with fresh eyes. Yet I couldn't picture her hands around Elle's neck or crushing Jonathan's skull.

Or was I dead wrong?

"What do you mean Elle found out? How do you know?"

She said nothing, just wiped at the mascara streaks on her cheeks.

"Olivia!"

"Because she saw us. Because she took photographs."

And there it was. The ugly truth.

"Photographs?"

A bitter laugh scraped from her throat as she dragged her phone from the back pocket of her figure-hugging indigo jeans and presented me with the money shot. There was Olivia in all her glory, staggering out of Bill and Cat's house just as dawn was breaking, one spaghetti strap of her dress hanging off her shoulder, bed head, bleary eyed and looking like hell.

The walk of shame.

"I received this the night before she died. Doesn't look good for me, does it?"

No, it does not.

The door swung open, and I nearly jumped out of my skin.

"Guys, what's going on?" Maddie hissed, her eyes searching Olivia's tear-stained face. "What are you doing in here?"

But it was written all over her face. Maddie had heard this story before.

"Jackie needs a drink," Cat yelled from the living room. "In fact, where's mine?"

"Coming Cat." *Please, Cat don't walk in here.* I couldn't stand it if she thought we were all enjoying a gossip at her expense.

"Olivia," I said. "Let's meet tomorrow to talk this through. Cat doesn't deserve to find out here, like this." I patted her hand. "We'll fix this. Somehow."

Maddie stood stock still, watching us.

Keep it together, Darcy.

"Grab Olivia's bag, Maddie. Let her touch up her make-up. Please," I urged Maddie to move into action.

Touch up? She looked like she'd been on a five day bender.

I shook off my dark thoughts and sauntered off to make nice with my guests.

After all, I was used to pretending.

***

I checked on Georgie and Henry and padded back downstairs to play another round of social charades, relishing the hour when I'd be rid of the ladies in my living room. Cat must have been on her tenth glass and was centre stage.

"I kid you not, she must be about twenty. Boobs out to here." Her hand swept over her fitted shirt. "No way those puppies are natural." Another sip. "So, there was she was, bending over a PowerPoint presentation on the smart board, tanned thighs on show! It's changed from the days when I was at school and our teachers had skirts to their ankles and hankies up their sleeves. Even Jack and Ben—you know, the gay couple from over on Cedar Road—were foaming at the mouth. But, make no mistake, she's as tough as nails. Rumour has it she had one of the whiny parents close to tears so she's an interesting addition to the school."

She shrugged her shoulders, and I had to smile.

"So anyway," she drained her glass, and with the dregs of her drink went her humour, "are we going to address the elephant in the room?"

All I could hear was the ticking of the clock. *Oh God. Please don't do this. Not here.*

Olivia looked ready to bolt.

"Elephant?" I said.

"Elle Bradshaw of course. What did you think I meant?"

And so, we began to pick over the bones of poor Elle's life.

"Talking of Everbrook," which we weren't, "I wonder if Cole will stay on given what's happened. Maddie, did you see anything unusual there on Friday morning? Something that I might have missed?" Of course, I was referring to her rummaging around Elle's drawers, but I waited to gauge her reaction.

Her gaze cut to the right. She was hiding something from me. Straight up. My good friend Maddie Clement. My friend who lived five houses down from Elle.

"Anything?" I said.

"But surely the police would have searched everywhere?" Jackie said.

And now I wanted to stuff a throw pillow in Jackie's mouth because I wanted Maddie to answer.

The front door opened and closed.

"Hey, ladies!"

Never had I believed I'd be more surprised to hear Bill Henderson's sleazy drawl as I was in that second. How many more times was this guy going to appear in my hallway?

"Hi, Kitty Cat. Had a little champers, have we?"

He slapped her thigh as he settled himself very comfortably on the sofa nodding at Olivia.

Olivia looked scared out of her mind and pretended to look for something in her bag. I knew she was avoiding his gaze.

Harry sauntered in, Cole on his heels, and threw me a look that translated as *not my fault*.

"Bill joined us the for the game. Cole's here too." He nodded at Cole as if I couldn't see him with my own eyes.

I forced a smile. "Did we win?"

"Och, did we hell."

Harry sank into the sofa. Scotland has a proud history of many things—unfortunately, winning football games was rarely one of them.

A sharp rap came at the front door. *What now?* We were one set of pyjamas away from a slumber party. I threw it open and reared back.

Sergeant Jim Burns stood on my doorstep...and he looked mad as hell.

"Can I help you?"

"Is Bill Henderson here?" Jim stood on his tiptoes, searching over my head as if expecting to find Bill swinging from a chandelier.

"What?"

"Henderson? Is he here? Not interrupting anything, am I?" The leer was back.

"Oh, he is, Sergeant." I pulled the door closer behind me and whispered, "You don't have to speak with him now, do you?"

He rubbed the bridge of his nose, apparently the default twitch when speaking with me. "Do I look as if I have time to waste, *Mrs* Sinclair. May I come in?"

His excitement of catching me in the act of getting it on with my neighbour was palpable so I put on a show, timidly stood aside and let him stride past me.

"Go straight through."

"Bill Henderson," he boomed.

"Be quiet," I hissed. "My children are asleep upstairs."

"Oh, are they now?"

A childish thrill trickled over me as, on seeing my living room filled with friends and neighbours, the self-righteousness slid off his face. But the thrill faded when Cat jumped to her feet.

"The girls! Are they alright?"

Shame on me. The thought that something terrible had happened hadn't even occurred to me.

"Calm yourself, Mrs Henderson. I'm here to ask your husband some questions about Elle Bradshaw. I don't have all night, so could you come along? I assume you don't want to chat in front of half the village."

Seven mouths dropped open. Cat reared back as if she'd been slapped in the face.

"Why do you need to speak with my husband? He barely knew Elle."

Almost half of the people in the room knew that to be a lie.

"Sergeant Burns," I said, "can I ask why you're barging into my house at almost ten at night? Couldn't you have contacted Bill in the morning? How did you even know he was here?"

"This is police business, Mrs Sinclair, and none of your concern. Mr Henderson, as I said, I don't have all night." He gestured with a rolling motion, clearly enjoying his little moment in the spotlight.

Bill's usual air of self-assurance had evaporated as quickly as his sleazy smile.

"Sure, Jim, let's go. But if you wouldn't mind letting my wife and I settle up with our babysitter first, I'll answer your questions. Come on, Cat."

He placed his hand on the small of her back, and she flinched. Maybe, finally, she'd reached her breaking point.

The drama disappeared out of our door and Jackie offered to drop Maddie and Olivia home.

Exhausted, I closed the door behind me. Cole sat forward as if debating whether to say something. I churned over the six ugly words in the text message, the bizarre goings-on in Mapleway Road, Olivia's breakdown, and the potential interrogation of Bill Henderson. I wasn't in a chatty mood. If I went upstairs and put my pyjamas on, he might take the hint.

"What do you know about my Uncle Richard?"

The question caught me by surprise, but I was all played out.

"I don't know him well, Cole, so it would be unfair of me to answer." A lawyer's answer but an answer, nonetheless.

"Just your observations then."

"Honestly? I don't think much of him at all. I don't want to upset you Cole, so I'd rather plead the fifth."

Cole looked at me thoughtfully. I could have sworn I saw a hint of amusement pass over his face.

"I had a feeling you might say that. Jess told me there was bad blood between my mother and Richard. Apparently, there was a scene at some fancy country club a few weeks ago. An argument that got out of hand. Do you know anything about that?" He held his head in his hands for a moment. "Could he be the one who hurt her?"

Harry began rubbing at his forehead as if chasing away an approaching headache.

"But why?" I asked. "Why hurt her now? What changed?"

A ragged sigh escaped his lips. "That's the problem, Darcy, I don't know. I haven't known either of them for such a long time." He stared at the wall. "I don't know anything about my own family."

Harry handed him a beer and he picked at the label on the bottle. "We'd grown so far apart I didn't even call her on her last birthday."

So, things had been a lot worse than Elle had ever alluded to.

"I don't know Richard well, never have, but he makes me...I don't know, uneasy? He quizzes me on what the police have told me, who they've been speaking to. It just feels more than a passing interest."

"Cole, I can't pretend that I was close to your mum. If I had been, I would give you every answer I could. Don't know anything about any scene at the club but I'm sure I can find out more. The sad thing? Jonathan would've been able to tell you everything but..." The lump in my throat was painful. "If I were you, I'd ask Richard straight out, cards on the table. Ask him everything you want to know and pray he answers you with some honesty."

There was nothing else to say.

As he stood, he cocked his head. "By the way, I'm sorry if our meeting earlier was a little awkward. I'm a bit embarrassed about that. I was feeling low and, well, you know, Gabby's a lovely girl but a bit intense. She wanted me to take her out again but I'm just not in the headspace for that right now. She did tell me there was nothing going on between her and Allen though. I just wanted to make that clear. I'm not that guy."

"Cole, you don't owe us any explanation. The main thing is to just look after yourself. There's a lunatic out there somewhere and God knows they might be closer than we think."

He hesitated at the door, looking a little lost.

"Why don't you come over for dinner? Anytime you feel like it. I love to cook, and our door is always open for friends, so the offer is there."

I waved goodnight and closed the door against the freezing wind.

Alone.

At last.

When I finally crawled into bed and switched off my bedside lamp, the darkness brought images of Elle crumpled on her floor, Jonathan in a puddle of red and a text message with words that made me want to slither out of my skin.

The dark was not my friend.

CHAPTER EIGHTEEN

Wednesday, 23 October

"**A**RE YOU FEELING ALRIGHT?" Harry said over the kids' bickering at the kitchen table. "You look like you have the flu."

"I feel like crap," I croaked. "Everything hurts."

"What does crap mean?" Henry asked.

I failed to hide a smile. "Nothing, Henry. Mummy's saying silly words."

"Silly Mummy!" Georgie yelled, and Pepper began to bark.

My skull was pounding as I shuffled towards the medicine basket and rummaged for headache relievers.

Harry swallowed the dregs of his coffee and finished packing up the kids' school bags. "Darcy, I'm worried sick about that text. I'm going to call Reece this morning, see what's happening." As he stomped upstairs, I followed behind like a puppy. "I'm working from home today." He patted a non-existent six-pack on his stomach and grinned. "Plus, don't forget, I'm a machine. If anyone comes calling, like the sender of that text message, I've got it covered."

***

Two hours later, I was sitting in Bob's office, listening to someone else's drama unfold.

"So here we are, six days later, and Grace is still holding on."

"Bob, your compassion is, well, rather underwhelming." I smirked, enjoying seeing my usually stoic boss squirm for a change.

He grumbled as if his mother-in-law clinging to life was an out-rageous inconvenience.

"Oh, bloody hell, you know what I mean."

Bob was tall, rail thin and silver haired. Blue eyes that shone with intelligence sat behind rimless glasses. A perpetual expression of contemplation belied a kind heart. He favoured tailored suits, sharp ties, crisp shirts and cufflinks so highly polished I could have touched up my make-up in them. I often quelled an urge to rumple his hair, just so something would be the tiniest bit askew.

Once, Stephen Barnes, one of the firm's associates, had sauntered into the office without a tie. Bob had asked him if his house had burned to the ground that morning, otherwise why would he be in such a state of undress?

Stephen was never seen without a tie again.

"How's Alison doing?" I asked.

Bob's wife was a doll, plump as a Christmas pudding and five foot in her bare feet. While Bob could be prickly as a cactus, Alison would pull you in for a full embrace and spill every detail of her personal life. Unless it was a legal conundrum, Bob didn't talk much. Alison, on the other hand, was as warm and inviting as a gooey chocolate cake.

Total opposites yet they seemed to adore each other, and I enjoyed them very much as a couple.

"You know Alison…staying positive and baking brownies for the nursing staff." He sighed and tossed a client file on his desk.

I dragged myself up from the comfy chair then sat back down. Seconds later I was spilling the whole sordid story to Bob—Elle, Jonathan's attack and the text message I'd received. In that moment I needed a friend.

He gawped, his expression a blend of horror and bewilderment, and let loose a string of expletives. For some warped reason I found this amusing.

"Are they sure?" he said, pacing the room. "I haven't heard much of anything because I've been stuck in that damn hospital. Someone really killed her? Elle? Well, my God."

"You knew her for years," I said. "What did you think of her?"

He snorted. "Elle Bradshaw was a bloody handful, but she was a good client, even though I wished she'd take her business elsewhere more times than I care to admit." Bob dragged his hand through his hair, causing it to stick up every which way.

Finally!

He leaned against the desk. "What kind of a sick bastard would attack Jonathan?"

I dropped my head into my hands and released a guttural sound I'd never heard before. Pure exhaustion mingled with fear perhaps.

"You know, if the person who attacked Jonathan meant to kill him, and I think we can assume he did, then how can we be sure they won't try again? How can he possibly be safe? And what the hell has it got to do with Elle?"

My stomach dropped. I felt like a fool because it hadn't occurred to me that danger might visit Jonathan a second time.

"Surely the police have thought of that."

"Never assume anything, Darcy. You should know that."

Bob was the teacher and his staff the pupils, regardless of age and experience. I didn't mind—my philosophy was to listen and learn.

When the misguided Stephen Barnes had asked Bob to consider a salary increase, Bob had paused for only a second, before saying, "Genius is born, not paid." Or so the story went. When Stephen had later recounted the tale to me, I hadn't had the heart to tell him not to hold his breath. The Oscar Wilde quote should have told him so.

"I knew Elle for years," Bob said. "Truth is, she could be a nasty piece of work if she wanted to be, but, my God, she was a beauty and, well…sometimes men just don't see past that."

I'd heard enough confessions. The idea of Bob frolicking with anyone, let alone Elle, was too much. My pained expression must have been obvious.

He released a sigh. "Oh no! Not me. But there were others beside Charles. That you can take to the bank."

Her dirty little secret, all laid out. *Bare.* Then again, was it ever that much of a secret?

I told Bob about the previous night's events, culminating in the questioning of Bill.

"Cat and Bill Henderson? No. I don't see it, Darcy. Bill's vain for sure and probably not the brightest bulb in the box, but I think he's harmless."

"Unless you're married to him."

"Well, sure, that's true. Even I've heard that there might have been a thing between Elle and Bill. Alison goes to the gym that Bill owns, not to work out, mind you. She goes for the social chit chat, or so she tells me, and she heard that rumour ages ago. Not a long-term affair by any means but, what is it you young people say, friends with benefits? Hook ups?"

Smiling at Bob, I let loose a soft laugh and it felt good. "Bob, no one has called me *young people* for years. You've cheered me up."

I thought about Elle's perfect image, and how those that spend the most time polishing the illusion of perfection usually have the most to hide—and the most to lose.

Thirty minutes later, I grabbed some files and headed towards Roast.

The hills in the distance were frost-tipped and the morning mist kissed the ground. As she often did when I sought her help, Mother Nature was rejuvenating me.

It soon crashed to a halt.

My eyes narrowed at Jessica as she sashayed across Firmont Road. Time to do battle.

***

Hand on cocked hip, Jessica barked orders at the barista as she scrolled through her phone, flicking her golden hair. Then she dropped her phone into her tote and snatched up her skinny whatever without a word of thanks and scanned the room.

She saw me, her eyes narrowed, and she threw herself into a chair like a toddler prepping for a tantrum.

I sat down at her table. The phone was back in her hand, a convenient prop.

"I hear you had a good chat with Cole Bradshaw." I folded my arms.

A full twenty seconds passed. Then she looked up, a malicious gleam in her eyes. "I knew you were jealous! Did you finally realise how drab your life is? Cole is *waaay* out your league."

"He's hot but not my type, I'm afraid. Happily married with two kids. I did all my messing about in my twenties. Now I'm all grown up."

She gave me a sad little shake of her head. "I doubt *you* were ever his type."

"So, I was with Cole last night and he told me an interesting story about Richard…about some showdown he had with Elle up at the club a while ago. Some sort of bad history there?"

Angry red blotches appeared on her pretty face. No doubt about it, this chick had issues.

"What is it with you poking your nose into my life? Jealous much?"

"I found Elle dead. On her floor. Murdered as it turns out."

"Oh, cry me a river. I thought you were some sort of tough lawyer."

Jerking back, I pulled away from the table to get as far away from the poisonous little bitch as possible. "You really are a piece of work, Jessica. Any information you have could shed some light on what's going on here."

If I'd hoped I could appeal to some sliver of humanity, I was mistaken.

Her face contorted. Not beautiful anymore. "Just look at you. Sitting in your bland clothes, holding your fifty-quid, crappy, vegan bag. All vegetarian and saving the fluffy animals. Nobody cares. Nobody! You're just irrelevant."

She couldn't have hurt me more than she had with those words if she'd tasered me.

"You're wrong. My family and friends care. My husband cares, and my kids care. I have them all close, in here," I tapped at my chest, "and in here." I tapped the side of my head. "And you're also wrong on one more point."

"What's that?"

"I didn't pay fifty quid for my bag. Only thirty."

"Cole and I are seeing each other, and you can't stand it. Look, I don't blame you – I couldn't stand sleeping with the same guy every night either. That must be a nightmare." She smiled, a graceful cat about to lunge for the poor bird she'd toyed with.

"I'm sure Cole will be delighted to hear you have no interest in finding his mother's killer."

"Shut up!" she spat. "You stay away from Cole."

"Or what? Stupid, vapid cow!"

Jessica reared back as if I'd slapped her.

I was mad as hell and furious with myself for losing my temper, but I couldn't stop. "I'll just bet you've never had a sleepless night in your life. I doubt you ever will. But our neighbour has been murdered. Our friend, Jonathan, was beaten to a pulp and left for dead. I saw what was left of him. If that doesn't give you nightmares, you must be the heartless little witch everyone thinks you to be."

Nothing.

Not a micro movement.

Time to use a different psychology.

"You do realise it's likely that someone we know is behind this? Think about it, someone in our, *your*, inner circle did this. Here. In the village. And since you're telling anyone who will listen about intimate details of the case and that you spotted Richard back at Jonathan's house you've kind of put yourself right in the middle of this mess so you better hope whoever is behind this doesn't come looking for you."

Her eyes widened.

Gotcha.

Not my heart-rending speech. Not my plea to her humanity. Not my insults. Rather, the idea that her contrived little world might be under threat—that's what got her mouth moving.

"I don't know much," she said, "my mother told me Elle and Richard had an ugly falling-out years ago. When Elle came back to the village, she never spoke one word to him again."

"What do you mean, came back?"

Her dainty shoulders shrugged. "My mother said Elle walked out on Charles many times, usually when she was spending too much. But that time she took off for months. When she finally came back, she kept her distance from both him and Richard. Her marriage was a shitshow."

And...

"A couple of weeks ago, Elle and Richard had a showdown at the club. I saw the whole thing. She grabbed his arm; he shook her off and she fell backwards. She was screaming, spitting venom. It caused a hell of a scene and she stormed out, mortified. Whatever it was about it was serious."

"What was she screaming?"

"It didn't make sense. She was accusing Richard of sending her something in the post. *A little reminder* she said."

I downed my coffee and made for the door, leaving the beautiful monster tapping on her phone.

***

An hour later, I held Jonathan's cold hand and listened to the depressing rhythm of the machines keeping him alive. *The past comes back to haunt you. Can it come back and kill you? After all, isn't the past a dangerous creature.*

Movement—just a twitch in my hand—jarred me. Had I imagined it? Again.

Ever so slightly.

"Jonathan! Can you hear me?"

Still the machines pulsed, but there was a definite flutter from the fingers I held in my hand.

I fumbled for the buzzer and a nurse appeared.

"His hand moved! Three times."

She took his hand in hers and stared at her watch. Her brow lifted. *She feels it too.*

In under a minute, nurses bustled around the room, then parted like the Red Sea when Andy Thomas strode in. "Mr Mitchell," he boomed, "Jonathan! Are you ready to join us?"

Charts were passed around the bed. Words filled the air. *Next MRI. Change in pattern. BP steadying.* I lingered in the corner, reminding myself to breathe.

"Sorry," Andy said to me, "you need to step out."

Nodding, I stumbled out of the room. The sound of orders being barked fading away.

I marvelled at how medical staff coped with situations like this—a person's life hanging by a thread. One slight tug in the wrong direction could change everything.

I didn't have the guts to do that job, that I knew for sure.

It seemed I didn't have the guts for much these days.

But times were changing.

The fire in my belly told me so.

***

I walked out of the hospital into a brewing storm. The wind howled around the buildings, creating an eerie whistle. The day was turning to dusk and passing cars and buses switched on their headlights to become mere lanterns in the fading light.

I weaved through the parking area to my car.

Another ping on my phone.

For God's sake, I just wanted to breathe but dragged the phone from my pocket in case it was anything kid related.

Unknown number.

Another six words: *I'm the agony. Never the ecstasy.*

Heat washed over me despite the cold and my skin began to crawl. My nervous system told me it was time to be scared. Time to wish I could change things because these words didn't feel as though they would have been typed by Jessica's manicured fingers.

No, not at all.

Scanning the parking lot, looking for shadows, the euphoria from Jonathan's twitching hand evaporated, leaving only cold, damp, fear.

A sound came from behind me.

I spun around and threw my arms out in a defensive pose. *Instincts.* A man, woman and a boy walked past me, seemingly confused by my reaction.

Bob's words came back to me: *How can he possibly be safe?*

***

I called Reece and filled him in while Harry paced. He was furious but so was I—at myself. I didn't need him adding fuel to my fire.

"Darcy! What the hell is going on? Why are you getting these messages? I thought I asked you to keep your head down."

"Will you be quiet!" I hissed back. Harry never yelled, so when he did, it pushed me right back to my dark place.

The kid hiding under her duvet.

Hands clamped over her ears.

Drowning out the noise.

Screaming.

The sound of a hand slapping skin.

Another sore face.

"I don't want the kids to hear. Harry, I know you're pissed but I'm sorry. I don't know why someone is doing this to me. I don't know anything! I haven't seen anything!"

Harry turned to face me. "I'm just, fuck...I'm angry. I'm scared. I love you, Darcy. I couldn't handle it if anything happened to you. Our kids couldn't handle it. You can't fix *everything*. You can't rescue *everyone*. I wish to hell you would realise that you cannot save the world. It isn't your job!"

"Not anymore. Is that what you mean? The past wasn't my fault Harry, I'm aware. But it's just the way I'm wired. I thought you knew that...I'm sorry if you can't handle it. The truth? I'll be damned if I change who I am!" The second the words left my mouth, I felt like crap.

At an early age I'd learned that self-pity was a waste of time.

Grow up, Darcy. Shit happens.

My hand flew to my mouth, the dam burst, and the floodgates opened. The tears that were now a familiar friend returned to visit.

Pretending to be tough was easy. Feeling it was a whole other beast.

Ten minutes later, I was all cried out and my sanity had returned. Harry was grateful for the reprieve of telling me *everything is going to be alright*.

The phone rang and Jackie screeched my name before I could breathe a word.

"I don't know what to do."

"Take a breath and tell me what's wrong."

"I had a half-day from the shop and decided to head to the church. As I told you, I wanted to check out Jonathan's desk but couldn't see anything unusual. So, I started with his dictations."

Jackie managed a small pool of volunteer secretaries who undertook administrative duties such as the typing of minutes.

"And?"

"Look," she whispered, "I shouldn't be telling you any of this, but I trust you Darcy and I know you're trying to help...Jonathan asked for an email to be drafted to the parish council. Elle lodged a formal complaint against Sarah Evans, alleging she had knowledge of inappropriate behaviour that amounted to gross misconduct of her duties.

Requested that she be immediately removed from her place on the board. What if Sarah found out and...what if she hurt Elle?"

Sarah would be a formidable enemy. Sarah held her position in the community with conviction, wholeheartedly believing it placed her on a higher pedestal than everyone else. How did she refer to herself? Ah, *the beating heart of the community*.

"And," Jackie continued, "I found a printed email sent by Elle to Jonathan two days before her death. She'd formally requested that an investigation be launched against Olivia Miller."

I drew in a sharp breath. "An investigation into what?"

"Well, that's the strange thing. There's only one page; the rest isn't here." There was a rustling of papers in the background. "I found it stuffed between utility bills. Now why would Elle ask for Olivia to be investigated?"

"I haven't a clue," I said, and then recalled the circled appointment on Jonathan's calendar and the picture of the spreadsheet I'd snapped with my phone.

Wait. Dammit, I'd snapped that on Harry's old phone—that's why I'd forgotten all about it.

"Darcy...Olivia's the treasurer of the parish funds. So, I mean... hell, I don't know what I mean. Do you think Sarah or Olivia could have anything to do with this?"

It was a loaded question; Jackie didn't really want an answer. She wanted me to tell her everything was going to be fine.

Five minutes after my conversation with her had ended, my phone blew up.

The second public shaming of Olivia Miller had begun.

CHAPTER NINETEEN

Thursday, 24 October

"**M**ummy, Mummy, where's my lunch box?" Georgie shrieked from the bottom of the stairs.

After ten minutes of searching, we found Henry giggling in his room, the item in question hidden under his pillow.

More shrieking, accusations and general bedlam ensued before we finally got both kids off to school. It was a typical, exhausting morning, and it was just what I needed, but my brain was throbbing again.

I swallowed two headache pills with a slug of diet whatever was handy and headed for the office. Today, I didn't want to think about death, about betrayal, about secrets. I didn't want to think about Olivia being escorted into the police station for questioning. I hadn't been able to reach her on the phone and my mind was wandering into dark and troubling places. And so, I combed through every file that required my attention, analysed every motion and dictated at double speed. I felt back in control.

When I'd cleared my desk and my diary, I powered down my PC, dragged on my coat and walked out the door with a clear head.

I was halfway home when the sensation hit me—a sense of unease that I couldn't quite put my finger on.

Gut instinct.

I turned, looked right, then behind me. The ring of my phone was shrill against the still, quiet air. Jackie again. We agreed to meet for coffee to discuss what she'd discovered at the church.

Then I sent a text to Cat asking how she was. I was curious about what had happened after Jim had dragged the Henderson's from my house. After that, I turned onto our street and my cosy little home.

Ragged breath behind me knocked the relief out of me.

Think, Darcy.

Keep moving.

I swiped to the Favourites screen on my phone, heart pounding.

Keep walking.

The breathing escalated, the sound nearer now.

Sweat gathered at my pores despite the cold of the night. The threat right behind me. I pressed Call, praying Harry would pick up.

He did.

I cut him off. "I'm outside. Open the door! Someone's behind me."

"What? What are you talking about? Wait a minute." An expletive drifted from my phone as I moved into my garden. I could see my house.

Safety.

So near yet so far.

"Darcy!"

Harry called my name and began charging down the path towards me. Only then did I muster up the courage to turn around.

A shadow retreated into the dark, a white plume of breath drifting behind.

"What the hell is going on?" Harry's eyes roamed over me as if looking for any injury. He then stepped around me, his head moving from side to side. Searching.

Turning back and cupping his hands around my face, his eyes looked for an answer I couldn't give him.

"Nothing Harry. I thought, well, I don't know what I thought. My nerves are shattered. I'm hearing things and honestly...I'm losing it. It was probably someone walking their dog and I'm thinking it's a serial killer behind me. Damn it."

Shaking like a leaf, I dragged my sweating palms against my thighs, bent my head and sucked in a breath.

"Come here." Harry pulled me in for a hug and held me for a full thirty seconds. "Got to stop scaring me like this, Darcy. I've aged ten years in the last few days."

We walked into the house together.

United.

"Mummy, are you alright?" Georgie padded into the kitchen, clutching her favourite bear. She looked at me fearfully.

I reached out for my daughter, and she fell into my arms. Breathing in the scent of her shampoo, I felt her little arms tighten around me, and just like that, my heart rate slowed.

"I'm fine sweet pea! I ran home to get some exercise and I'm out of breath. How silly of me to run with heels on."

She giggled and nestled her bear into the crook of her arm—all was well.

I trudged upstairs and scrubbed my face, washing away the fear.

Over the next half an hour, four more phone calls proffered increasingly more elaborate versions of the police's interest in Olivia Miller.

"I knew it…" "She must have done it…" "Never did like her…" On and on it went. The scarlet letter had been pinned to Olivia's chest and the kindling for the bonfire was being stockpiled. My stomach was churning,

Harry tucked into toast, avocado and tomatoes and a cup of disgusting herbal tea. I was on the hard stuff—straight-up caffeine. Before this week I'd only drunk decaf after five p.m. Like all my other good intentions, that rule had been chucked by the wayside.

"What do you think the police wanted with Bill last night?"

Harry's eyes softened, and corners of his mouth crinkled. "Well… Your expression right now is comical."

I blinked, ready to snap because I was tired and irritated to hell. I counted to ten. "What do you mean?"

"You're like a character in one of your crazy TV shows. Like you want to assemble all our neighbours and reveal whodunit."

Instead of laughing along, I felt my cheeks burn with guilt and regret. Had I been treating this as a game? One person was dead, and another lay in intensive care, and I had a kaleidoscope of images that I'd never be able to erase. The weight of my own inadequacies suddenly felt very heavy.

I'd felt inadequate since I was a kid. Why couldn't I protect my mum? Stupid. But it didn't make the feeling burn any less.

That's the thing about the past. Buried memories eventually spill out everywhere. Dark and twisted and messy. Ready to stab you in the heart when you least expect it

"Hey," Harry grabbed my hand. "I was only messing with you. Stop overanalysing, Darcy. If the police don't have an answer yet, then how could you?"

Stop with the self-pity, the self-indulgence.

This was getting to be a habit.

"My TV shows are awesome. You're just too stupid to guess who-dunit." I smirked and reached for his hand.

My lifeline.

"Alright! And we're back!"

Could I choke down my inadequacies and bury the self-doubt?

Of course, I could. I'd been doing it for years.

***

Friday, 25 October

Dawn had brought a breath-taking scarlet sky, and I'd leaned against my open front door for a full twenty-minutes soaking up the sight and breathing in the early morning air.

I felt calmer than I had in days, but now ominous grey clouds loomed in the distance as I gazed out of the coffee shop window.

Jackie and I were in Roast, hugging hot drinks.

"I'm heading straight over the hospital," she said. "I'll feel better once I see him."

I nodded and she locked her fingers, rubbing them together.

I did the same thing.

Kindred spirits.

"I've written everything down. I've made an appointment to see Reece McDonald. I'll give him the originals. Darcy, I'm exhausted. I've been up all night, worried sick, but I think I'm doing the right thing."

She pushed a sheet of paper towards me, looked over my shoulder and whispered, "This is strictly between us."

Jackie was looking at me as if I might be wearing a wire. I bit back a grin.

"Promise, not a word. I know you like Olivia, so do I. And for what it's worth I don't think she could have hurt Jonathan. Or Elle. But let Reece sort through this mess, at least this part of it."

I gave her an encouraging smile before taking my leave.

Olivia waved at me from across the road. "Darcy! Wait!"

I buttoned my coat while she weaved through the traffic. Her face was crimson, from either rushing, the cold or stress. I looked into her eyes and settled on the latter.

"Can't talk," she said, her breathing ragged. "Have to be at the station again to meet with Reece." She grabbed my arm, and her voice raised a few octaves. "I didn't do this, Darcy. Any of it. I swear to you. Meet me later. Please. My head's all over the place. I'll tell you everything."

"Sure, Olivia. I want to help you. Please let me. Call me."

She looked at her watch, squeezed my arm and hurried back across Firmont Road. All around me there were busy commuters, tired customers standing in line to get their first, or tenth, caffeine hit.

Cars and buses roared by. Puddle water sprayed into the air. Rain began to drizzle.

Just another normal day.

And yet it wasn't.

Even though Olivia was now some distance from me, the slump of shoulders betrayed the load she bore, a reminder of the calamity that had visited our town.

Beauty and optimism, ugliness and tragedy, the carefree and the burdened.

It's a fine line that we walk.

***

The clock on my computer told me it was nine-fifteen a.m. The words blurred on the screen. *Explained, averred, applicants, respondents*—all legalese I dealt with on a typical working day. The answers to the motion to appeal had to be lodged by Monday, but today the work felt excruciating. Instead, the bag in which the illicit papers were stashed called to me.

My office phone trilled. Bob relayed to me, "I just had an interesting call from Richard. He mentioned a visit from Reece McDonald. Apparently, his long-standing relationship with Elle, or lack thereof, has piqued the Detective Inspector's interest. He told McDonald to back it up or he'd be contacting his solicitor."

"Surely that's standard."

"That's what I told him. Anyway, he's meeting Rick Barton, the criminal-defence guy, up at the club where he's treating Cole and Jessica Evans to dinner."

I snorted. "Sarah pretty much pimped Jessica out, she was that desperate to matchmake them. Like a Venus flytrap."

"Seems odd to me. His mother barely cold a week and he's running around with the local trollop."

"Trollop?" *Please tell.*

"You know what I mean. She's awful, much like her mother. I can take Sarah in very small doses. If Eric Evans didn't deliver a good retainer each year, I wouldn't give any of them the time of day. Forgive me, I'm just exhausted. Sitting in that hospital every bloody night on those godawful chairs is making me a grumpy old man. There must be electric chairs in the state of Florida more comfortable. I feel old, Darcy, and I don't like it."

"Here's a thought, why don't you take a day off?"

"I will. When I'm dead."

He hung up leaving me pondering my next move.

Now then. Who might I rope in for a spy's dinner at the Cedarwood Country Club?

I snatched up my phone and told Gia exactly what I needed. She knew the guy who ran the club restaurant. Ten minutes later she called me back and confirmed a reservation at Palermo's.

We'd have a table next to Richard Bradshaw's.

The game was afoot.

What the hell was I thinking?

***

Even in the dark of the night, the club screamed old money, as did the expensive cars parked outside.

On a clear day, the view was a gift. Perfection. An eighteen-hole golf course snaked around the red sandstone building, which sat directly on the banks of Loch Donnach. The Saltire and the Union Jack fluttered in the freezing October wind atop two soaring flagpoles. Stunning floor-to-ceiling bay windows graced the façade, each draped with magnificent ochre embroidered curtains.

Gia tottered in her heels towards the bar, and I stumbled behind like Quasimodo escaping the bell tower. Gia chatted to some acquaintances at the bar while I scanned the room for our targets.

"I see the girls are out with us tonight," I eyed her plunging neckline. Damn. I wanted to run home and change into something a little more...provocative? Sexy? Fun?

She grinned and raised her gin and tonic. "They are indeed. If you're aiming for the sexy-librarian look, you probably should have gone for an updo."

I glanced down at my black dress. "Sexy librarian?"

"Alright, just librarian. You need to get your sexy back, girl."

Did I ever.

Feeling a little deflated I drained my glass quicker than I should have and ambled over to the restaurant.

My chest thumped when I spotted Cat and Bill at the small bar in the restaurant. So, Bill wasn't in a jumpsuit yet.

Richard's discordant voice drifted across the floor. I caught a waft of Cole's aftershave as he passed our table, and took a second to appreciate it, and the charcoal-grey suit and dazzling white dress shirt, no tie.

Sue me.

Jessica looked stunning in a minuscule little black dress, hair spilling down her back, make-up flawless, from the champagne sparkle on her lids to the pop of fire engine red on her pouting lips. I wanted to poke her with the fork in my hand. Those plump lips turned into a sneer as she spotted us at the next table.

"Did you escape the compound tonight, Darcy?"

Smirking, I nodded. "Good one. I see both your brain cells are working tonight. Where are you off to? Studio 54's been closed for quite some time."

She frowned and her flawless complexion flushed. Cole pulled a chair out for her.

Gia was already four gin and tonics in, and I was beginning to doubt the wisdom of my plan. The last thing I needed was Gia kicking off.

She extended her hand. "Lovely to meet you, Cole. I've heard quite the buzz about town about you, and I have to say, you don't disappoint."

Jessica looked like she was about to have a stroke.

"Great to meet you, Gia. You out for a girl's night?"

She shot him a toothy grin. "No tequila shots tonight. Darcy's a bore. How about you? How are you holding up?

"He's holding up just fine. He has me," Jessica snapped.

In the background, Elvis Presley sang about suspicious minds. The irony wasn't lost on me.

Richard cleared his throat.

"Are you alright, Richard?" Gia said. "You should take a sip of water—you sound quite hoarse. I heard that nice Reece McDonald has been putting you through the wringer. It's all over the village."

I wanted to crawl under the table, even in my unsexy dress. When God was handing out the filter gene, Gia had wandered out of the queue in her five-inch heels, skipped town and never looked back.

She turned to Jessica. "Have you been questioned yet? I mean, after the scene between Elle and your mum a few weeks ago I was expecting the cops to be crawling all over your place."

Richard threw down his linen napkin, and mercifully a waiter appeared. Gia returned to our table beaming.

"What the hell are you doing?" I whispered.

She batted her lashes and smirked. "That dinner will be boring as hell. Might as well spice it up for them."

"Just cool it, will you. I know I said I wanted to have a snoop session tonight, but I don't want to get into a brawl with Jessica so just leave her be. I can't take any more stress Gia. If anything gets back to Harry, I think he'll lock me in the basement."

"Might not be a bad idea." Gia poked her tongue out at me.

"Real mature." Smiling I sipped at my drink, something catching at the corner of my eye.

Cat caught my eye and waved to me. Then again, like an air traffic controller.

What the ...

We met halfway.

"I have something to show you, but not here!"

"What are you talking about? What is it?"

"I'll call you tomorrow."

"Cat, just tell me what it is."

"Can't. Let's just say Fifty Shades of Wrong. Tomorrow."

More like *Fifty Shades of What the Hell.* "At least tell me if everything's alright with Bill."

"He's been grilled like a steak on a barbeque. Fill you in tomorrow."

She headed back into the arms of greasy Bill, who was posing at the bar.

I watched her settle into her drink as I wondered just what on earth she wanted to *show* me.

Sarah and Eric Evans strode through the door and made a beeline for Cat and Bill. Once Sarah was seated, Eric made the rounds like a mafia don.

Charisma and money. It never failed to impress.

Eric chatted it up with friends, whisky glass in hand, relaxed and in his element, and Richard and Cole soon joined him. The way they worked the floor intrigued me; they each enjoyed the limelight, and all became the stars of the show.

I couldn't help but wonder what on earth was I doing here? Should I have got Isla to babysit and enjoyed a bowl of pasta with Harry instead? Of course I should have. Instead I was wasting my time trying to finish a puzzle missing half its pieces.

Fool.

Cole headed towards the rest room, and I moved as fast as I could on my spikes from hell. After all was said and done, I did desperately want resolution for Elle and Jonathan.

"Cole! How are you? Have you heard anything from the police?" I asked, cringing. The desperation in my voice sounded foolish.

He appraised me with a strained expression, then said, "No, nothing of any importance. They spoke with Richard; I have to say, he's pissed. He doesn't like people poking their noses into his business."

I took a little step back. Had that been an insult or a threat? It felt like both. But then the unfamiliar expression evaporated and morphed into a small smile. "Things have been...tense. Richard is, well, he's hard work and I haven't even begun grieving my mum because I don't know how to start. How sad is that?"

"It's a cliché, Cole, but you do have to give yourself time. Look at everything that's happened in less than a week. You've lost your mum, in the most horrific way. You're back home when you didn't expect to be. You've left your friends behind. Your whole world has been turned upside down. Just slow down and go easy on yourself."

He reached out and touched my hand. "Thanks Darcy. I appreciate that more than you know. I like Jessica but, well... we don't really talk deep, and Richard is difficult at best, so I appreciate it. Maybe I'll get one of my friends to come up north, I think I need that. Maybe the four of us could have dinner."

"Sure, do that. Come over to our house. As I told you I love to cook, and Harry can force some tequila down your throat."

"Sounds like the perfect night."

"Oh, there's Maddie and Dave! I think the whole of Cedarwood is here tonight. I'll go say hi. Catch you later, Cole."

Dave waved and walked over to a table where Maddie and Olivia and Allen Miller were sitting.

Dave whispered, "Save me from this excruciating dinner."

"Hi everyone. Are you all well?" My gaze settled on Olivia.

"I'm a little better thanks, Darcy. Allen asked me out for dinner tonight." She titled her head towards her ex-husband as if I couldn't see him sitting at the table. Allen looked relaxed, happy.

He put his hand over Olivia's and squeezed. "Remember what I said about making amends, Darcy?" Allen raised at glass at me, and I returned a heartfelt smile. He looked happy. Olivia looked happy. I just hoped she could stay out of handcuffs long enough to enjoy whatever this was.

"Well, I won't keep you guys any longer. Enjoy. Mads, buzz me tomorrow."

For the next two hours, I picked at my pasta, Gia traded dirty looks with Jessica, and men shook hands and slapped backs with Cole and Richard. With each visit to their table, Cole fell into relaxed conversation and Richard's ego swelled. Jessica resorted to taking selfies.

And then the mood shifted.

It took only a split second.

"Enough! I don't want to talk about my mother," Cole's deep voice boomed.

Jessica put her phone down and Richard barked at the waiter, demanding the bill. I shot the guy a look of sympathy.

I'd learned nothing other than the Bradshaw's were as screwed up as any other family.

Jessica pouted, trying to persuade Cole to take her for a cocktail. His bored expression interested me. His weary sigh didn't go unnoticed. What was going on there? But then, Jessica stood and smoothed her tiny black dress, it settled mid-thigh and clung to every perfect curve and Cole reached out to her. I guessed it didn't take Jessica Fletcher to solve that mystery. It was obvious what the attraction was, even to me.

I'd have made my escape had Richard not gone over to Dave and loomed over him. Dave's pleasant face flushed an ugly shade of purple. Even from ten feet away I could feel a change in atmosphere. Anger, resentment, possibly rage.

Dave sprang to his feet, slamming his whisky down on the table so fiercely that half the liquid sloshed over the tablecloth.

"You really are an arrogant prick, aren't you!" Dave leant into Richard; their faces almost touching, Dave looked ready to throw a punch.

Maddie shot out of her chair so fast it tipped backwards. "Sit down, Dave! Richard, please leave."

I held my breath. The standoff continued. There was an inch between the men's faces.

"Don't ever breathe my wife's name again or I swear I will kill you!" Dave spat.

Maddie raised her voice ever so slightly, just loud enough to break the spell.

"Dave, I asked you to sit down. And Richard, again, please leave our table."

Allen stood and placed two hands on Richard's shoulders, steering him away. Richard shook him off like he was shedding himself of a disease and sauntered towards the bar seemingly without a care in the world. *The mask back in place.*

Allen strode after him. "You know what, Richard? You really are a dick. I know that you started the rumours about Olivia. I know you lied to me. Why? Did she turn you down?"

A string of expletives followed. "Turn *me* down? You think I'd be interested in that old tramp? Allen, she's been around the block more times than me! I wouldn't screw her if you paid me."

Allen reared back as Eric appeared behind him like the grim reaper.

The restaurant manager emerged from the shadows and ushered Richard towards the door. Cole had retreated to the bar downing a glass of what looked like neat whisky, Jessica draped over him like an untidy shawl.

Sarah signalled for Eric to get their coats.

Bill Henderson drained his brandy and waved for Cat to get moving.

The table where I'd stood began to settle, albeit uneasily.

It was the last time I saw Richard Bradshaw alive.

CHAPTER TWENTY

Saturday, 26 October

"**M**UMMY, THE SWAN STOLE my bread!" Georgie squealed as Henry threw shredded bread into the air and ran through it, coating himself with crumbs.

We were bundled up in coats, hats, and gloves, braced against the freezing-cold but glorious morning.

My phone vibrated.

I groaned.

Maddie.

So much for family time.

"How are you this beautiful morning?" I said.

She answered with ragged breath, and I moved away from our little group.

"Shit, Darcy, what do I do? Richard's dead and Dave's being asked questioned by that awful Sergeant Burns, and I don't know what to do."

"Wait...*What?*" I had an urge to lie down on the ground where I stood and sob. This couldn't be real. It just couldn't be.

Pressing the phone painfully against my ear, listening to Maddie fall apart, I looked around at the beautiful loch, at the sailboats bobbing on the frigid water, at the children zooming by on bikes and scooters, at mums and dads and family dogs trotting alongside.

Beauty and tragedy. All rolled into one.

I stared at the cerulean sky dotted with clouds. Richard Bradshaw. The handsome monster I was sure all along had played his role in the cruelty dealt out these past few days.

Dead.

"I'm so sorry, Maddie. I don't know what to do anymore."

We left the swans and the ducks and the happy people behind and landed on Maddie's doorstep.

She looked as if she hadn't slept for a week and had aged ten years. Her usual glossy locks had been scraped back into a limp ponytail. She ushered us inside while I settled the kids on the floor with a toy medical set we'd bought Dave as a Christmas gag gift. I poured coffee, dumped four sugars in Maddie's cup and a shot of brandy and told her to start from the beginning.

"We were up at seven having breakfast. Next thing I know that asshole Jim Burns is in my kitchen, asking Dave where he was early this morning. He knew about the fight at Palermo's last night and the threat Dave made." Her lip trembled, and tears pooled in her eyes. "Richard was found dead this morning...Oh my God, Dave wouldn't hurt anyone! Jim was accusing him of...oh my God, it was just ugly! He would never!"

"What happened last night, Maddie? I know Dave didn't do this, so you don't have to convince us, but he was livid with Richard. What did Richard say to him?"

Fear, repulsion, anger. All three crawled over her face. She wrapped her arms around her body and began to rock backwards and forward.

"Maddie? What the hell did he say?"

"I can't, Darcy. It makes me feel sick." She covered her face and took a deep breath.

"Maddie! You know you can tell me anything."

"He said I'd offered to open my legs for him. He said I wanted him inside me. He said he screwed..."

I threw my arms around her and whispered, "Don't say anymore. You don't have to."

"Darcy, I didn't. I swear I didn't touch him. I'd never cheat on Dave. God, I feel sick!" Her hands flew to her mouth.

"Maddie, calm down. Nobody will believe *any* of this." I nodded at Harry, implored him into action.

He patted Maddie's back. Awkward as hell. "Come on Maddie, everything's going to be fine."

Empty words, but I knew he meant them.

Richard Bradshaw had been an awful human being—no news there—but to voice a lie so disgusting that it could end a marriage, simply for the fun of it, and then enjoy your work as you watched it unfold...that took a certain kind of sick.

Richard had been more dangerous than I'd imagined.

But now he was gone.

And a deadlier monster was still out there.

***

On the way out of the police station, we bumped into a weary Reece McDonald.

He gazed somewhere past us. "I'll never understand the depths of depravity humans will sink to...Sorry, tough morning. Listen, you were at Palermo's last night. Can you make yourself available for a statement?"

It wasn't a request.

"Of course."

Jim was creeping about in the shadows by the front desk, so I lowered my voice, "Can I have a quick word?"

We stepped away from the bustle.

"Tell me if it's none of my business, but how was Richard killed?"

Reece studied me for a few beats. "You're right—it is none of your business, but it'll be public knowledge soon enough and Cole has just been informed, so...It was almost identical to the attack on Jonathan, only this time he made sure the job was finished. Twenty-three blows to his skull."

Twenty-three.

I closed my eyes for a moment, but it did nothing to cushion the jolt of fear and repulsion from his words.

Overkill.

Rage.

Personal.

Someone close.

"Look, Reece, we can agree that the same person is responsible for what happened to Jonathan and Richard. But Elle was different."

"How so?"

"Well, the attacks on Jonathan and Richard were brutal, crazed, unrelenting, but Elle? That was methodical, planned. If the floor hadn't shown obvious signs of someone else having been in her property at her approximate time of death, and there hadn't been the indications of a struggle at the top of the stairs, her death would have never been investigated. We'd have assumed it was a tragic fall and that would have been that."

Reece nodded along with every word I said. He'd already arrived at the same conclusion. "Elle was the primary target. I agree. Make it look like an accident, job done and move on."

"Exactly. So, my point is, it all begins with Elle."

"Reece. Telephone," a woman's voice called over from the desk.

My hand reached for his arm. "One last thing. Why did Jonathan call me? I don't understand that part of the puzzle. We're friends but not super close, he's closer to many others. There has to be a reason he chose me."

Was it because I'd been at the lunch and had witnessed something? Heard something? Or was I seeing shadows?

As I exited the station and took a hit of cold air, it was then that I remembered the photograph I'd taken in Jonathan's house.

"Damn it. Harry, I took a picture of a spreadsheet with your old phone. Can you cast your scientific, math-loving eye over it for me?"

Someone called out his name and we both turned. James and Carol Ashford were coming out of the police station. James played five-a-side football with Harry every Wednesday night and worked in the city, so they often shared a train journey. And I'd met Carol at a barbecue over the summer and had got to know her a little.

Carol looked like she'd been dragged through hell and back and a sliver of alarm swept through me. Black mascara stained her cheeks, her blonde hair sticking out every which way as if she'd been standing in a wind tunnel and her eyes were swollen and red. Then I recalled that she ran a small cleaning and housekeeping service, and I connected the dots.

"Carol! What's happened?"

"I'll never get over it." She released an anguished sob. "I'll never unsee what was left of him. What that psychopath did."

She grabbed my hand and squeezed so hard that I winced.

"Did you find Richard?"

"It wasn't even supposed to be me at his house this morning, though thank God I was because Tessa would have collapsed. She called me yesterday to say she was ill. I was dreading it – haven't visited a client's house in years, too used to being stuck behind my desk now." She stared somewhere past me. "The second I opened that door? I knew something awful had happened. I could feel it—the anger I mean. It sort of hung in the air. Vases were smashed everywhere; it was a huge mess. I thought maybe there'd been a burglary and Richard was away for the weekend. And then I went into the living room and…" Her pupils dilated and her eyes widened as if she were seeing it all for the first time. "It took me a second to see Richard. All I could see was the blood…The walls, the ceiling, his beautiful furniture, it was drenched. I couldn't even tell it was him lying there."

James wrapped his arms around her and made soothing noises.

"I need to get her home," he said, "she's still in shock."

My God, it was worse than I'd ever imagined.

CHAPTER TWENTY-ONE

"**D**ODGY ACCOUNTING, THAT'S FOR sure."

"Really?" I asked. "You can tell?"

"Yup. My best guess is that Elle spotted it. If she took it to Jonathan, it's related to the church."

And the treasurer was none other than Olivia Miller. Hmm.

My phone vibrated. Gia.

"It's the village of the damned."

The shriek was so loud I pulled the phone away from my ear.

"Gia, I can hear you. I'm not deaf."

"What the fuck's going on, Darcy? It's like *Friday the 13th* around here, bodies piling up all over the place!"

I winced at her glibness. "Are you talking about Richard?"

"No, I'm talking about JFK. Of course I'm talking about Richard! I'm almost hyperventilating. I was out shopping, came home and saw Richard's house cordoned off and the hazmat boys swarming all over the place. There are cop cars everywhere, and I mean everywhere! Callum took a call from that cute Reece earlier. You know, the Daniel Craig lookalike. Said to make sure I'm available to give a statement. If he turns up in a Bond tux, I'll give him more than a statement."

She sounded positively ecstatic. The chiming of my doorbell sounded.

"Gia, I have to go. Someone's at the door."

I swung the door open and immediately regretted doing so.

"Tell me everything and start from the beginning!" Sarah barged past me, swept down the hallway and into the living room.

Harry glanced longingly at the door, no doubt hoping for a sharp exit, but the glare I produced would have frozen water, so he stayed put. I needed a witness.

Sarah surveyed our décor with a critical eye. "Fine."

High praise indeed.

"Sarah, I'm exhausted. I'm really not in the mood to talk."

She dismissed the comment with a flick of her hand. "Be that as it may, Darcy, but my baby is distraught. Can you imagine? Jessica and Cole are in a close relationship. She's doing everything she can to console Cole."

I could only imagine the tricks she was pulling out of her bag.

"I've known Richard for years," she said. "We didn't even get a chance to chat with him last night. Eric can't believe it either. We just feel sick about it. They were golfing buddies, you know; in fact, they played a few rounds just the other day."

I took the bait. "I know. I was at your house when they came back from the club, remember? How did Richard seem to Eric? Did he seem worried about anything?"

"No, quite the opposite really. Eric said he was planning a trip. No doubt spending the cash he'd get once Elle's estate was settled. Not that he needed the money of course. He was loaded in his own right, but you can never have enough. Richard was so pleased that Cole was home. Two peas in a pod."

That was certainly a different version of the story that Cole had told us only a few nights ago. Cole seemed to have been wondering if Richard had had a hand in the death of his mother.

"Who was Richard planning a trip with?"

Sarah patted at her perfect honey-blonde hair. "Who knows who he's been messing around with lately? He mentioned a few liaisons to Eric, but you know men, they never get the finer details. So, I'm afraid I can't elaborate."

She glared at Harry as if somehow it was his fault.

"Liaisons?"

An evil little smile danced over her face. "Oh, don't be so naïve, Darcy. You know damn well what I mean. Richard was a handsome, rich, single man. In remarkably high demand."

"I'm not being naive," I snapped. "I'm just wondering who'd be stupid enough to sleep with a sociopath."

She tried to raise an eyebrow on her frozen forehead. "Oh, come on now. Look closer to home. Some of the people you pal around with have found him very entertaining."

If she meant Maddie, I was going to throw her out the door. "Who?"

"I'm not going to tattle on anyone who needs a little pick-me-up. It's none of my business. But I will tell you that Olivia was very friendly with Richard from what I hear, and he had a thing for Maddie Clement that may or may not have been reciprocated."

"Don't even go there, Sarah! I'm serious. Maddie never hooked up with Richard."

Sarah shrugged but still managed to look smug. I wanted to wrestle her into a headlock.

"Ah, but the best is still to come. Jackie McPherson." A malicious smile spread over her face and she leant back into the sofa.

"What?"

"Don't let that little church-mouse act fool you. I hear she has a very different side to her come nightfall. That's all I'm saying."

"Alrighty, Sarah." Harry stood, no doubt spotting the crazed look in my eyes and clapped his hands. "We have to get the kids ready for homework, so unless you want a coffee or anything we're going to have to get moving."

Sarah had planted the seeds, and like a sucker, I was letting them take root and grow. But then, for just one insane second, I wondered. What if there was some truth in her story? She'd also claimed that Jackie was in love with Jonathan, even obsessed with him.

No, Jackie wasn't involved in any of this. She couldn't be. But then again…

204

Surely, I'd learned by now that it only takes a thin veneer to mask malignant intent.

Harry saw Sarah out and sank into the chair next to me. "This is insane. Is it a serial killer? I mean, really? The chances of that happening here must be minuscule."

"Spoken like a true scientist," I said, and shook my head. "But, no, that's not what's going on here, Harry. There's a reason for all this misery. Something triggered this. Revenge, money, love, hate. Someone close to Elle, Jonathan and Richard is behind this, I can feel it."

Harry turned to me. "That could be anyone though. I mean even we knew all three."

"Absolutely. So that leads me to the horrific conclusion that it has to be someone we know."

Enough speculation.

Time for an expert opinion.

***

Twenty minutes later, Isla stood in my doorway, shaking raindrops from her hair.

"I've just cleaned my floor!"

"Oh, lock your OCD in a cupboard, will you?" she said, and planted a kiss square on my cheek. "Right, let's see what you've got for me."

I waved her into the living room and showed her the hideous texts I'd received. Print outs of screenshots. I wanted to burn them and get them the hell out of my sight.

"I took screenshots so you could read them together."

"Good for you. You're learning." Isla slid a pair of glasses onto her nose. "Narcissistic little bastard, isn't he?"

"He?"

"Could be she. I'm no profiler but I've covered my fair share of stories showcasing the dregs of humanity. My best guess is that these were written by someone who's truly angry at you for inserting yourself into recent events. This person feels disrespected, hence my reference to narcissism."

But I was already one step ahead. What I needed was clarity

"Christ, Isla, we're surrounded by narcissists."

"Indeed. The agony-and-ecstasy reference is interesting. Irving Stone's biography on Michelangelo perhaps."

What?

"You're a smart cookie, Isla McAllister, but I don't get it. Michelangelo?"

"My bet would be it refers to the great artist suffering for their art. Back around to narcissism." She snapped her fingers. "Not a sufferer of the Dunning–Kruger effect, which is what I'd expected before I read these. Look, the use of the word *agony* is chilling, packs a punch just as he intended. I reckon we're dealing with a malignant narcissist, the king cobra of them all."

My chest tightened. "Isla, you're freaking me out. Malignant? You really think so. Shit! I knew it."

"I mean it Darcy. That…" she pointed at the print outs, "that right there is either a sociopath or a psychopath."

But I'd known it all along.

My past.

My up close and personal relationship with a cruel monster.

I'd seen it all before.

My venture into the world of true crime.

My observation of and reading human psychology had already told me so.

"Yep, the sadist, the egomaniac, the seeker of pain. My gut tells me these came from the hand of someone who has grand delusions about their own self-importance. The egotist with violent tendencies. A lethal combination. This isn't someone you ever want to come up against."

My gut knew it.

It was already too late.

Sociopath or psychopath?

In the end it didn't matter.

One of them was hunting me.

***

Shredding every ounce of sense I had left, as soon as I'd seen Isla off, I decided to fire off a text to Sarah, asking her to meet at lunchtime the next day.

In the meantime, I had Cat's Fifty Shades of Wrong to look forward to.

"Cat," I said, "if you know anything about what happened to Richard, I'm not the person you need to be speaking to."

She sighed. "No, it's nothing like that, but I can't sit on this any longer, and I trust you. Get me a Patron and fresh lime if you have it."

I glanced heavenward, hoping for divine intervention. Nada.

"Sure, let me get that for you."

This better be worth it, I thought as I stomped into the kitchen.

And it was.

"Here." Cat pushed her phone towards me. "Press play."

"What is this? Is this something weird?"

"Oh, it's weird alright, but it's relevant. Play it."

A grainy video appeared, the image gradually sharpening. I recognised the backdrop—the Cedarwood Country Club. Popular for the finest fundraisers and fancy weddings. A party was in full swing in the main hall. Eric Evans' fiftieth perhaps. Whatever the celebration was, I hadn't been invited.

The camera swept round a table of people. Some I knew, some I didn't. The shot landed on Jessica. She was draped over an older man who was enjoying the peep show she was delivering.

The video moved to the dance floor, where revellers were gyrating to a tinny version of *Twist and Shout*.

The lens slipped to the floor, and then we were outside the hall. I recognised the flocked cream paper against the walnut panelling.

A man and a woman were pressed against the wall, groping each other feverishly. Intimate and frantic. Heads back, necks strained. The man slipped a hand under the woman's dress, and she moaned. Pleasure being delivered.

"What the hell is this? Who is it? And why am I watching it?"

Joy Division's *Love Will Tear Us Apart* drifted from a speaker in the nearby hall. The make-out session became more feverish.

The sound of enjoyment being shared made me shift uncomfortably in my chair. The camera zoomed in, and the characters faces became clear as day. I couldn't help but gasp.

Sarah Evans and Richard Bradshaw.

What the hell?

Sarah turned and stared straight into the camera. Her expensive lipstick wasn't smudge-proof after all, and her eyes were glassy with booze and passion. They flashed, now cold as ice.

"What the hell are you doing, you bitch?" She slapped Richard's hand away and lunged like a cobra.

"Sarah! I always knew you were a slut."

I couldn't see the speaker's face, but I knew her voice.

Elle Bradshaw.

The screen went blank.

CHAPTER TWENTY-TWO

I WANTED TO SCRUB MY hands. "When was this? How did you get a hold of it? Why are you showing it to me?"

My voice sounded a little high, a little confused, a little disgusted. I wasn't sure why, maybe because I felt like I was looking at a shattered mirror.

"Darcy, calm down. It wasn't a porn flick, for goodness sake."

"It's not that. It's just...there's too many secrets, too much betrayal. I don't know how they can stand it. Fuck! I can't keep my head straight."

"Here, let me get *you* a drink and I'll share a some of my wisdom with you."

We went into the kitchen and Cat put a glass in front of me. I didn't touch it; my head was already swimming.

"This is a small town," Cat said. "People have a lot of money and too much time on their hands. Believe it or not, that sometimes breeds unhappiness."

Who were these people that had too much time? If I could have, I'd have bought time by the truckload because I never had enough of it.

"That's the way it is. So, happiness is sought in other ways, whatever fulfils them; but, and never forget, appearances are everything and people don't like to be caught indulging in a little play."

God, it was depressing.

"I'm not saying Cedarwood is a fancy knocking shop, far from it, but you know what they say—the devil makes short work for idle hands."

"What about you, Cat?"

She laughed. It was a harsh sound. "I try to make it work. Every day I try. I love my girls. I love my Bill, but I'm not a fool. He loves me, that I know, but he needs to feel important. He's the insecure one in our relationship, not me."

"Cat, I don't know you well, but I think we're becoming friends. Please don't settle just because it's easy. You deserve better than that."

"I know. But my girls are happy, Darcy. They thrive in the school Bill and I can afford to send them to. Bill's happy. And I guess I am too, in my own way. And that's that."

That's that.

I took her hand and squeezed it. In that moment my heart broke a little, but I'd never let her see it. "I understand. More than you know."

And in my own way I did. I'd seen the pain people would endure to keep a family together. Even when everything was ripping apart in front of their eyes.

I'd lived that nightmare when I was a kid.

Some of my friends lived in loveless marriages because it was easy. Was it worth it?

The hell it was, but changing things was always easier said than done.

"Someday I'll tell you my story, Cat, then you might rethink your last statement. If you have any doubts, then get the hell out."

A look of empathy passed between us and in that moment, I hoped Cat knew there'd never be further judgement from me.

"Funny thing Darcy. Whatever has gone down in this village over the last week seems to have frightened Bill. I think he might have finally grown up. He's been attentive, he's different. Maybe he's finally realised that the grass isn't greener. In fact, it can be muddy, dirty, and spoiled. So maybe I'll get my happy ending after all."

"I truly hope you do, Cat. Now about that video?" I said.

"Well, it was about six weeks ago. Eric's fiftieth. Sarah and Elle were bitching at each other all night and Richard was in the middle. Don't know what it was about but there were a lot of dirty looks and nasty words flying about." She stared at the wall. "There was something between the three of them, but I can't put my finger on what. I'd heard through the grapevine that Sarah and Richard had hooked up in the past. I've known her for years; she's a friend and it was none of my business."

She'd put air quotes around the word *friend*. It didn't surprise me. Sarah was a friend to no one.

"Elle told me she was going to take Sarah down. I laughed because it sounded so ridiculous, but she wasn't kidding, she was mad as hell, and I was glad I wasn't on her radar." She sighed again. "Sarah and Richard had been getting handsy with each other at the bar, and then they disappeared. I didn't give it a second thought until... Elle called me a few days later, and I went over for a G and T and a catch-up. She had all her evidence laid out in technicolour. Even sent me a copy and urged me to send it to all my friends. 'Give the PTA something to talk about at their next meeting' was what she said."

"Did you send it to anyone?"

"No!" Cat said. "I might be many things but I'm not a homewrecker. Sarah's marriage is her business, and let's just say if any of the stories about Eric have been true then you can't blame a girl. I told Elle she was playing with fire, that she should delete the video and never speak of it again, but she was enraged. She hated Richard—couldn't let go of whatever was between them. Of that, I'm sure. The thought that she had a ticking time bomb in her hand just delighted her. I mean, it was crazy."

"So?"

"So, my point is that the video is proof that Sarah had every reason in the world to want both Elle and Richard dead. She'll do anything to protect what she has, make no mistake."

"Do you think Elle showed it to anyone?"

"I know she did. She showed it to Sarah."

Whoa.

"Sarah knew Elle could send this video everywhere if she wanted to. Elle told her so. I can't imagine Eric would have turned a blind eye, too proud for that. And Jessica? The psychopath in the making. I wouldn't want to tangle up close and personal with either of them."

"So, you find Jessica just as scary as I do?"

"Cold as ice. Empty in the heart."

Well, well. It was all spilling out today.

Sarah and Richard. Affair or one night stand?

Why was Elle in the middle? Jealous perhaps?

If she was, then what the hell did that mean? She wanted something intimate with Richard herself. Or she simply hated Sarah touching things that she thought belonged to her.

I needed to clear my head.

Wrapping things up with Cat, I decided to walk. It was the next best thing to chilling in front of the TV with a mystery marathon and a bag of crisps. And I'd had quite enough subterfuge for one day.

Harry loves to run—helps him decompress from the day and he enjoys the side dish of health benefits that come with it. I prefer my side dishes with chips drenched in salt and vinegar, but I love to walk so I strode down the road with Pepper in front, tugging hard on his lead, snuffling the pavement. The clocks would go back tonight, meaning nightfall would come earlier and the kids and I would have an excuse to get into our jammies as soon as we could.

Dusk was settling.

Pumpkins and ghosts adorned doorsteps and gardens.

Again, Pepper dragged me to Mapleway Road and the open gates of Everbrook. I was beginning to hate this place.

On a whim I marched up the driveway and rang the doorbell. The chime exploded against the silence of the night. Why was I here? Why wasn't I home with my kids? Pepper danced around in circles and my heart broke for him.

She's not there, Pepper.

Cole greeted me in low-slung jeans and no shirt, hair all rumpled. Hot as hell – like he'd just fallen out of bed. If Jessica popped out behind him in skimpy undies, I'd break my exercise rule and sprint back down the driveway.

"Did I wake you up? I was just passing and…please accept my condolences." My words sounded limp given the brutality of his uncle's death.

He shook his head. "You didn't wake me. I was sitting staring into space, drinking a beer." He stood aside and opened the door wider. "Come in."

I cringed as I passed the spot where Elle had lain only days before. Three empty beer bottles and a sheaf of papers were spread out on the living-room floor. The TV was on but muted.

Cole waved me into a chair while Pepper strained at the lead.

"Do you mind if I let him off? I think he feels at home."

Cole stared at Pepper. Not a hint of compassion. It bugged the hell out of me.

"Sure," he mumbled.

I unclipped Pepper and let him snuffle about. "I heard what happened to Richard. It's…it's unfathomable. Do the police have any idea what the hell's going on?"

"He was killed late last night or in the early hours of this morning. The last time I saw him was at Palermo's, and that was late, so it must have happened after that. The police have just left. Been here for bloody hours because, of course, I don't have an alibi. The one night I send Jess home, and this happens. And I thought he was involved."

So had I.

"Dave Clement didn't hurt Richard," I said.

"How do you know that, Darcy? People are capable of the most amazing things."

"True, but he's the wrong guy, Cole. I know it."

He threw the remote onto the coffee table. It skittered across and fell onto the polished floor. "Then maybe *you* should head up the investigation. You seem to have all the damn answers!"

He jumped to his feet. I reared back, clenching my fists…gut reaction.

"Darcy! I'm so sorry, I didn't mean that. I don't know what the hell I'm feeling. Or doing."

Gauging his demeanour, I took a second to settle myself. "Cole, you've been through more in the past few days than most people do in a lifetime. Don't apologise." As I spoke, I could feel my cheeks flame

He left the room returning a minute later with two cold beers.

I figured he needed to talk so I sat back and took a sip. Then another.

"It's time for me to leave," he said. "I can't stay here anymore. As soon as mum's affairs are settled, I'm off. Maybe sooner. This house is huge, but I feel claustrophobic. Doesn't make sense but it's how I feel. I can't stand it anymore."

"You're grieving. In the worst possible circumstances. If *I* can't get my head around this nightmare, then I have no idea how you must be feeling right now."

He gazed around the room. "That's the one thing keeping me here. This house. I hate this place, yet it makes me feel connected to my mum…but I can't lie, it would be great to walk away from this mess."

My phone buzzed. Harry.

"Darcy! You'll never guess what."

Cold dread.

I couldn't stand any more heartache.

"It's Jonathan! He's opened his eyes. He's responding."

"He's awake?"

Cole's head snapped up and he jumped to his feet.

"I don't know any more details than that," Harry said. "It's still early days but a huge step forward. I told you this is going to work out."

I disconnected and stared at Cole.

"Call them, call the hospital." Cole gestured towards my phone. "That's great news!"

"I'd rather wait. I want to speak to Dave first, get the real story."

Sitting my empty beer bottle down I got to my feet, desperate to get home. To sleep.

"Now, listen, anytime you need to talk just give us a call. And I do mean that. I'll let you know what I hear about Jonathan."

As I called to Pepper, my eye caught a picture of Elle in an elegant silver frame. She was younger in the photo but still just as beautiful. More so even.

A memory clawed at the surface, but it was an itch I couldn't quite scratch.

I didn't know why but it made me apprehensive.

***

Pepper scampered down the hallway in search of Georgie and Henry. The chorus of giggles and barks told me he'd found them.

"Harry, I have something to show you. Prepare to enter the circle of hell." I waggled my phone.

He grabbed it. "What is it?"

"Just play it."

His expression shifted from surprise to horror while he watched the video.

"Where the hell did you get this? God, I will never erase that from my mind."

"That, Harry, is motive."

"You can't be serious! You really think Sarah would kill Elle and Richard over this video?"

"Why did Elle record that? For one reason only—to blackmail Sarah."

"Blackmail?" he said, incredulous. "Darcy, what the hell are you talking about?"

"Not for money but for power. Look, Eric makes a fortune. She's worth a mint in her own right, but I cannot imagine what's on that video would be good for business. Eric's business or Sarah's for that matter. I'm sure her mother still sits on the bench. Her father mingles with the Whitehall crowd or so I've heard! Letting anyone get a glimpse of that would be like signing her own social death warrant."

"Darcy, this is crazy! Should we show it to Reece?"

"He must have seen it. Wouldn't they have taken Elle's phone and computers from the house? It fits. It actually all fits."

"But it doesn't fit. Because of Jonathan."

Jonathan. How could I have forgotten? He was the piece of the puzzle that didn't finish the picture.

Damn it.

Ten minutes later, I was finishing off a bag of Doritos while Gia interrogated me over the phone.

"So, any intel?"

"Intel? Gia, have you been watching reruns of *24* again?"

"Why, yes, I have since you ask but stop changing the subject. What's the latest?"

I brushed crumbs from my hands and watched them fall onto the floor. No way was I spilling; it would be all over the village before dawn. As much as I loved my friend, she couldn't keep her mouth shut to save her life and there was too much at stake to blabber these secrets all over town. Messing with people's personal lives and reputations didn't sit too well with me.

A call from Dave put a little spring in my step. Jonathan's vital signs were stronger, and he'd opened his eyes briefly. Another MRI was scheduled for first thing in the morning.

I spent the next half hour at the table with my two kids, a pink teddy and a toy monkey. All four were a salve for my soul. No matter what was going on in the real world, they could bring normalcy and innocence back to my life in a heartbeat.

I crawled into bed, tried to catch up on *Unmasking a Killer*, but switched it off less than a minute later.

No more death. No more destruction.

Instead, I breathed softly in the dark, waiting for sleep to take me.

CHAPTER TWENTY-THREE

Sunday, 27 October

THE KNIFE DRAGGED BUTTER over the toast, and I was so lost in thought that I almost sliced my finger. I stared at my hands. They were present but my mind was elsewhere, churning over the events of the past few days.

Henry wailed for me to hurry up. Georgie began to fret about fractions.

"I have to get my sums right, Mum. Mrs Sanderson's going to read out our results in front of the whole class!"

"Georgie, you've got this. With hard work and practice, you'll nail it."

I didn't add that fractions were my nemesis and that I'd soon be passing her off to Harry to deal with.

The phone rang, startling me. I didn't need a therapist to tell me I'd developed a dread of unexpected calls and unanticipated visitors.

"Dave's home!" Maddie said as if he'd returned from a tour of duty.

I let go of the breath I'd been holding since the phone chimed and felt the tension lift from my shoulders.

"We were stuck at that damn station for hours. We saw Allen on the way out and he was arguing with Jim. He was pissed, like super belligerent. What a mess this is. I feel like I'm freefalling."

Weren't we all?

***

I stood just outside Jonathan's room, unabashedly eavesdropping on the medical debrief taking place just feet away from where I lingered while pretending to scroll through my phone.

"The prognosis was poor, but we've made progress," Andy said. "His vital signs are stabilising. Latest MRI showed the swelling is reducing so I've begun reversing the induced coma. He's been breathing on his own for almost ten hours."

Hands clapped and I almost jumped out my skin.

"Make no mistake, if Jonathan comes out of this, he'll likely have a challenging rehabilitation in front of him. But for now, this is all positive news."

"Appreciate your honesty," Dave's voice sounded tired. "That you got him stable is nothing short of a damn miracle so I'm feeling optimistic. Trust me, for my own selfish reasons I need some good news."

As both doctors turned towards the door, I pretended something enthralling had appeared on my screen. Andy cocked an eyebrow at me, then smiled.

"You can go in now."

Dave seemed unsure where to put himself. Jonathan lay motionless and expressionless.

"Snap out of it, Dave. You've had a hell of a few days, but it sounds like a little progress has been made here. That's good, right?"

He dragged a hand over his face. "I'm sorry, I'm just...I don't know, freaking the hell out? What the fuck happened to Richard? I swear I had nothing to do with it."

"Dave, nobody—"

"I wanted to rip my hair out in that interview room. Claustrophobic. Over and over, the same questions. Didn't matter how many times I answered them, straight back to the beginning again. I couldn't think straight. They said overkill."

His fear and disbelief were evident.

"What?"

"I heard them talking outside the room. That's what they said. Overkill."

One word, but one that delivered a hell of a punch.

Overkill.

It usually established rage and passion. Hatred and disgust. But I'd already guessed that.

Dave's anxiety seemed off the charts. Something else was going on.

He exhaled, a ragged and painful sound. "Have you noticed anything wrong with Maddie recently?"

Have I ever.

"In what way?" I said as innocently as I could pull off.

"I don't know...she's jittery, nervous. She says everything's fine, but I know something's off, I can feel it. I guess it all started when Olivia and ..."

"Go on."

"It's not my place. I shouldn't have said anything. Sorry. Forget it. I'm stressed out of my brain right now, and probably looking for things that aren't there." He exhaled and it sounded laboured, weary.

But he was back-peddling, and it annoyed the hell out of me.

"Hand to God, Dave, I'm way past stressed. I want to crawl into my bed and stay there for a month. I'm not sure I'll ever get over what I've witnessed over the past few days. I can't sleep, I'm jumping at every little sound I hear, I can't relax for the life of me. Every time I step a foot over my front door, I feel someone is watching me." I'd reached boiling point. "Just the other night I swore that someone followed me home from the office. I'm losing my damn mind. So, I think it's time we all laid our cards on the table. The more we paper over the truth the easier it is for whoever is behind this to stay in the shadows. So, be honest. What's going with Maddie and Olivia? Because, believe me, I know..."

A soft knock at the door startled me. I spun around and Jackie peered around the door.

"Can I come in?"

As frustrated as I was by the interruption, I didn't have the heart to be pissed at Jackie.

I waved her in. "Jonathan's intubation's been removed."

Her tentative smile split into a wide grin. "He looks so much better!"

Dave opened his mouth, but she waved him off. "I know, small steps, but what a difference."

We played musical chairs and chatted about Jonathan's recovery for ten minutes or so, me throwing Dave the occasional sulky glance. I'd make damn sure I brought up our conversation the next chance I got.

He went for coffee, and I focused on Jonathan's face, trying to stay awake.

And then his lips moved. At least I thought they had.

I scrambled out of my chair. "Look. Jackie, look!"

Her phone clattered to the floor and a soft moan escaped his lips.

"Jonathan! It's Darcy! Jackie's here too."

His eyelids fluttered and he made another sound. Was he trying to speak? I went to him and repeated my name, told him he was safe.

"*Sand,*" he whispered, and his right hand twitched.

A micro movement, but movement, nevertheless. I placed my hand on his and listened hard.

"*Sand.*"

Another stray piece of the puzzle? Or the mumbling of a man numbed with pain and medication?

"Jonathan," Andy boomed. He'd appeared out of nowhere. "Time for your visitors to go but they'll be back tomorrow. Now then…"

I was so tightly wound, I wanted to barf.

What had just happened?

What had Jonathan said?

Just an incoherent mumble? No, something more; I felt it in my bones. He'd been trying to tell me something. The question was, what?

I drove home.

Like life, the journey passed too quickly.

CHAPTER TWENTY-FOUR

THE CLICK-CLACK OF HEELS echoed ominously, then Sarah opened her front door.

Get it together, Darcy. Hold your nerve.

Sarah chattered all the way down the long hallway and led me into her sitting room—white walls with notes of hazel and bronze courtesy of the soft furnishings. Dominating the room was a huge white fireplace flanked by two colossal, bronzed vases, each containing a riot of autumnal flowers. She gestured to a plush overstuffed sofa. A bottle of Bollinger sweated in an ice bucket on a small maple table. Next to it, a tray of Italian smoked hams completed the culinary extravaganza. A gleaming sterling-silver tea service offered dainty, bite-sized macarons.

I wanted to move in—lion's den or not.

Sarah popped the fizz and filled our glasses. Had it not been for the sleazy video on my phone somewhere at the bottom of my bag, it might have been a somewhat pleasant afternoon.

Sarah took a long sip—no Lucrezia Borgia antics at play here—and gestured to the tray of nibbles.

"Thanks, Sarah, but I don't eat meat."

She flinched as I if I'd casually alluded to enjoying an afternoon of S and M. "Go on, I'll never tell."

I shook my head and updated her on Jonathan's progress. Her reaction was one of relief. If she was acting, she was damned good.

"I need to talk to you about something," I said. "Something rather personal. I'm not quite sure how to bring it up."

"Either have the backbone to say what's on your mind or don't. I despise simpering."

"I saw the video."

Sarah downed half her drink, her expression blank. "What video?"

"It's none of my business but…"

"Damn right," she said, and picked up the bottle.

I gripped the arm of the chair. "Sarah, I have zero intention of breathing a word about this…unless it has something to do with Elle's death."

"Elle's death? What the hell are you talking about?"

"I know it was Elle filming the video. It was a spiteful thing to do."

"Spiteful? Fuck. It was pure, damn evil. That bitch held it over my head for weeks. I couldn't believe it. She literally held my life in her hands. She thought she was playing with me, but she played with fire, didn't she?"

Oh, sweet Jesus, I hadn't thought this through. I looked around the room for the quickest exit.

She cackled and her cold eyes lit up, seemingly delighted by my reaction. Why had I showed fear?

So stupid.

I wouldn't make that mistake twice.

"Have you lost your mind? Do you honestly think I killed that miserable bitch? Oh, Darcy, I wish I could take the credit, but I didn't do it. They don't do cashmere jumpsuits in prison. If they did, I'd have chucked her down a flight of stairs years ago." She snapped her fingers in my face. Her aggression showing as clear as the dawn starting each day. "Look at me. There are only a few things in life I take seriously. My money, my daughter, my comforts and my home. I really don't care about anything else. Got to look after yourself in this big bad world, and I do it without a blush. No one will ever stand in my way and that stupid bitch was trying to do exactly that. But by the grace of God, before I could do anything desperate, Cat Henderson answered my prayers the minute she called me last

Friday with the news that Elle was being stretchered out in a body bag. Imagine my surprise." Her empty eyes searched my face. "My questions to you are how do you know about the video and where did you get it?"

"It doesn't matter who showed it to me, but you can imagine *my* surprise when I realised that both the person filming it and the male star of the show are now dead."

"It sure as hell matters to me. I like to know where all the snakes in the grass are slithering."

We sat in uncomfortable silence.

I'd sit there all day if I needed to. No way would I be delivering Cat's name to her on a silver platter.

"I'm no killer," Sarah said. "If I was, I can assure you that Eric would have left this mortal world years ago. He really is the most insufferable man. Whatever's at play here has nothing to do with that video. Richard and I had a fling. It meant nothing but a good time. He knew how to push my buttons if you know what I mean."

A little of the Bollinger made its way back up my throat.

"But, Elle, oh my God, she held it over my head like a guillotine. Threatened to send it to Eric, who might be a lot of things, but understanding is not one of them. I like things the way they are, Darcy, and if you try to adjust them then ending up at the bottom of the stairs will be the least of your problems. Don't play with me."

Time to act the scene of my life.

I threw my head back and laughed. "As you so often remind me, Sarah, I wasn't brought up here in Cedarwood. Not pampered, not catered to so I can handle myself. Don't underestimate me. I'm not here to upset you. Only the truth matters. And, frankly, I don't care if you get your kicks with half the village. I don't mess with people's lives, that you can take to the bank."

Her shoulders eased a little.

"But," I said, "if I find out that you had anything to do with what happened to Jonathan then I'll sail you down the river in a heartbeat."

A small smile tugged at her lips, and she lifted her glass. "Then we have an understanding."

"So," I said, "tell me what happened with Elle and Richard at the club."

"Ah, you heard about that, did you? Truth is, I'm not sure. God, I'd have killed to know that story." Her laugh was so brittle it could have shattered into a thousand pieces. "Bad choice of words. Elle pounced on Richard like a raging bull, ranting on about receiving something in the post. I got the feeling Elle believed Richard had raked up some old story to mess with her. Honestly, she wasn't that interesting. He told her she'd lost her damn mind and she lunged at him. I couldn't believe my eyes. He pushed her away, and she stumbled backwards and almost landed on her arse. Elle was many things, but she never would have dreamed of making a scene like that in public unless it was serious. Whatever it is was, it had cut her to the core, even I could see that. It was all anyone could talk about for weeks."

"Why did they hate each other so much?"

"She never spoke about it, but something happened years ago between her, Charles and Richard. Money, sex, take your pick. I tried for years to get to the bottom of that trifecta—a little leverage goes a long way in this town—but she held her secrets close. I always admired her for that." She crossed her legs and stared beyond me. "She had a huge fight with Charles, or so I was told, disappeared for a few months. Then one night, she appeared at the club, dressed to the nines and raring to go. Naturally, we all assumed she was divorcing Charles."

My mind was spinning in so many directions I felt dizzy. "Money or sex?"

"Huh?"

"Money or sex. That's what you said. What one did you think it was?"

"Knowing Elle, both."

I gasped. "You mean Elle and Richard?"

Sarah smirked. "Why not? Elle was a beauty, even I can't deny that. And Richard, well, what can I say? He knew his craft. You should have seen him back in the day."

Her lips parted, and I longed for a shower.

"Don't look so surprised, Darcy. Charles was a dud by all accounts."

The more I looked at the picture the more fractured it seemed to become.

Sarah tapped the side of her glass. "Did you ever wonder why Allen shed Olivia like a disease?"

I shook my head, dreading the answer.

"She welcomed Richard into her bed. Or so the story goes. There you have it—ugly as it is. Drink up, Darcy. To our new friendship." She raised her glass and smiled cunningly. "If I can help you with any titbits, call me anytime, but always remember I don't like snakes in my grass. I slice their heads clean off."

I gripped my glass and held it still.

I wasn't stupid enough to toast with the devil.

***

"Do you remember the story Jessica told us at dinner? That Richard's car was parked in Jonathan's driveway after we'd all left after lunch?"

Harry and I were in the kitchen, stacking the dinner plates.

"Yep. What about it?"

"I've been noodling on that, and one of two things must be the truth."

I ignored my husband's anguished sigh.

"Either Richard did go back there and unwittingly dragged Jonathan into the middle of whatever ugly mess was going on between him and Elle, or Jessica made the whole story up."

"Why would she?"

"For attention or, to throw some shade at Richard for getting it on with her mother and putting her pampered life at chez Evans at risk. It's plausible."

Harry nodded. "If she's anywhere as scary as I think she is, then it's absolutely plausible."

"So how do I get to the truth?"

A soft knock on the door made me jump.

"Will you calm down," Harry said, "you're jumping out of your skin at every noise." He squeezed my arms and landed a kiss on my forehead before sauntering off to the door. "Calm down. I'm right here with you."

Reece McDonald. I led him to the living room.

"I had my officers comb through every second of security footage from the hospital just in case anyone was on your heels. Nothing. Both texts were sent from a burner. For now, it's untraceable. I know all of this is disappointing, but I have to say, I'm concerned. Our perpetrator has been incredibly careful."

Harry slapped his forehead. "I really want to punch this coward out."

Reece nodded. "I spoke with Jonathan's doctor earlier. He sounded positive. It'll be a real blessing if he comes out of this."

He twisted his wedding band, and I couldn't help myself.

"Does your wife worry about you doing this type of job? You must really lose your faith in humanity."

"Sometimes I do." Reece sighed. He exhaled and stared at floor but continued to twist his wedding band. "My wife passed two years ago. Breast cancer."

"Reece, I'm so sorry! She must have been young."

"Thirty-eight and full of life. Kate and I were trying to start a family when she got the diagnosis—stage four."

His pain was almost tangible, and it hung in the air. I yearned to reach out and comfort him but held back. I didn't know him well enough.

"To be honest," he said, "it almost killed me, too. I sank myself into work instead of a bottle. I try and live in the present, but some days are just so bloody hard. My friends are trying to get me to date but I'm not sure I'm ready."

My heart ached for him, for his loss.

Another victim robbed of his future.

I reached for his hand and patted it, delivering my comfort, wanted or not.

CHAPTER TWENTY-FIVE

Monday, 28 October

"THE NEXT THING I know, he tells me he's a reporter and asks can I give him a comment! I told him to get the hell out of my shop!"

Mel Young was still as outraged as she'd been twenty minutes earlier when she started her story.

I imagined cramming one of her famous cinnamon buns in her mouth to shut her up. Instead, I nodded and said for what seemed like the hundredth time, "Good for you, Mel."

"I mean, can you imagine? A reporter!"

I almost cried with relief when the barista handed me the skinny latte and lemon muffin. I snagged an empty table next to the window and dropped into the chair.

"Get me an Americano, black." The grating whine drifted over and the signature theme tune from *The Omen* started to play again in my head.

"Hi, Jessica." I faked a smile as I leaned over to greet her.

Her pout turned into a sneer. "Are you following me? You're like everywhere!"

"I live here, and you're not that interesting. How's Cole?"

He stood in line at the counter, yawning and rubbing his face.

"He looks tired."

She smiled salaciously. "He should be. I had him up half the night, if you know what I mean."

"I meant after what happened to Richard."

Jessica shrugged and grinned. "He doesn't feel like talking much when he's with me. There are much more interesting things to do."

"Therapy not your strong suit then?"

"Huh?"

Oh dear.

I was on a roll and decided to go all in.

"Did you make up the story about seeing Richard's car in Jonathan's driveway?"

"What are you talking about?" she spat.

"Tell me the truth before Cole comes over here. I reckon you've got about five seconds before I lose my shit."

"Jesus, so what? Who cares? Richard upset my mother and he needed to be taught a lesson. I look after my family."

"So, you're Don Corleone now?"

Confusion snaked across her beautiful face, and that made me smile. I'd known she was an idiot all along.

"I wouldn't let you look after a disease," I said. "Do you realise what you've done?"

"Everything alright here?" Cole said.

My eyes didn't leave Jessica's face. "How are you doing, Cole? I'm just having a chat with your friend. Not a morning person, is she?"

I tore my eyes from Jessica and looked at him. Still breath-taking, but something was different. He looked a little lost, maybe? Something in his eyes. I held his gaze for a few beats then offered a heartfelt expression of sympathy.

"You look exhausted."

He looked away. "You have no idea, Darcy."

I pushed past Jessica and said, "You should try being a human being for once. Speak to him, make sure he's alright."

I couldn't stand to be in her presence a moment longer and headed out onto Firmont Road.

"Mrs Sinclair. Mrs Sinclair!"

The broad Glaswegian accent belonged to a woman I didn't recognise. Plump, late fifties, early sixties. Short, no-nonsense faded blonde hair. Disarmingly cheery toothy grin.

She limped towards me with the aid of two elbow crutches. One clattered to the ground when she offered me her hand. I retrieved it and rewarded her with a smile.

"Can I help you?"

"I'm right sorry to bother you, but I wonder if you might be able to help me?"

"Bye, Darcy," Cole said as he walked past me.

I glanced through the window. Jessica sat slumped in her chair. A childish feeling of victory bubbled up inside me.

I turned back to the woman. "Of course. Excuse me, but do I know you?"

She shook her head. "No, hen, you don't, but Laura who works in your office told me all about you and said you might be to help me."

"Do you need some legal advice, Mrs...?"

"Davidson, hen, but call me Moira. Anyway," she blew air from her flushed cheeks, "it's about these terrible murders. Right shocking it's been."

I nodded.

"You see, my son Tom went to university with Cole Bradshaw. So proud of Tom we are, first in our family to ever go to university. His father and I still can't get over how good he is at maths. Never seen anything like it. People used to joke about him being the milkman's son because his dad never had a head for numbers."

She clucked her tongue at the memory, and I couldn't help but smile. Tom's mum was a talker.

"That boy just sailed through his exams. Got accepted by Glasgow and St Andrews, but he went to St Andrews. Broke my heart that he was so far away." Her hand went to her chest. "Broke it in two."

I was beginning to understand why Tom had chosen St Andrews.

"Anyway, we stayed in Kilmakern back then," she said.

Kilmakern was a smaller village about twenty minutes away. It was pretty but wouldn't ever house the likes of my good chum Sarah Evans.

"Tom helped his dad and I buy a small house here for our retirement. I'm telling you, that boy is a saint! Never been so happy. And the garden! Well, it's paradise. I tend to it every day. Well, I did until I got my new knee replacement. What a surgery that is! Don't ever get old, pet. It sucks, let me tell you."

"I'll bet your garden's beautiful."

"Sorry, hen, I do tend to prattle! Well, you see Mrs Sinclair..."

"Moira, I'm Darcy." I gestured for her to resume her story.

She nodded. "Och, it's right lovely to meet you. Anyway, my Tom is just about to take some time off work. See, it's his own business. Runs it with a partner—money stuff, you understand. He's coming home for two weeks to help us out because I can't do much for the first few weeks, you see, and my Jimmy has a bad back, so we're a bit stuck doing the day-to-day chores. Truth be told, though, I think he just wants a break from his wife. Melinda is such a talker; the poor boy never gets a word in."

Freud would have had a field day with Tom.

"The thing is, he heard about the terrible goings-on here. I fill him in on the local goings-on, you see, and, well, he wants to attend Mrs Bradshaw's funeral and pay his respects to Cole. He hasn't seen him in so many years, but it's the right thing to do and I always brought Tom up to do the right thing."

I pulled my coat tighter against the biting wind and wondered if I should offer Moira a coffee. I didn't get a chance.

"Truth is, I suspect he wants a few beers—you know what boys are like." She rolled her eyes. "Anyway, Laura, the girl that works in your office, well, her mum lives next door to me so we always get to talking and she told me that it was you that found Mrs Bradshaw, you poor thing." She enveloped my hand in her large one. "She told me you've become good friends with him, and so I wondered if you might put my Tom in touch with Cole, seeing that they're old pals. Tom's arriving later today."

"Of course, Moira. I'd be happy to."

I wasn't comfortable handing out Cole's private number, so I fished a business card from my bag. "Tell Tom to give me a buzz and we'll take it from there. I'll let Cole know. Bet he'll be delighted."

"Och, bless you, Darcy. Laura was right, you're a lovely girl."

She parted with a beaming grin and hobbled off down the road just as my monstrous new sparring partner exited Roast. Jessica's hair buffeted Medusa-like all around her in the howling wind.

This was turning out to be a doozy of a morning.

"Round two, Jessica?" I asked.

"What was that woman saying about Cole?"

"None of your business."

She stamped her foot.

Even Georgie had stopped that nonsense several years earlier.

"He's *my* boyfriend. I have a right to know."

"You really don't, Jessica. Let's continue this another time. I've a job to get to. Some of us have to work for a living."

"Must suck to be you," she said, and a little smirk tugged at her pouting lips.

Sometimes more than you know.

I turned and walked away, head tucked into the wind, humming *California Dreaming* by The Mamas and Papas because all the leaves were brown.

Slowly, the tension in my shoulders melted away. I reminded myself that I needed to spend more time appreciating what was around me rather than rushing blindly through the day just to get from beginning to end.

Mother Nature's hand had served me well today. The trees had shed their leaves and the ground was a carpet of gold and bronze. Harry and I had been married in the autumn—a beautiful wedding, small and intimate —and it was the stunning backdrop, not the bride, that had stolen the show.

By the time I'd reached the office, I felt refreshed and revitalised.

"I just bumped into Moira," I said to Laura. "I gave her my number and I'll put Tom in touch with Cole."

Laura tossed her hair. "Thanks. Gets my mum off my back. I told her she'd probably catch you in Roast as you do love your morning coffee, don't you? And I knew…"

"No problem, Laura," I said, imaging a conversation between Moira and Laura—like some Wimbledon final with never-ending rallies.

Bob and I spent a couple of hours going over a case, then Laura tossed the mail on my desk. Just as I grabbed for it, Bob settled his files on his lap as he leaned back in the chair. "Heard there's been reporters milling around town, asking questions."

"Were you in Roast this morning by any chance?"

Bob nodded. "I can't get my head around the news that Richard was murdered. I've known him for years. What the hell is going on, Darcy? Elle. Jonathan. Now Richard. If you would have told me two weeks ago something this wicked could happen here in Cedarwood, I would've told you take a few personal days. There must be a link. Something connecting them. Something more than just family ties and friendship. I've gone over and over it in my head, and I just can't grasp it. You know when I started the firm all those years ago Charles Bradshaw was one of my first clients."

"Really?"

"He was. He sent a lot of work my way and made sure Richard used the firm. Sent his own clients here too. I owed a lot to Charles. He might have been a quiet guy, but he was a good guy. Never understood how the hell he ended up with Elle. She was a hell of a woman, you know that, but I can't think of any one specific reason someone would kill her. It can't be financial. I mean she was loaded, but other than bequeaths to charities, most of her estate goes to Cole. But he's loaded too, made a mint in his career. Anyway, he wasn't even here when she died. Charles is dead so no life insurance issues there, and Richard's gone so who the hell could it be? If not a financial reason, then what? Jealousy? Payback?"

I opened my mouth to reply but quickly closed it, as Bob continued to talk, "And what possible reason would there be to hurt Jonathan? Now there's Richard. Richard was a bad guy, a real piece of work. That I can tell you without remorse. Can I see someone wanting to pop him one? Sure, I can. I wanted to punch him many times over the years. But to bludgeon him to death. Good God! What do you think Darcy?"

Before I could answer my phone pinged. Checking it wasn't a text from the kids' school, it read as an unknown number. Sweat erupted on my skin. I clicked on it.

Hunting is my pleasure, but the catch is my thrill.

Isla's words came back to me.

Malignant sociopath.

Bile climbed up my throat.

Burning.

Searing.

"Bob, it's another one," My voice sounded mechanical, detached.

"Another what?" He was off the chair and over to my side in a heartbeat, gently taking my phone from me.

Bob drew in a breath that sounded painful.

My hand reached for the phone.

Call Reece.

***

When I'd arrived home from the office early, Harry had lost his shit. I spiralled because Harry was the calm and rational balance in our relationship. His words were angry, but I could see the fear in his eyes and that scared me more than anything. I had no idea who was behind this misery.

How can you fight an invisible monster?

I flew into a rage. A mixture of exhaustion, fear and being totally pissed off. Harry had eventually backed down. It felt like a win until I broke down in tears and apologised. After all, it was all my fault.

Self-pity and I were becoming old friends.

We spent an hour patching things up.

"Harry, can you take the kids upstairs to play? Maddie and Olivia are coming over for...well I don't know what for, but we've a lot to talk about and I don't want the kids around. God, I miss my old, boring, orderly life."

"And I miss Netflix and us in our PJs, not having a clue who in this damned village is sleeping with who, who's cheating on who, or who has the biggest bank balance. I've never met so many narcissists and hustlers in my life, and I don't want them in my living room."

Narcissists and hustlers. But which of them was malignant? I squeezed Harry's hand. Just his touch gave me strength for the night ahead.

Maddie arrived carrying what appeared to be the weight of the world on her shoulders. Olivia was a beat behind her, looking like a scared rabbit. I ushered them into the living room.

Let the interrogation begin.

Before I could draw breath, Olivia burst like a dam.

"I'm a whore and a thief. Take your pick."

Maddie released an anguished sigh.

"It's true," Olivia said. "I'm both those things, but I didn't kill anyone."

Was this happening? Would I finally be able to slip the last few pieces into the puzzle?

"Here, Olivia." I placed a glass of Prosecco in her hands.

"It was my own cross to bear. I should never have gotten Maddie involved and now she might be in trouble with the police, but maybe I can fix this."

Her voice was wrapped in pain, making the air feel heavy.

"You know all about Bill Henderson. You know we slept together. It was a hideous mistake that I can't undo. If that makes me a whore, then I can accept it."

"Doesn't make you a whore, Olivia. I'm guessing it made you feel even lonelier."

"Loneliness and desperation are dreadful places, and I've lived in them both. They make you do the most incredible things. I slept with a friend's husband, and I stole money. I stole it from Jonathan."

CHAPTER TWENTY-SIX

"**I**'VE BEEN SITTING IN a dark place for an awfully long time," Olivia said. "I missed Allen, my house, everything. Didn't have a penny to my name and couldn't pay my rent for the dump I was hiding in, so I stole money from the church's treasury fund. I'm a thief and I'm pathetic, and any shred of self-worth I was grasping onto went down the drain the second Jonathan was attacked. I can't stand the guilt."

I glanced at Maddie and knew in an instant she'd heard this all before. She'd been smack bang in the middle of it all along.

Poor Maddie.

Poor Olivia.

"I couldn't pay it back!" Olivia said. "I had nothing. And just when I was wondering how much lower I could sink, I got a call from Elle. She'd spotted my grubby lie a mile off—knew I'd doctored the monthly budget accounts. It wasn't the moral high ground; she wanted the scarlet letter pinned to my chest and for me to be paraded all through the town."

Olivia lowered her head into her hands.

"I found her," Maddie said so softly I almost missed the words.

"Found who?"

"Olivia."

"I was in an ugly way, Darcy. I'd swallowed a handful of pills but, as always, I'd not had the backbone to go through with it. Too scared to die, too embarrassed to go to the hospital…I called Maddie, begged for Dave's help the second I swallowed the last pill."

I slid onto my knees and took Olivia's hand. She didn't seem to mind. "Olivia, how could you linger in such a dark place and not reach out to me? I could've helped you."

A prickle of shame crawled over me. How could I not have seen this?

"Too proud, too weak, too embarrassed…take your pick. Dave made sure I'd vomited everything up and took me to the hospital. He even got me to speak to a therapist. Maddie paid everything back to the church and I promised her I'd pay her back every penny. God, I felt so light, so unburdened. And then…"

And then Elle had entered the picture.

"Elle sent me the photo she'd taken of me leaving Cat and Bill's house and told Maddie she was going to pass the real figures to Jonathan. The whole village would know I was a thief. And a slut."

A sob so painful fell from Olivia's mouth that I winced.

"At first, I was devastated, and then…then I was angry. Hope was all I had left, and she wanted to take it away from me. I wanted to kill her."

No. Don't say it. I yearned to cover my ears.

"But I didn't hurt her, I swear it!"

Olivia looked me dead in the eyes, and I believed her.

I believed every damned word.

"I know how bad this looks for me, and I'm scared out of my mind I'm going to get the blame. For all of it. I could have paid Elle back by throwing her down the stairs. I could have hurt Jonathan to stop him calling the police. And then there's Richard," she spat his name.

Another little piece about to click into place.

"My old friend Richard who told Allen that he'd had me in the gent's toilet at the club. Allen believed every disgusting word. That's why my marriage ended. That's why I was left with nothing. I never knew because Allen refused to utter one word to me. He got out of bed one morning and told me it was over. He wanted a divorce, he had the prenup and I was on the kerb before noon, hand to God. And I never knew why."

Olivia laughed but there was no joy in the sound.

Richard. Damn him. The man had been a cancer. Dangerous and malignant, spreading ugly disease everywhere he'd gone just for the fun of it. I hoped he rotted in hell.

"So that's three strikes for me, isn't it? I'll be in the dock before long, and I've probably dragged Maddie right along with me."

Maddie flinched at the words. "Reece found my calls to Elle on the night she died and the night before that. I believe a few people have alluded to the fact that I couldn't stand her—not so easy to explain why I repeatedly called her. The police also know I was planning to meet Jonathan and Olivia the day after he was attacked. It was marked on his calendar. Here's the thing, Darcy; I'd paid the money back on Olivia's behalf, so no one ever had to know. If Elle had left it alone, we wouldn't be in this shitstorm."

"That's on me, Maddie," Olivia said, her voice breaking a little.

"No, it's not. It was Elle's doing. She told Jonathan. She was the catalyst. Elle even told Jonathan about Sarah's fling with Richard."

I stared at Maddie. "*You* know about that?"

"Elle told me. She took great pleasure in letting me know that Olivia and Sarah would be off the board and that Olivia would be sitting in a jail cell for embezzlement. Embezzlement? She had taken enough to pay her rent, that was it. And then there was our little showdown at Palermo's on Friday night with Richard. So, you see, it doesn't look too good for me either."

No, it did not.

"Maddie, what were you looking for in Elle's house the morning we found her?"

"Oh God." She buried her face in her hands. "I can't believe I did that. Rummaging through her drawers like a thief in the night. Her body cold just feet away. I just wanted to find whatever it was she had on Olivia. A spreadsheet was my best guess, but it was probably on her phone all along. Dave will kill me when he hears this. That's why I was at her house the morning we found her. I was going over there to beg her one more time to leave Olivia in peace. And then we found her."

And then we found her. Broken and discarded.

"Does Reece know any of this? Olivia, when he pulled you in for questioning what happened? What did you tell him?"

"Reece had found the photo of me on her phone. Found the text that Elle had sent me. I had to tell him the truth. Had no way out. I couldn't have made up a story that morning to save my life. I was in bits, and I just couldn't stand any more lies. I don't want to live in the darkness anymore."

Living in the darkness. It was exactly how I felt.

"What did he say?"

"Oh, he kept me there for hours. Same questions over and over. Where was I Thursday night? Where was I Sunday afternoon? My one saving grace was that I had an hour-long phone call with Saffron on Thursday night, around the same time they think Elle was killed so I think that helped my cause. Just a little. Maddie had come over earlier to tell me that her last call with Elle didn't go too well, that she was probably going to start spitting venom all over town. I didn't want to slip into a dark place, so I called Saffron and told her I missed her and that I needed some daughter time."

"What about you, Maddie. Do you have an alibi for Thursday night?" I held my palms up. "Not that I think for a second that you hurt Elle but I'm just trying to get everything straight in my head."

"Nope. I hung up the phone with Elle absolutely seething, grabbed my car keys and went to Olivia's, told her the bad news and came straight home. I remember thinking I was going to drive straight off the road in that rain, held my breath the whole way home. I came from Cedar Way, so I didn't pass Elle's house. The road was deserted. Dave didn't get home until after one in the morning, he was performing an emergency surgery. Other than seeing Olivia that night I have no alibi. Didn't make any calls. Didn't speak with Dave until he got home. Didn't do much of anything, except have a stiff drink."

"Why do you think Richard fed his story to Dave at the restaurant? What was his end game?"

Maddie shrugged. "My best guess is he was pissed when he saw us sitting with Allen and Olivia and wanted to terrorise us some more. No other explanation for it. That's what I can't get over Darcy. It's just the pure and utter ugliness of it all. Why? Why do this to Dave and I? Why did he do this to Allen and Olivia?"

Because he could. Simple as that. Another sociopath had been among us all along.

"If I went back to him, to Allen, would you think poorly of me, Darcy? Would you think I'd lost my mind?" Olivia asked in a voice that begged for reassurance.

"Why on earth would you think that? Of course I wouldn't judge you. Do what's right for you, what makes you happy. Just always know your own self-worth. My God, I must remind myself of that every day. My self-worth has been in the gutter more times than I care to mention. Don't settle for anything less, Olivia. Promise me."

Maddie slugged the dregs of her drink and I skittered to the kitchen to grab another bottle. I was surprised to feel a little hope swelling in my chest. Now that many of the ugly truths had been laid out bare in my living room, I felt cleansed. The picture had become a little clearer.

"So, ladies," I handed out the drinks, "what comes next?"

***

Two hours later, Harry paused over his cereal bowl, spoon midway to his mouth. "Richard did that? Are you serious?"

"Sick, isn't it?"

"I can't believe Olivia went through that. I'm proud of you Darcy. I mean it. You've dragged all these half-truths out into the open and got everyone talking. I know I've been on edge recently but it's only because I love you and sometimes…well, you can be like a dog with a bone and that makes me nervous. But always know I'm proud of you."

Tears gathered at my eyes, but I was certain these were happy tears. It made for a nice change.

"Now that's out of the way, does it mean my living room will be free of sobbing women? There's only so much a man can take."

He ruffled my hair and sloped past me, leaving me to wash the discarded bowl.

Exhausted, I made my way upstairs and crawled into bed. Opening my book, I read the same sentence twenty times then gave up.

I tossed. I turned. I fought with my pillow. Harry snored softly beside me…

I opened my eyes, sat bolt upright and squinted at the clock.

Two-thirty-nine a.m. *What the…*

Pepper's violent barks reached a crescendo.

I yanked out Harry's earbuds. "Get up! Grab your phone."

"What? No, wait, I'll go," he said.

I checked the kids and ran downstairs, almost losing my footing on the stairs.

Shit scared or not I was first down at the front door.

Ready or not.

Light exploded in the hallway and Harry grabbed Pepper by his collar. "Hold him."

I soothed the dog, my hands trembling, while Harry opened the door letting in a burst of freezing-cold air. I held my breath and I moved towards him.

"Nothing here. Maybe he heard a fox." His hand massaged his chest. "My heart's pounding!"

I stood and listened.

Silence.

I could feel the presence, the threat in the air, just out of reach.

I looked to my right.

Something glinted in the moonlight.

The head of a hammer.

Its edges sticky with pumpkin flesh.

What remained of the fruit lay spewed all over our front step, beaten to a pulpy mess.

CHAPTER TWENTY-SEVEN

Tuesday, 29 October

S OME SAY THEY KNOW when something catastrophic is about to happen.

I didn't.

Not that morning.

And for the life of me, I cannot imagine why.

"Thanks, Bob. I can barely keep my eyes open. If Laura can email me the amendments, I'll go through them."

In the background, Harry was on his phone.

"Listen," Bob said, "for some reason, this sick bastard thinks you're involved in this. It's dangerous now. Too much at stake. Those babies need you in one piece. Keep your head down and stay safe."

I was touched by his words. Felt myself welling up.

Harry waggled his phone. "That was Reece—he's coming over later. This is way past scary, Darcy. Why you? Why is this lunatic singling you out? I don't get it. None of this make any sense because, and don't take this the wrong way, I doubt you are any match for this psycho. You don't know anything. So why you? For fun? And if it is for fun that scares the shit out of me."

His handsome face was drawn and tired. Bone weary. His eyes troubled. That scared me. That made me feel sick to my stomach because in one way or another I had caused this.

Big intentions.

Big mouth.

Big fool.

"Right, I'm going to get the kids to school and then come straight back home. I'm picking the kids up from school today, not taking any chances. I hope you're heading for bed. You look like hell."

I winced. Every fibre of my being ached. But I was restless. I was anxious and unable to sit still. If I kept moving forward then everything would be fine, wouldn't it? "I couldn't sleep if you shot me with a tranquiliser. I'm meeting Jackie for coffee, then Maddie and I are going to Jonathan's to water the plants, clear out his fridge and get some things for the hospital. I'll be in company all day. Harry, I don't want to take any risks either. I'm tired of this, and for what it's worth I'm sorry if I caused all of this. Whatever the hell it is that's going on around here."

I waited for a verbal spar, but none came. Harry enveloped me in a hug. "You didn't cause any of this. Listen to me, none of this is your fault, none of it. When you get home, you're not stepping one foot over the door until Reece has this resolved and nailed this bastard. I'm serious Darcy. I'm done with this. Be quick and be safe."

I should have listened.

***

"What do you know about Richard Bradshaw?"

I was in Roast with Jackie, nursing a coffee having filled her in on the latest text I'd received and our visitor in the dead of night.

"And I don't mean his death. I mean him—his life."

"Not much. Only what I've heard in the village. I hate to speak ill of him after…well, you know."

"But the truth is still the truth."

"The truth is I avoided him at all costs. He was the catalyst to several divorces over the years. Who needs that cancer in your life?"

"I heard that he and Elle had quite the altercation at the club a few weeks ago."

Jackie clucked. "Oh, that was something."

My pulse picked up. "Were you there?"

"Lucy and I were at Palermo's then went into the bar. Richard was holding court at a table with Sarah and Jessica and several other people. Next thing I knew, Elle stormed in, screaming at him for sending her something in the post, something about the past. I couldn't believe what I was seeing, she'd lost her mind."

Same story.

Different mouth.

What happened, Elle?

"It didn't make sense. Something about a certificate. She didn't say what, but my guess is a death or birth certificate, something like that. She told him it was a cruel joke to play on her." She snapped her fingers. "I can't believe I forgot that."

"So, Elle received some sort of certificate through the post, and it sent her into a rage. And she blamed Richard. Why?"

"Whatever it was, it brought back a painful memory for her. Something she hadn't dealt with. And you know what they say?"

"What?"

"That the past always comes back to haunt you."

Fear snaked up my spine. Was she right?

The answers were grazing my fingertips; I just couldn't grasp them.

"I found the loveliest photo," Jackie said as I stood. "You, Maddie, Jonathan, me, and Carla and her gorgeous wee baby at the charity fun run in March."

I remembered.

It'd been for Breast Cancer Awareness. It had been a good day.

"I've popped it in a little frame and put in on Jonathan's desk. He'll see it when he comes back to work."

Something in my mind tugged so hard that I sat back down.

Elle's white and lemon bedroom. The photograph I'd found on the floor. The only thing out of place. Elle beautiful and carefree, pregnant, maybe even hopeful. Someone standing next to her just out of focus. Charles? Then a third person in the background, kneeling or crouching. What was my brain trying to tell me?

Jackie chattered on about how all the photos had been cluttering up the filing cabinets since Sally had passed away.

"I think I'll go through them all and pick out some of their holiday photos."

"Wait," I said. "What did you say about photographs?"

Jackie smiled. "Sally drove Jonathan crazy. She'd never just keep their photographs on their phones or in the cloud. She had folders and albums everywhere. After she passed, Jonathan brought a load over to the church. The idea was that sorting through them would give him something to do while he was grieving but, typical Jonathan, he never got around to it."

"Where are they? Can I look through them?"

Surprise then confusion skittered across Jackie's face. "Sure. Now?"

I nodded.

Now.

***

We crossed Redwood Grove to the tune of the primary school bell ringing in the distance. I waited for the inevitable eruption of yells and giggles from the kids escaping their desks. I smiled, hoping Georgie and Henry were having a good day.

Built in the early nineteenth century, a gift to the community of Cedarwood from the wealthy Maxwell family, the church stood proud against the heavy grey sky. James Maxwell was said to have been strict, stern, and ill-tempered, a true follower of the teachings of John Knox. The sandstone building was a stunning centrepiece to the village, and had hosted many a wedding, funeral and christening over the years.

There was history in this place. A privately funded archaeology group linked to the university were even investigating evidence of a burial site in the grounds, including a former church gifted by David I to the Knights Templars.

Harriet Farmer strode up the flagstone path, waving a blue folder.

"I was in having a nosy in advance of the McFarlane wedding. Jackie, I need to speak with your partner Kay immediately." She tossed her chocolate curls and placed a hand on her hip. "Kay's such a scatterbrain."

She dropped the comment at Jackie's feet as if Kay's shortcomings were somehow Jackie's fault.

Bella Rosa supplied the bouquets and floral arrangements for every wealthy Cedarwood bride for miles around. It kept Jackie in regular communication with Harriet, a successful wedding planner who, by all accounts, ran each special day like a drill sergeant. I liked Harriet, but in small doses. She could be a riot after a few cocktails, and her sarcasm was delicious.

"Have you met Ben McFarlane's wife to be?" Harriet said. "Kim Kardashian lookalike that goes by the name of Sea or Lake or some such nonsense. Flip flops and not a bra in sight. He must have picked her up in a commune or—"

"Do you mean River?" Jackie said.

Harriet snapped her fingers. "That's the one. Ben's mother's pitching a fit; River is demanding a vegan wedding breakfast. Can you imagine?" She rolled her eyes. "Anyhow, enough of this chit-chat. I need to investigate the missing fuchsia mystery! I can thank Kay for this nightmare. Bye, ladies."

I grinned and turned to Jackie. "You dodged a bullet there. Bet you're glad it's your morning off."

"You've no idea. She's a nightmare—each day brings fresh hell."

We entered Jonathan's office and a wave of sadness washed over me. I'd never stepped foot in the room, yet somehow it still felt cavernous and cold without him. Jackie dropped old leather books and photo albums on Jonathan's desk.

"I don't know what you're looking for. This is a complete mishmash. Jonathan's parents, God rest them, are even in here. Sally, too. Some of Elle and the usual suspects from back in the day. And even his old crowd from university."

Now we were getting somewhere.

After ten minutes I felt a headache looming.

I'd looked at hundreds of pictures, mostly faces I'd never met and never would.

And then I hit the jackpot.

Familiarity at last.

In one picture, Jonathan's arm was casually draped around Elle. She was smiling directly at the camera. Charles was in the background like he didn't belong.

In another, Elle was wearing a stunning crystal-encrusted ivory wedding gown. She was breath-taking. Loose blond waves fell sensually over her tanned shoulders. A sultry smile played on her lips for the camera. Charles stood to her left, and even through the lens I could sense his discomfort. Richard looked wickedly handsome in his morning suit, gazing at Elle as if he wanted to pounce on her.

Sarah had been bang on the money.

And in a third, Elle stood against a bay window, holding what looked like a glass of brandy. Off to the right was what had to be a ten-foot Christmas tree adorned with crystal and white baubles and hundreds of tiny white lights. She wore a full-length ruby-red evening dress. The shot could have been ripped from the pages of an interior-design photo shoot.

Except for the child.

He looked so out of place, sitting on the floor, a bandage encasing his hand and wrist. He stared sullenly into the distance.

Cole? This was Cole Bradshaw?

His brown hair shone, and his dark eyes brooded, but this was not a happy child. Sympathy welled up inside me. No cuddle or chocolate bar would assuage the discontent that seeped from that child's eyes.

I couldn't take my eyes off the photo but couldn't work out what was bothering me.

When Jackie was rummaging through another drawer, I slipped
the photograph into my packet
  If only I could thread it all together.
  The truth was near.
  As ugly as it was.

CHAPTER TWENTY-EIGHT

M Y PHONE RANG AS I left the church. Gia.

"Guess who I'm spying on right now?"

"Trump?"

"Callum and I are having a rare weekday lunch together over at The Farmhouse and guess who just strolled in?" She didn't wait for a response. "Sonny and Cher, of course I mean Cole and his shadow. Anyway, we've not ordered yet so get over here if you're free and we can quiz them."

"About what?"

"I don't know. Just come over."

"Why? Is Callum not entertaining you?"

"No, he wants to entertain me later."

I rubbed at my aching temple. This conversation was making my headache worse.

"I need an afternoon nap so hurry up before he starts getting handsy."

"Gia, I'm not coming over to play third wheel on your creepy date."

"Just move your arse."

***

I swung into the car park next to a cosy little whitewash building that had been renovated from a working farmhouse. The restaurant housed no more than thirty patrons at a time and was always packed. The atmosphere was warm and familiar, the food fantastic, and the view a poetic backdrop of rolling hills laden with mist.

In the nearby field, several horses flicked chestnut manes, warm breath billowing from their nostrils.

I yearned to join them. I wanted to lie down on the frozen grass and blow puffs of air from my lungs and stare at the sky and think of nothing. I did not want to spend any time with Jessica, so what was I doing here?

Fool.

Tripping over the doorstep, many heads swivelled in my direction and my cheeks burned. *Why am I so damn clumsy?*

Gia waved me over. Callum stood and pecked my cheek while Gia twitched her head towards a tiny table where Jessica had draped herself over Cole. He was hunched over a menu and his body language told me he might be tiring of his unshakable shadow.

"Hey, Cole. How are you?" Gia said turning in her chair. "Any word from the police?"

I cringed at her lack of subtlety, and Cole blew out a long, laboured sigh. His five o'clock shadow was turning into something more substantial...and if anything, it made him even more attractive.

"Nothing," he said, and looked over at me. "Can I have a quick word?"

I went over to their table. Jessica snatched her phone up and Cole shot her a glare.

"I have a meeting with a Katie McAndrew about my mum's will this afternoon. I need to start getting my affairs in order. Should I be meeting with Bob Anderson too? Richard mentioned his name."

I nodded. "He's the best, but he's a litigator. Is something wrong?"

He laughed but it was humourless. "Just about everything. I've decided to put Everbrook on the market. I just can't stay there anymore."

"What the hell are you talking about?" Jessica gasped. "I thought we'd decided—"

"*We* haven't decided anything. I want to sell it, put it behind me."

I nodded. "I can understand that."

Jessica shot me a spiteful look. "Oh, shut up, Darcy. You're such a meddling cow."

"I'm only saying—"

"Well, don't."

I turned back to Cole. "Bob wouldn't deal with the sale himself—as I said he's a litigator—but Katie will sort you out. That's her wheelhouse."

"Thanks. The quicker I get the wheels in motion the better. I need to get the estate settled. I need closure."

"Enjoy your lunch, guys. I'm sorting through a few things at Jonathan's and need to hustle. We're planning to visit the hospital tomorrow." An idea popped into my head. "Do you want to come with us, Cole?"

He smiled and nodded. "I'd love to. How's he doing? Any change?"

"A little. His neurologist is cautiously optimistic."

"Don't you want to go, Jessica?" Gia said. "I bet you have a naughty-nurse outfit stashed away somewhere."

While my lunch date had been a bust, I'd learned something: Cole was selling the house and was tiring of Jessica Evans.

I climbed in my car and turned up the volume on *Time of the Season* by The Zombies—quintessential sixties, which just happened to be my favourite decade of music and fashion. My spirits began to climb.

I was just getting into the chorus when I glanced up at my rear-view mirror. A large black SUV was right behind me. Had it been on my tail since leaving The Farmhouse?

Get a grip, Darcy.

My phone rang. I answered, and a male voice I didn't recognise spoke. It was pleasant and soft.

"I'm sorry to bother you, but I got your number from my mum, Moira Davidson. My name's Tom."

The penny dropped. "Your mum explained everything yesterday. Nice to talk with you."

Even over the Bluetooth I could sense him cringing. "Mum's a talker. I'm surprised she didn't whip out my baby photos. I bet you got my whole life story. Sorry about that."

We both laughed.

"I couldn't believe it when I heard what's been happening here," he said. "I mean Cedarwood's a swanky place with zero crime to speak of. That's why I helped Mum and Dad retire here. And I had a few friends from this neck of the woods when I was a kid; it's always where I wanted to live, you know what I mean?"

"I know exactly what you mean. My own story is not so different. So, you know Cole, right? From way back?"

I slapped my forehead; I'd forgotten to mention any of this to Cole.

"I haven't seen him since university but thought it only right to pay my respects. And my mum says you've been kinda close with him since he got home."

"I can't even tell you what a strain he's been under—it's been a horror story."

I heard an intake of breath.

"Maybe I can take him out for a beer and a catch-up, try to take his mind off things for a few hours. He never did deal with things well."

My ears pricked up. "What do you mean?"

Tom hesitated, "Er, just that he was a bit of a loner, you know?"

This didn't sound at all like the Cole Bradshaw I knew—the centre of everyone's universe. No, it didn't sound like him at all.

"Well, I bet he'll be chuffed to see you. I'll text him and give him your number. Is that alright?"

"Of course. Thanks. I can't wait to see him. Mum tells me he's been breaking hearts all over town."

I laughed. "I don't think he'll be short of dates on a Saturday night, let's put it like that. In fact, one of the local hotties has already tried to snap him up."

"Good for him. It's so weird, though; he never pulled once during our whole time at St Andrews. I always felt sorry for the guy. He was so self-conscious about his hand. No confidence whatsoever. No social skills either. I can't believe how different he sounds. I bet he'll feel sorry for me now—time's not been kind to my hairline."

I struggled to imagine a time when Cole hadn't been a player. "God, he has changed then. Listen, I've got a great picture of us that was taken the first day I met him. I'll send it to you so you can see what you're up against."

Tom's soft laugh tinkled through the speakers, and we hung up. I checked the rear-view mirror again, relieved to see that the black SUV was gone.

I relaxed my grip on the steering wheel. *You fool, Darcy.*

Feeling a niggle of hunger spin to a stomach grumble, I knew I was famished. Time to head to Roast for some fuel before heading to Jonathan's. If I didn't eat, I would be of no use to Maddie later.

The lunchtime crowd had long since gone, so snagging a table was no issue. Mel brought me a cheese, tomato, and jalapeno panini with a large skinny latte

"How bloody cold is it today?" she said. "I can't wait to get away on holiday. Two weeks today I'll be sitting in the sun, supping cocktails and warming my feet in the sand."

The word hit me like a ton of bricks. *Sand.* Jonathan had been trying to tell me something. I willed the solution to come to me but got nothing.

I called Harry—he sounded relived I was alive. We decided I'd call when I was done at Jonathan's, and he'd order pizza. Then I pinged the group photo over to Tom like I'd promised.

Deep in thought, my heart thumped when a tug at my coat sleeve roused me from my ponderings.

"Darcy? Sorry, I didn't mean to frighten you. We're all a bit jumpy these days I guess, huh? I just wanted to say hi and ask…eh, well, how's Cole?"

I stared at Gabby as I scrambled to find my manners. "Gabby! I'm so sorry, I was a million miles away there. I haven't seen you since… well, since I bumped into you and Cole that night. How's things?"

She held my gaze until I folded first. Lifting my empty coffee cup to give me something to do I waited for a few beats until I couldn't stand the silence, and said, "Is everything alright?" I thought back to her expression that night. The one that had bothered me so much.

"Fine. Just, well, have you seen much of Cole recently?"

Ah, so that's why she had stopped by my table. To get the lowdown on Cole Bradshaw. I couldn't blame her.

"Yeah, I've bumped into him here and there. In fact, I saw him a couple of hours ago."

"Is he still hanging out with Jessica?" Her expression was unreadable. It surprised me because I was usually good at reading faces.

Was she upset? Annoyed? Jealous? Relieved? I honestly had no idea.

The words that fell from her mouth next stopped my rumination cold.

"I wanted to talk to her. To warn her but I don't know her well enough, so she'll take it the wrong way. Guaranteed."

The little hairs in the back of my neck stirred and began standing to attention. Something in my gut stirred too. Intuition? Dread? I didn't know which.

"Look, one thing I want to clear up first. You don't know me. I don't know you. But I still want to tell you I wasn't *with* Allen that night in Sarah's house. My ex plays golf with him, I've known Allen for a couple of years, but not in *that* way. Sarah seemed desperate for him to show up with a date, so he just asked me to tag along. I knew the split second his ex-wife walked in that I was a patsy. Honestly? I was mad as hell. But I didn't want to embarrass Allen, so I said nothing. I should have told the lot of them exactly where to go. I hate feeling used. And I felt grubby as hell standing in that room."

Didn't we all but I wasn't surprised by Sarah's antics. I felt bad for Gabby, and I felt a little shame on my behalf for assuming that she had been hooking up with Allen. It wasn't fair she had been mixed up in whatever devious chess game Sarah was playing with Olivia. But Gabby seemed eager to talk so I offered a few heartfelt platitudes and let her settle into her story.

"The only good thing that happened that night was meeting Cole."

And there it was.

"Until it wasn't."

Wait. What?

Her expression from that night I bumped into her and Cole floated back to me again. What did I see? Bliss? Lust? Fear? Or a combination of all three.

"What happened Gabby?"

A sliver of fear, dread, anxiety, I wasn't sure which, snaked up my spine. I felt freezing cold.

"Cole and I swapped numbers at Sarah's house. Honestly? I thought he was as hot as hell. He called me twenty minutes after I left Sarah's house and invited me over to his house for drinks. Look, it's been a while since I've dated so I jumped at the chance. I mean, you've seen him! Who wouldn't, right?"

"Gabby, I'd have been there in a heartbeat. If I wasn't married."

Her smile reached her eyes but just as quickly they dimmed. She leaned forward. My heart rate accelerated. "Everything was great. I mean it was the best night I've had in years and honestly, I didn't want to leave. I could have stayed curled up with him forever. He was so unlike any guy I've ever met. So charming, so clever, and those eyes! But…" She dropped her heads into her hands and when she looked back up at me her smile was gone. "We were messing around. Playing. Joking. I said we better have another go because I wasn't convinced that he was that best that I'd ever had. I was being playful. Silly. Stupid. I thought he'd reach for me and we would continue where we left off. It was like I had flipped a switch. Darcy, I've never seen anything like it."

"Oh God, Gabby, what happened? What did he do to you? I knew something was up with you that night. I saw it written all over your face."

"He screamed in my face that I was a whore! Threw my clothes at me. Ordered me to get the fuck up and out of his bed. He said I was nothing more than a time filler for what was a boring night, and that he could guarantee that he was the best I'd ever had. I was terrified.

Then I tried to rationalise it thinking I'd hurt his feelings, so I tried to convince him that I was joking; he was amazing and that I was sorry. He blew up! I mean he went insane. Smashed a glass against the wall and screamed at me to get the hell out of his bed. Almost lunged at me. I was shit scared. I threw my clothes on and crept down the hall to the front door. Then he came at me. But, not like *that*...it was like some other wire had tripped. He grabbed me and kissed me. It was soft, tender, as if he'd been craving me his whole life. As if nothing had ever happened."

I swallowed painfully. My mouth was so dry my tongue couldn't get traction.

The narcissist.

Gabby had just described the narcissist. More than that, she had just described a dangerous one.

Malignant.

"I didn't know what the fuck was happening. I was in shock, but the kiss was so tender I thought I'd imagined it all, overreacted, you know? He'd just lost him mum in such a dreadful way, and I was judging him too harshly. So, I apologised to *him. I* reached for *him and* let him touch *me.* How sick is that? He had the upper hand, and, in that moment, I would've believed anything that came out of his mouth. Then, of course, we ran into you and your friend and something inside me snapped. Like the spell had been broken. I got home and bolted my door. Been keeping a low profile since. I can't explain it, he scared the hell out of me."

A tinkle of bells chiming made her reach inside her bag and snatch up her phone. "Sorry, it's my friend. I'm meeting her at The Fir Tree for drinks so I'd better hustle. If you are good friends with Cole, then I'm sorry if I've upset you...not my intention. I just wanted to you to know. Keep your guard up, that's all."

"Gabby, I appreciate you sharing this more than you know. I'm glad you got home safe that night. Trust me, I think your gut intuition is bang on the money. Take care."

She disappeared out the door leaving me in a state of confusion bundled with growing anxiety. In that moment I wanted nothing more than to get home to Harry and my kids.

I yelled a goodbye behind me as I left Roast and pulled my coat around me. The wind was beginning to howl, cold rain drizzled, and sodden leaves blew around my legs. Streetlights cast an eerie glow onto the rain-spattered street.

I was about to put on my gloves when my phone rang.

CHAPTER TWENTY-NINE

"**D**ARCY?"

I couldn't make out the voice in the wind.

"I can hardly hear you. It's Tom Davidson."

"Sorry, the weather's awful."

"Listen, I'm really sorry to bother you but I'm a bit confused."

My gut clenched.

He continued talking but I caught just a few words—*photo*, *text*, *Cole*.

"Sorry, Tom. Can you repeat that?"

"I said I'm not sure what photo you texted me, but that guy isn't Cole Bradshaw."

"What?"

"The tall guy with the dark hair? That's not Cole Bradshaw. I mean he looks like him but no way, man. I was holed up with the guy for five years at uni. That's not him."

The words knocked the wind clean out of me. My pulse quickened. *No.*

"Thanks," I whispered. "My mistake."

I pulled up the picture I'd sent to Tom and stared.

Me, Maddie, Jonathan...

And a smiling stranger.

I took out the picture of the little boy nursing his disfigured hand.

The hand that had ended up so scarred in the accident on the broken slide.

The football game in the park with Jonathan.

The story Jonathan had shared at lunch.

On the day a bat had been smashed against his skull.

The photograph had been trying to tell me the truth.

This child was the third person in the photograph from Elle's bedroom.

The one she'd clasped just before her face was smashed, her neck was snapped, and she was thrown down the stairs.

No one had been sitting or crouching or kneeling in the background—it had been little Cole Bradshaw staring at the ground all along.

So, if the real Cole had been in the photograph, then who was the child that Elle was so obviously pregnant with? She'd had no other children.

Only she had.

And I'd considered him to be a new friend.

I fought back a wave of nausea. The Cole I knew, the one who made every girl's heart beat a little faster, every guy a little more aware, the one whose strong, perfectly, tanned hands had gripped mine, had no hint of scarring. No puckering of the skin. No reminders of a childhood accident.

Not *sand. Hand.* That's what Jonathan had been trying to tell me.

I recalled his frown that day in the driveway. That's when he'd realised something was wrong.

Terribly wrong.

And so had Cole.

It had been about revenge and retribution all along.

Elle, Jonathan, and Richard. I should have looked closer at the victimology.

Elle had been his first kill—his only intended target. Then Jonathan had revealed a little of his past. That had put him in harm's way. And Richard? I thought I knew what ugly part of the puzzle he was.

The jigsaw was finally complete. The stray pieces had clicked into place. The picture at long last revealed was a devastating one.

I fumbled with my phone, dropped it, cursed, picked it up and found Reece's number.

It connected—straight to voicemail.

"It's Cole Bradshaw. He's the killer. Only he isn't really Cole. Please call me back. I don't know where he is, and I'm scared."

I counted to ten, then called the station.

"Burns," a gruff voice said.

I rattled off my plea to speak to Reece.

"DI McDonald's not here, Mrs Sinclair. Can you calm down and tell me what's is going on?"

"Listen! It's Cole Bradshaw. He's an impostor...I, I have proof. He killed Elle and Richard. Find Reece and tell him to call me. I'm going to Jonathan Mitchell's house. My friend's already there and she's alone. I need to make sure she's safe."

I hung up leaving Jim sputtering disbelief and ran to my car, scanning the street around me.

Nothing.

Thankful for once for my true crime obsession, I skirted the perimeter of my car, checked the back seat was empty, then jumped inside and locked all the doors. I breathed deep, in and out until the rushing in my ears had subsided.

New plan: Call Harry, get Maddie and connect with Reece. Safe and sound.

Tick tock.

"Are you on your way home yet?" Harry whined. "I'm starving."

"Harry, listen. It's Cole Bradshaw. Don't speak, just listen to me!"

"Cole? What are you talking about?"

"Harry, I don't have time to explain all of this. Trust me. Cole Bradshaw is the killer. He killed all of them. But he isn't really Cole! I'm not making any sense, I know this. I'm right Harry. I know I'm right."The words tumbling from my mouth made my head spin. "I'm stopping at Jonathan's to get Maddie."

"What the...Have you lost your damn mind? Come home right now! I'm calling Reece."

"I'm almost at Jonathan's."

"You have two kids here. Home. Now!"

"Ten minutes tops. Lock the door and stay with the kids. Call Reece. Call the police. Call anybody who'll listen. I love you."

I disconnected. Tried to slow my breathing. The pounding in my ears was back.

Are you sure?

Do you know what you're doing?

What if you're wrong?

***

I turned in a circle, surveying the street around me.

Spruce Drive was cold, dark, silent.

Good or bad, I didn't know.

The house was lit up like a dinner party was in full swing. Thank God – Maddie was still here. I listened at the door.

Silence.

I pushed open the door and called her name.

Still nothing.

I called out again.

"Darcy? Is that you? Why are you yelling? What's wrong?" She popped up from behind the upstairs balustrade. She tucked her raven hair behind her ears and frowned. "Are you alright?"

"We have to get out. Now."

"What's…"

"Cole! It's Cole. He killed them. Come on!"

She laughed, incredulous. "That can't be."

"I'll explain on the way." A stench hit my nostrils and caught at the back of my throat. I gagged. "What's that smell?"

"Sorry, I forgot to throw it out," Maddie said. "It's been sitting there for over an hour—just rotten food and curdled milk from the fridge."

"I'll toss it in the garden. Just hurry up. Please Maddie."

I dropped the bag by the recycling bin, then ran back to the house.

I felt the presence.

Sensed the rage.

A searing pain exploded inside my skull.

My hair was grabbed, my neck yanked back, my head slammed against the door...

Then the darkness came.

CHAPTER THIRTY

EVERY NERVE SCREAMED.

Where was I? Why was I on the floor?

"I said get up."

The boot connected with my rib cage. Pain, fear, and adrenaline surged through me, and vomit spewed from my mouth.

In my hair.

On the floor.

Move!

I began to crawl forward. Moaning sounded from somewhere near me. It took me a few seconds to realise the sound was coming my own throat.

Move!

I pushed up on my hands but collapsed straight back onto the floor.

"Get up now or I'll kill you where you lie, you little bitch."

The voice was a distorted voice but familiar.

It belonged to the beautiful man I'd known as Cole Bradshaw.

Harry. Georgie. Henry. Get up!

I gulped in air, pushing up on my hands and dragged one knee forward, then the other until I was kneeling. Bile dropped from my hair. I squinted through my swollen lids.

The room had been ripped apart.

"Welcome back, you stupid bitch. I said up!"

One strong hand wound its way through my matted hair. Another punched the side of my face. My head whipped around, and white-hot pain cut through my neck and lanced down my back.

"Please, stop."

He mimicked me in a sing-song voice.

Shame crawled over me first.

Guilt slithered over me next.

I'd put myself right in the middle of this nightmare. All my own fault.

A small fire began to burn deep within my belly, then spread to my chest. Shattered pieces of my past whirled through my brain.

A distorted picture.

Fractured.

My mum.

Screaming. Crying. Bleeding.

No dignity.

No hope.

The noise of pain and destruction.

A lifetime of trying to make everything alright.

Guilt.

Despair.

Enough violence.

Not going down with a fight, Darcy. Got to find a way out.

My gut knew that this moment, this very moment, would be the fight of my life.

Get ready, Darcy.

He grabbed my face with both hands. "Look at me!" Spittle sprayed over my skin. "You're going to hell tonight, and then I'll be gone. The dark is my friend, Darcy. Always has been."

I raised my head and looked at him. Dead in the centre of those beautiful eyes. The ones that had fooled everyone. "You're not Cole. You never were."

He lifted his hands, and I shrank back. Instead of striking me he clapped.

"Well done!" He wagged his finger. "See, I knew you were trouble. A nosy little bitch. But now you'll have a front-row seat for all the pleasures I inflict on those who get in my way. I tried to warn you. Why didn't you listen? This is all your own fault."

He paced like a caged animal. Reminding me of my father. Coiled and ready to strike. I knew the signs. I'd seen them before. So I sucked in a breath and steeled myself.

"All your own fault. All your own fault." He muttered over and over. I'd heard those words so many times before.

My father had uttered them every day. It was always *our* fault. They washed over me, making my temper boil.

This is good. Ignore the pain. Get ready.

"Who are you?"

CHAPTER THIRTY-ONE

M Y QUESTION BROKE THE spell and he stopped dead.
"I'm Cole Bradshaw," he roared and jabbed his torso. "I
should always have been Cole Bradshaw. I came home and took what
was mine. It should all have been mine!"

"You're Elle's other son," I said. "But she didn't want you."

He lunged towards me and landed a fist against my cheek. A sickening crack rang out a split second before the ache started.

I cradled my face. The pain was indescribable. The throb came in
pounding waves, like an excruciating heartbeat.

Pound. Pound. Pound.

No way out. No way home.

"No, that spoiled bitch didn't want me. She threw me away and
kept that weak, pathetic little bastard she called a son. Oh, you should
have seen him, a fucking sad sack of shit. He made me sick."

I tried to draw in air, but it was too painful.

So breathless.

Panic spiralling out of control.

I wrapped my arms around my body in a pathetic attempt to protect
myself from whatever came next.

"So shut your mouth! *I'm* Cole. It should have been *me*." Saliva flew
from his mouth, and he clawed at his hair. Any lasting trace of beauty
on his distorted face faded, leaving nothing but a blank canvas.

He's gone.

"Do you know what became of my pathetic brother? The great
Wall Street success? He died in a puddle of his own piss. And I…" his

hand pounded the wall, "I was there. I injected him with the double shot of heroin. Yes, that's right. The real Cole Bradshaw was a junkie."

My tongue was swelling; I wouldn't be able to talk for much longer.

"I could never have done that to my child. My *own* child? I don't understand how she could have done that... Why didn't she keep you?" I asked, trying to break through the shell and connect with his humanity.

He turned and stared at me.

And I knew.

There was nothing left.

Futile.

"Mummy was a dirty whore who got herself knocked up by her husband's brother. That's right," his eyes glittered with madness, "Daddy dearest was good old Richard. That monster was my dad. Guess I didn't stand much of a chance, did I? It was already in my DNA."

Of course.

It was as clear as the morning dawn.

The brown-black eyes, the handsome face, the alpha-male stance, the narcissistic charmer who fooled everyone around him.

The malignant sociopath.

It had been there in front of me, and I'd missed it.

But Eric Evans had seen it: *"You look just like your uncle,"* he'd said that night at Sarah's soirée.

So that's why Elle had disappeared for several months all those years ago. To give birth to this monster.

"He didn't want me, and she couldn't be bothered to raise another kid, so she threw me away. I was adopted when I was a week old."

Keep him talking. He loves to talk about himself. It was the only weapon left in my armour.

"Did you have a bad childhood? Is that why you wanted to make them pay?" Almost afraid to hear the answer, I barely dared to breathe.

"Bad? No, it wasn't bad. Fuck, that would have been interesting at least. Two stupid fools following me around all day. Tending to my every need. In our ordinary shitty little house, on our ordinary crappy street…and if we worked hard, we could go to dead-end seaside towns in our ordinary, shitty little car. When I finally escaped that prison and landed at university, they'd send me food packages like I was incompetent. Am I incompetent, Darcy?" His fingers touched my chin and tilted it upwards to meet his stare.

Shame washed over me as I shook my head. "No, Cole." I had to play his game.

"I'm fucking extraordinary!"The pacing resumed. "You've seen it, haven't you? The way a whole room shifts when I walk in."

The pain in my skull was unbearable so I nodded slowly.

The dazzling smile slipped back into place as he remembered, recalling every moment in his own spotlight. "The parting of their lips, the slight movement of their hair, the shift of their posture, so eager to please me, to be picked by me. Wanting to be my friend, needing my approval. I have that power over everyone, Darcy, and it's just so damned good. I wish for just one second you could feel that sort of control. It consumes you, eats you alive, because you can do anything. Anything at all."

Back and forth.

Around and around.

He stared at me. "I just can't help myself. It's too easy. Women, men, money, power. It's all there in the palm of my hand—every day! And I just take it. The rush, that feeling when you have complete control, it's…it's indescribable."

The bastard in front of me had seemingly had everything handed to him on a plate for his entire existence and still he killed. He didn't have a bad childhood. He didn't have pain and suffering and wicked memories. *He didn't have to make everything right.*

And yet here we were.

Just like before.

Just like always.

The innocent get destroyed and beaten to a pulp.

Something deep inside me snapped.

I wanted to hurl myself at him and rip his head clean off his body.

This is good.

Let the anger gather strength.

Let him talk.

On and on and on.

"And Jessica?" I asked.

He dissolved into hysterical laughter. "Nasty little creature, isn't she? The worst kind—spoiled and empty but with no real skill, no talent. Just stupid, just there to be manipulated. I had her in my bed before she took a sip of her first drink. But you..." He crept towards me, wagging his finger. "You were different. I could feel it, sense it. You didn't trust me, did you? I liked that. The way you looked at me. Not desire, not awe, just interest. Damn, I enjoyed that. Found it arousing Darcy, I must admit."

My spine straightened. Getting ready for the fight.

"I let my guard down a little with Gabby though. Stupid cow got right on my nerves that night, and I couldn't have that. Not quite as dumb as Jessica because she knew she was in danger. She sensed it. I had to give her just a little taste. I saw you watching her that night we met you outside my house. The way you stared right through her, as if you knew. That intrigued me."

He crouched down in front of me. Face inches from mine. Then he placed his lips on my swollen and bloodied ones. I wanted to crawl out of my skin.

He had taken enough from me. He'd brutalised me. If this was next, then I'd fucking claw and fight with every sliver left in my body... which wasn't much.

"So, tell me your story. Why did you take such an interest in me? I'd love to know."

"Not my best work, Cole. Or whatever your name is." I spat blood from my mouth. The metallic taste was adding to my nausea. *So thirsty.* How I wanted a cold drink. "I was raised by someone a lot like you.

Not quite as demonic perhaps, he mostly tormented his own family. I've seen up close and personal the kind of damage monsters like you cause. But you do hide it well. I'll give you that. You almost fooled me…not quite though."

My answer angered him. I could see it in the movement of his facial muscles. The twitch in his jaw as he ground away at his teeth. I eyed his fists waiting for another blow. Instead, he pressed his mouth hard against mine again and resumed pacing.

As painful as it was, I dragged my teeth over my swollen bottom lip to scrub the taste of him away.

"That night you came to my house and told me straight to my face that Dave couldn't be the guy? I wanted to kill you right there in my mother's living room—well, after some play of course." He stared at me dead in the eye. "I would have enjoyed that part." Back in my face, he traced his finger over my bottom swollen lip. "People don't often tell me what I don't want to hear. My God, it was just so, I don't know…exciting." He reached for a strand of my hair and gave it a slight tug.

I swallowed the bile clawing up my throat.

His hand stroked my cheek.

Moved back to my lips.

Holding my breath until my lungs screamed, I let my eyes wander to look anywhere but at him.

Scanning the room, I searched for a weapon, anything that might give me a fighting chance.

Nothing.

He continued to stroke my hair.

A single, hot tear slid down my face.

I'd lost the fight. I was sure.

"Why send me those texts? The hammer? I was never a real threat to you. Never."

"Couldn't help myself. I missed the thrill of the chase, and you were begging for attention, weren't you? I followed you so many times, watched your every move for days. I could have had you anytime I wanted to, but I didn't. Don't you want to thank me for sparing you for so long? Don't you feel grateful?"

Staring at the floor I didn't respond. Instead, I spat more blood onto my legs. I didn't want to ruin Jonathan's floor any more than I had too. That thought almost made me laugh.

Silly me.

Always trying to make it right.

Even now.

He screamed in my face, "I said don't you feel grateful?"

I nodded, ashamed of my acquiesce, and let out a desperate sob.

"But in the end, here you are. Right where I want you."

"Why Jonathan?"

"It all got away from me. I hate to admit it, but I made a mistake. Just one. And it's the butterfly effect, isn't it? The calm waters rippled, and that became a wave, and then, well, I had to protect myself. I'd planned it all so carefully. But you, well you just had to go looking, didn't you? That day you told me at Jonathan's that you thought someone had been in the house with Elle, oh Darcy, I could have punished you right there on the spot."

Punish me.

There it was.

That desperate desire to punish.

Just like my father.

"What went wrong? The police said you were in London. How could you have killed Elle? You had an alibi." I asked.

Everything hurt. I wanted to vomit again, and time was running out. He wouldn't talk for much longer.

"I only ever intended to kill *her*. Mummy dearest. I'd know for a few years who'd created me, but when I found out what they were worth, the power they had... Well, that got me angry, and bad things happen when I'm angry. My alibi was easy. When you look like me you can get any stupid woman to do the most amazing things... even lie to the police. Creating that alibi didn't even break a sweat. I had no intention of being here for more than a few days. Even I knew I couldn't pull off being Cole for more than a week. It would have been so sweet, until it all went fucking south."

Damn, I should have guessed. It was all so easy.

"The Bradshaw money should have been mine. It should *all* have been mine, not his, not Cole's. I tracked him down easily enough. With the right people you can find out the most incredible things. He was hanging out in some dump in Chelsea with a pack of rich-kid degenerates. So predictable. Every night shooting heroin into his arm with its deformed little hand. Christ, had our mother done a number on him. Doubt he'd ever had an erection in his life. Pitiful."

I nodded, still looking around me, still trying to break through the pain and muster some strength.

"Gained his trust, learned all the family secrets, emptied his bank accounts and shot him up a double. Simple as that. I swapped my wallet for his and left him dead on a rail track in a crappy part of London. The train took care of the rest. I popped a copy of my original birth certificate in the post to Elle and then headed up here to keep a watchful eye over the village and torment her for a while. It kept me amused. Gave me a chance to get used to the people who'd be in my life every day."

The planning, the waiting, the execution.

More diabolical than I could ever have imagined.

The different versions told to me of the story of the showdown between Elle and Richard over *a letter* or *a certificate* swan into my mind. It hadn't been sent by Richard at all.

"It was supposed to look like an accident, you know. I wanted her zipped up in a body bag, disposed of cleanly. Then I would have had every damn penny, gotten out of town, sold the house from afar and spend what I wanted. But no! The stupid cow made me so angry that I throttled her and snapped her damned neck. It was all her fault. All her fault!"

He kicked out at a large copper-coloured standing vase. It shattered into a thousand pieces.

"And Jonathan! That stupid bastard! He really spoiled my plans. The second, no, the *instant* he took my hands in his kitchen, I could see it in his eyes. A flicker, a recognition that something was different. He knew it. He *knew* I wasn't Cole. Because you see, Darcy, I'd forgotten about Cole's pathetic little hand. Even I couldn't fake that. I mean look at me—I'm perfect. Jonathan called me that afternoon, begged me to tell him the truth—told me that he felt it in his gut. He knew... don't ask me how he knew but he sensed it; some Godly other world shit going on there, I think. Over and over, he kept saying you're not him, tell me who you are—why are you here? Of course, I was only too happy to oblige and pay him a visit. I told him some ridiculous story about acting on Cole's behalf and, you know, he bought it... let me walk straight through the door. I couldn't believe it when you told me the next morning that he was alive. He did put up a hell of a fight. Heard his arm crack in half and still he fought me."

I wanted to lunge at him, hurt him, punch the mouth uttering those disgusting words. The rage fuelled the fire in my belly and my pain eased ever so slightly. And then it hit me.

That was my only chance.

Channel my years of pain and anger and stamping down my emotions.

Let them come tumbling out.

Let them blossom and spiral and be as ugly as he was.

Fight back.

Focus.

"And Richard?"

"Funny thing about Richard—the split second we shook hands, I knew that he, and not Charles, was my father. I'm a different breed, after all. A different species. And I can recognise my own. So poor old dad didn't stand a chance. That night at Richard's? It was brutal, like the Colosseum. His face, oh Darcy, the expression on his face when

I told him who I really was. His son. And I knew he'd forgotten that I'd ever existed. Well, that made me fucking mad. He begged and begged. He pleaded and cried. It was just so...intoxicating."

He looked somewhere past me, into the abyss, eyes misting as he relived every brutal, vicious, cruel, unrelenting blow.

And now I understood.

He'd been good, but not quite good enough. Yes, he'd mimicked empathy, fear, devastation. And almost perfectly. But he didn't understand those emotions. It's why I'd caught those moments of disinterest; the indifference when he was with Jessica, the amusement when she crawled all over him, even the way he'd stared at Pepper that night in Elle's home.

There was simply nothing there.

My gut had tried to tell me, and I'd ignored it.

"And every fool in this pathetic village welcomed me home with open arms. The stranger that walks amongst you. Everybody wanted a piece...everyone wanted to be my guide, my friend, my lover. Take your pick."

He was almost at the end of his story.

I was running out of time.

"She recognised me; you know." He crouched down on the floor and grabbed my hands. I recoiled, then forced my body go limp; I couldn't risk the chance of sending him deeper into his rage.

"Did she?" I whispered, my swollen tongue catching on my teeth.

"In that last second of her life. She knew it was me that had come back for her. She saw it in my eyes, and I saw it in hers. I'll never forget that."

Poor Elle. Giving up her baby over a foolish fling with a narcissist who'd discarded her like every other woman he'd encountered. Putting her own needs first. Only to have him hunt her down and execute her so many years later. That realisation must have been even worse than the violence that followed.

He patted my hands. "You really shouldn't have done this to yourself. I tried to warn you. Why didn't you listen? I'm sorry I fixated on you but, well, you were riling people up, asking questions, and I just couldn't have that. Poor Darcy." His hand went to my hair again, stroking it softly. He ran his finger gently down the side of my aching cheek. Tenderly he touched my swollen lips.

He waited for the inevitable minuscule release of anxiety from my shoulders, and the snarling laugh was back in place.

"See? See how easy it is? You thought I was going to let you go. In the end you're all the same."

He wound his fingers through my hair and snapped my neck back.

His face loomed down on mine.

My past crashed into my present.

No. More. Violence.

Every brutal night I'd lived as a child came flooding back to me.

Flashback after flashback.

Raised fists, grabbing of hair, shedding of blood, stripping of dignity.

I screamed into the air, releasing one emotional spew of anguish.

I couldn't take one more hit.

I wouldn't.

He saw it in my eyes, and I also saw the split second of confusion in his.

Grabbing my opportunity, I exploded into a ball of fury, fear, desperation, madness. I swung my arms towards his face, clawed with my fingers, shredded with my nails, pounded with my balled fists, butted with my forehead.

A sound ripped from his mouth.

Primal.

Something I'd never heard before from a human.

I was going to die.

Right here.

In this room.

I squeezed my fingers into one last fist.

In the corner my eye, I caught a flash.

Movement.

Maddie.

Beautiful Maddie.

Huge green eyes filled with absolute terror.

A trembling finger at her lips begged me to stay silent.

Throwing my entire body weight against him, I punched him in the solar plexus. I fell onto the floor, dragged him with me.

I clawed, I kicked, I gouged.

Everything I'd ever learned at Krav Maga all those years ago seemingly useless now. Against a real predator. Against an inhumane monster...but it was all I had.

With every flail of my arm his rage grew.

"You little bitch."

His strong, beautiful hands encircled my neck, and he squeezed.

The pain was blinding, and panic exploded in my chest.

A guttural scream sounded far in the distance. "Stop it! You're going to kill her."

Cole's neck snapped around.

He released me and pushed himself off the floor.

The hunt for Maddie was on.

I rolled over, gulping in air.

Get up.

Help Maddie.

Now.

I dragged myself to a standing position and a wave of dizziness nearly landed me back on the floor. My legs burned as I stumbled towards the hall.

Maddie was on the third step.

Cole lunged, grabbed her hair and snapped her head back.

"Stop!" she screamed.

I recognised the terror in her voice; I'd heard it in my own.

She was on the floor, on the second step.

He raised his arm and delivered a blow to the side of her head.

I ran into the kitchen, threw drawers and cabinet doors open.

Finally.

I grabbed a large kitchen knife. It fell from my sweat-soaked hands and skittered across to the floor. I picked it up and moved back into the hallway, towards the stairs. Could I really use it? Bile rushed up my throat.

Gagging, I moved towards the chaos.

Cole's arm swung back once more.

The front door splintered.

"Get down! Back it up, Cole. On the floor!"

A roar of voices filled the hallway.

Reece? Who's talking? What's happening?

My legs buckled.

Black boots flew past me. More voices. Reece...the police? My gag reflex kicked in again, this time I was sure it was with relief.

Screaming.

Sounds and smells and chaos.

I felt so cold.

Back on my knees, my eyes searched for Maddie.

Cole dragged Maddie by her hair up the remaining stairs and onto the landing. She snapped her head back and headbutted him.

His hands flew to his face. "Bitch!" he roared and lunged for his prey.

She dropped to the floor, knocking him off balance and propelling him towards the balustrade. His arms flailed; his hands reached for purchase but found none.

Over the edge he plummeted to the ground.

He landed with a sickening thud.

A pool of crimson oozed from his head and leaked from his lips, and the light faded from his beautiful black eyes.

The monster that had walked among us was dead.

CHAPTER THIRTY-TWO

Thursday, 31 October, 10.32 a.m.

I STARED AT MY BRUISED reflection, still trying to come to terms with everything, fix the fractured shards. While my body was healing, my psyche was not—but I'd make damn sure to put it back together, piece by little piece. If I didn't, then the predator who'd pretended to be Cole Bradshaw would take another part of me with him.

I couldn't allow that.

He'd taken enough already.

Flinching as I patted concealer on my face, I traced a finger under my swollen eye, then snatched my hand away. Not because of the pain, but because I could still feel his touch and it made me feel sick.

Who knew how long it would take to erase that memory?

My whole body ached—with pain, with exhaustion.

Going to bed meant staring at the ceiling in the dark, and the dark brought the demons to life. Instead, I was content to lie on the sofa, every light blazing and the TV playing in the background. Noise and chatter—the sounds of life. That's what I needed to clutter my brain with...not silence.

Because silence brought back memories not only of Cole, but of my past. I'd spent so many years trying to bury them in the dark of the night.

"Darcy," Harry called for the fifth time.

I moved downstairs, breathing in with each step, and opened the living room door. Several heads swivelled my way, and the air grew a little tight. Unshed tears pooled behind my swollen eyes.

"You really don't know how good it is to see you all."

Several voices spoke at once and my tension melted.

My memory of that night was neither muddled nor confused. It was damn near perfect. Every detail vivid, every sound amplified. When I closed my eyes, I was haunted by the startled expression on Cole Bradshaw's face as he'd drawn his last breath. The macabre scene, accompanied by the tortured theme tune of Maddie's screams.

I'd spent one night in hospital.

Harry had gripped my hand as I'd staggered over the threshold of our home, to safety once more, and held me like he was afraid he would lose me. We had sat like that for a long time.

I'd made it home.

We'd told the kids I'd slipped on the ice—'*don't worry kids, I just slipped, silly Mummy*'. It was for their own good. They needed a reason for why I didn't look like myself anymore. A reason that would satisfy their innocent minds and not reveal any of the horrors of the real world. Fortunately they had all the time in the world to find that out. But for now, I wanted them to grasp every thread of childhood they could and savour it.

Statements, phone calls, and pills had followed.

Then more.

Pills. So many pills.

Around and around.

But now it was time to shine a little light into the darkness.

"What was his name? His real name?"

Reece looked at the floor then met my gaze. "Rob Preston."

I crossed the room and sat on the sofa next to Isla.

Of course, he'd always be Cole Bradshaw to me.

"I have his birth certificate," Reece said. "Elle was his biological mother—no doubt. The father's name is listed as unknown, but I've ordered comparative DNA samples. There's no doubt in my mind that Richard was his biological father."

"He was." I swallowed and winced. The motion was painful against my swollen trachea. "Rob told me so. You know, Richard never even suspected that Rob wasn't Cole and he sure as hell didn't imagine that Rob was his son. I guess he never thought much about it at all over the last twenty odd years. Rob took his time to kill Richard. I guess the apple didn't fall too far from the tree."

"The sick bastard was honest about that much. There wasn't much left of Richard by the time he'd finished."

"So, Elle had an affair with Richard all those years ago?" Isla asked. "Didn't see that one coming, but I should have. I remember being with them years ago and the chemistry between them was electric. Charles, of course, pretended he hadn't seen anything. But I did. I think we all did. Elle had that effect on men you see, so I guess I didn't ponder too much about it. It was all so long ago. She did disappear for months, but everyone assumed she was just pissed at Charles."

I nodded. "Elle really did love Richard. I do believe that. She'd kept the photograph of when she was pregnant with Co...I mean Rob. It was weathered, cherished, I could feel it. I think Richard destroyed what was left of her. I'm just not sure if there ever was a whole lot to begin with. I never really knew Elle, but I feel I understand her a little better now."

"I've submitted a request order to the relevant local authorities to exhume the body of the real Cole Bradshaw. The original post-mortem determined the body was that of Rob Preston, who, they believed, had collapsed and died of a self-administered heroin dose on a train track in an industrial area of London. The condition of the body made a full ID impossible, but they had evidence of drug use, track marks all over him apparently. And they had his wallet and phone, which we now know Preston planted. Honestly? They didn't look too hard—too many of these cases and underfunding make a hell of a combination."

"And the money?"

"Gone. Whatever chunk Cole had left, and it appears to have been substantial, had been transferred into another account. Seems like

Rob Preston went on a hell of a spending spree after Cole died. But, of course, his goal was to empty the entire Bradshaw estate and move on to greener pastures."

Regain his crown and conquer a brave, new world.

"Jonathan? Where does he fit into all of this?" Isla was perched so far on the edge of the chair I was afraid she'd topple onto Reece's lap.

"Poor Jonathan," I said. "He really put himself in the eye of the storm. He knew something was off the second he saw Rob's hands. Maddie, do you remember? In the kitchen that day at lunch? Jonathan grabbed both his hands to comfort him. Those hands were strong, perfect, no scars. Nothing like the story that he had just recounted of Cole's ghastly injury. Jonathan called him a little later demanding to know what was going on. Rob told me Jonathan knew he wasn't Cole, it wasn't just the lack of scarring, it was something deep inside him...he just felt it. Remember, Jonathan and Sally had spent a lot of time with Cole when he was a toddler. Maybe it was just gut instinct. We won't know for sure until Jonathan starts talking. I just wish to hell he hadn't called Rob that day. Rob had promised him that it wasn't anything underhanded and said he'd pop round and explain."

"I remember Jonathan's face that day. Standing on his doorstep. Like he'd seen a ghost." Maddie gazed somewhere into the past.

"It had bothered me—why Jonathan called me instead of a long-time close friend or even the police. He called me because I'd been there that afternoon and I'm a lawyer. I'm sure of it. I think he wanted to ask me if Rob could get into a lot of trouble for impersonating Cole Bradshaw. He probably didn't want him arrested with a slew of charges. I'm certain Jonathan genuinely believed it was no big deal, it could all be explained. I honestly don't think he felt in any real danger. And so, Jonathan let him walk right inside his home and, well, you know the rest." I thought back to my meeting on Firmont Road with Moira. "If it weren't for Tom, I'd never have pieced it all together. That was Rob's big problem...the longer he stayed in Cedarwood, the longer he was running a high risk of being found out and that's exactly what happened when Tom Davidson turned up. Reece, you must reach out to him and let him know."

Reece nodded. "Already done."

His phone pinged and he glanced down at it. A little smile danced across his lips.

"I've told Dave everything," Maddie said, almost vomiting the words.

"You and Olivia nearly bought yourself a ticket to a cell," Reece said. "I couldn't have lined up better suspects if you'd served them to me on a platter. Good thing I don't simply follow the evidence. Thing is," he turned towards me, "I was halfway there. I'd already found so many red flags out there about the real Cole Bradshaw that I was having a hard time connecting him with the guy I'd interviewed. I had an interesting chat with his last employer, who painted a vastly different picture of the cocky, self-assured player I was getting to know, and it wasn't sitting right with me. That was his one mistake. Rob Preston was just too perfect to ever have pulled off being the real Cole Bradshaw for long. Cole by all accounts was a highly intelligent man, exceptionally skilled but struggled daily with severe depression and social anxiety. He couldn't have been more different from Rob. If we hadn't conducted a post-mortem on Elle, I do believe he might have walked away with the estate and disappeared before anyone realised and had a chance to nail the bastard. Won't be the first time it's happened, and I have no doubt it won't be the last."

"What about his parents?" Dave asked quietly. "His adopted parents."

"They're a mess. Devastated." Reece rubbed the back of his neck. "Bad enough that they thought their perfect son was a junkie six months ago...but this? Best guess is they'll fall into a dark hole and be lucky to crawl out of it somewhere down the line."

Two more lives shattered into a million pieces.

We wrapped our little pity party up with promises to meet next week for dinner and drinks and lighter conversation.

Keeping up the pretence.

"Darcy, I hate to even bring this up, especially now but…" Reece leant in close and whispered, "Would you find it at all weird if I met Jackie for dinner? I kinda like her, I mean really like her, and…"

I slapped him on the arm. "Why are you even asking me that? I'd love for you two to hit it off. Jackie's lovely, so go, eat, be merry—but just promise to give me the low-down."

I smiled and my throbbing jaw protested, but it was worth it.

"Got it. Now, make sure you rest up, switch that brain off and chill, or I'll haul you down to the station for an interview with Jim Burns."

I couldn't help it, I shuddered. I'd lived through quite enough this past week. Another meeting with Jim would have sent me over the edge.

Our visitors drifted out the door and Harry clapped his hands.

"Name any food you want, and I shall make it happen."

"Well, we never did get our pizza so a veggie supreme please, heavy on the cheese."

"You've got it, but only if you promise me one thing." He sat on the edge of the coffee table and took my hands.

I was so exhausted; I'd have agreed to anything.

"Never, ever scare me like that again Darcy. I thought I'd lost you. That was the worst night of my life. You can't even begin to imagine what was going through my mind. Not to mention the kids and everything we've built together. It could have all been gone…in an instant. I'd never have gotten over that."

He cupped his hands round my face and kissed me lightly, mindful of my injuries.

"I'm fine Harry. We're fine. I promise you that. Now go and get that pizza cooking."

Harry disappeared into the kitchen, and I stared out at the evergreens bending majestically in the wind.

My heart felt a little lighter.

Still.

I was lying to him.

There was pain lodged deep.

I wasn't sure how long it would stay there.

Maybe one week. Maybe forever.

I'd never forget Cole. I'd never forget his face or the sound of his voice. Like a first love, he would be forever part of me, whether I wanted him to be or not.

Something told me that every year when the first leaf changed colour and drifted down from the tree, when the first thread of gold melted into bronze, when the first little chill crawled over my body heralding the change of the season, I'd think of *him*.

Always.

Roll on winter, I thought, and rubbed the goosebumps on my arms.

I really should have known better.

The end

Darcy Sinclair will return in *A Deadly Shade of Winter*

ABOUT THE AUTHOR

Nic Winter was born and raised in Glasgow, Scotland. After leaving University, Nic has worked in the legal field.

Her earliest influences in writing truly began after discovering Agatha Christie and she raced through her entire collection of books in record time, cementing her love of the mystery genre.

Nic developed an intense interest of psychology, borne from reading a plethora of true crime books, which has helped inspire many characters in her books.

Also a horror movie buff, Nic can easily say that *Halloween* must be her favourite horror film of all time, although many come a close second.

Nic has rescued animals her entire life and believes that she is a cat whisperer. She is also a strict vegetarian.

Now a mum of two kids, Nic is never seen without a coffee in one hand and a notebook in the other, whilst hunched over her laptop muttering to herself.

When not writing, Nic loves to read beautiful words penned by other authors, cook and treat her family to many new culinary concoctions, enjoy mother nature and then treat herself to a delicious cocktail.

ACKNOWLEDGMENTS

Agatha Christie once said, *"that the best time to plan a book is whilst doing the dishes"*.

As a mum of two kids, I took Dame Agatha's advice and turned the mundane into the murderous. To write this book has been a joy. Sure, there were times when I wanted to cry, but to stick with it and see it through to the end, meant more to me than I ever thought possible. To eventually write the words *The End* was an incredible feeling. I finally did it Mum!

There are so many people that I want to thank that have been part of this journey, but first I must thank my mum to whom this book is dedicated.

Mum, you gave me my love of books, of the written word. You gave me my love of the mystery genre when you placed *Agatha Christie's Death on the Nile* in my hands at the age of ten. I'm heartbroken you aren't here to see the finished book. You loved the first draft, so I know you would be cheering me on. Thank you always for being the best mum a girl could ask for.

I must also thank Stuart. We've had so many adventures together and this was another chapter, no pun intended. You did the impossible and kept the kids away from the computer before they could delete every draft written.

To my beautiful kids, Sophie and Jamie. You have given me so much joy since the day you were born, you have also given me so many wrinkles, but I wear them with pride (and a lot of concealer). May you both have endless adventures, fun, and most of all, utter happiness.

I hope that this proves to you that you should always put in the hard work and follow your dreams. I also hope that you enjoy the book when you are both old enough to read it.

A heartfelt thank you to my big brother Graham. Thanks for listening to my million plot holes and reading the early drafts. We did good big bro.

Another heartfelt thank you to Irene and Liz, for always encouraging me to keep going and never give up! Your encouragement has meant the world to me.

A huge thank you to my friend Gordon Bissell, who was there from the first draft and must have read this book a gazillion times! I wish you every success with your books, I know it's going to be an incredible journey for you.

Another thank you to my friend, Dr Stuart Knott, who took time out of his own busy writing schedule to read through *A Season to Kill* and listen to my plots for book two.

Thank you to my friend Julia Slack for taking the time to not only ARC read *A Season to Kill* but to help with the last tweaks. You have an incredible eye for detail and I wish you every success in your own writing journey.

Thank you to Elizabeth Moore Kraus...where do I begin dear friend? Not only did you stay up all night to ARC read *A Season to Kill* in a matter of hours, but you also wore your Professor Liz hat and helped me dissect those last issues keeping me awake. That is the definition of a true friend. Thank you for your support, your guidance, your gift of making me laugh when I'm too tired to think straight...and for making me an honorary Sister! You have brought the California sun into my life.

Thank you, Louise, for being such an incredible editor. You took every word I wrote and polished it until they shone, and I couldn't have done it without you.

To all my dear writer friends who kept me going with all the support a girl could need (you guys know who you are) and I thank you from the bottom of my heart.

Finally, a huge thank you to all the readers out there. If you took the time to read my book, I thank you deeply, and I truly hope that you enjoyed it.

Without readers there would be no story worth telling.

Love, Nic

Printed in Great Britain
by Amazon

41283307R00169